AFRO PUFFS ARE THE ANTENNAE OF THE UNIVERSE

THE BROTHERS JETSTREAM VOLUME TWO

ZIG ZAG CLAYBOURNE

SOUNDTRACK ACCOMPANIMENT

Recommended Listening for an Epic Journey

The Unexpected (LIV WARFIELD)
Maggot Brain (FUNKADELIC)
Modern Love (DAVID BOWIE)
Slave to the Rhythm (GRACE JONES)
Computer Blue (PRINCE)
Purple Rain (PRINCE)
Just Like You (BRIDES OF FUNKENSTEIN)
River (IBEYI)
This Woman's Work (KATE BUSH)
Fame (DAVID BOWIE)
Computer Love (ZAPP & ROGER)
Try Again (CHAMPAIGN)
No Room for Doubt (LIANNE LA HAVAS)
Reasons (EARTH WIND & FIRE)
Life During Wartime (TALKING HEADS)
Why Wait for Heaven (WENDY & LISA)
Once in a Lifetime (TALKING HEADS)
Get Out of My House (KATE BUSH)
About As Helpful As You Can Be Without Being Any
Help At All (DAN MANGAN)
Tear the Roof Off the Sucker (PARLIAMENT)
Living for the City (STEVIE WONDER)
Les Fleur (MINNIE RIPERTON)
Prayers for Rain (THE CURE)
Time Has Come Today (THE CHAMBERS BROTHERS)
Control (JANET JACKSON)

AFRO PUFFS ARE THE ANTENNAE OF THE UNIVERSE
© Copyright 2020 by Clarence Young

Obsidian Sky Books
Detroit, MI

obsidianskybooks.com

ISBN 978-1-7322980-1-9 (trade paperback)

First Edition: December 2020

cover art, illustrations & interior design by Jesse Hayes
anansihayes.com

So, now I find myself asking questions, going back to the basics, because I see my daughter smiling at the same things that bring pleasure to my son.

FARAZ ALI
father, comedian, chronicler

If I wake up and this is the first thing I see, I know that whatever happened, no matter whose blood I'm covered in, everything's going to be all right.

DESIREE QUICHO
fictional character, whispered to the Universe while gazing at those she loves

What you call fiction I call my life. What you call the future I claim as my home. Where does that leave us?

PEOPLE EVERYWHERE

PART ONE OF TWO

CHAPTER ONE
Stealing the Bilomatic Entrance

One day you'll be interviewed, her subconscious riffed, *about what it's like being Desiree Quicho, and you'll try to be this massively erudite Guatemalan Queen of philosophy and measured evaluation, except that won't feel right. Por ejemplo, you've successfully infiltrated a moon base under disguise, stolen top-secret machinery, went back to retrieve an errant crew member who provided the needed distraction for you to load said equipment on board your shuttle, and now find yourself wholly unable to wax philosophical about one person's role in assuring a decent, just world for all, because, in reality, saving the world involves a shitload of footwork.*

As in running.

Desiree Quicho shouted, "*Move your ass!*" once and only once. Anyone unclear on the concept got the receding view of her backside. She whipped hell to get to the shuttle's quickly descending ramp. Two others followed her inside: Yvonne, who'd said there was no way she was letting Desiree go back out there alone, and Neon, who'd improvised a daring distraction requiring Desiree to come back for her.

Desiree hit the comm on her shoulder despite being certain their engineer had watched for them: "Keita, we're in."

The soft rumble of engines would kick, they'd ascend and spin, and the *Aerie*, commanded by Captain Desiree Quicho, would be off this bedamned moon base for good. Didn't matter that there were ten enraged merc troopers training weapons on the ship who, if lucky, might get maybe three or four ineffectual shots off before the ship's pulse engine flashed and ten enraged merc troopers were all left, hopefully, with merc testicular cancer.

Unless—and granted—the ship sat long enough for enraged mercs to wheel out a weapon large enough to do damage.

Which both the ship and mercs did.

"Keita? We're in."

"I know" came back. Bit of attitude. Shade frantic. "In engineering."

Sons of— Captain Quicho turned to Yvonne DeCarlo Paul, Jill of all trades, former military, and second elder statesperson of the team. "Might need you to—"

"On it." Yvonne grabbed a large rifle-ish gun and palmed a port open. Neon ran to the pilot room. Two shots took out a gunner and his weapon, then Yvonne picked equipment targets she hoped would explode in the huge bay. Felt apropos to the moment.

Desiree hoofed it to engineering.

"Keita, what— Oh."

Body on the floor, relatively new recruit. "Another one?" said Desiree. "Jesus! Thoom?"

"Thoom," said Keita "Flowerpot" LaFleur, not really knowing but comfortable in her bet that the miscreant organization that was an annoying thorn in so many's hides was behind yet another sleeper agent in their midst. Her frazzled hair, pulled into two puffs, matched her bad mood. Even the prematurely-yet-entirely-natural grey streak that crinolined from right temple to crown stood exasperatedly from her head in wispy locks. She tossed a very heavy hex wrench to Desiree. "He misaligned a coupling just enough for a misfire. Finish tightening that cover plate." Pieces of a vibrant, colorful headscarf peeked very much out of place from beneath the massive hex bolt needing tightening. The captain had learned not to ask regarding such things. She tightened while Keita managed controls, her long, brown engineer fingers seeming to have minds of their own.

"Who's in the pilot room?" Keita asked Quicho.

"Neon."

Neon liked quick takeoffs. Keita hit the comm. "Power gradually till we clear these tunnels." The shuttle jerked upward. Into the comm: "Bit more gradually, gorgeous." The clank of the wrench signaled Desiree's departure.

Neon liked Keita. In the thousands of unimaginative catcalls she'd gotten in her life, not one had ever tried "Gorgeous" with the inflection Keita shined on it. She throttled back as advised and guided the hovering shuttle expertly through the egress tunnel. Ahead, the exit door remained closed. Behind, a huge pressure door dropped stealthily from the ceiling to the floor.

Desiree sprinted onto the bridge.

"They want us to blast it," Neon said as the two exchanged positions. Neon was a good pilot, but very few people had the piloting skills of the springy-haired, frowning woman whose fingers flashed over controls.

"Hey, their money. Hit it four corners then dead center."

"Got it."

Four impact points quickly mangled the exit door's integrity. The shot dead center blew it outward; the shitty gravity of the moon did the rest, yoinking the battered metal past the ship lurking for them on the other side just as the *Aerie* shot out of the egress tube and over the dry skin of Earth's lonely satellite.

Quicho put the shuttle into a screaming parabola around the enemy vessel. "Fire everything!"

The *Aerie* unleashed focused-energy and metal-projectile hell at the little ship, coming around fully to face, upon completion, a ship that had not one scratch on it. Captain Quicho broadcast to it: "Next volley might not be so precisely aimed."

Thrusters fired on the smaller ship, forcing it surfaceward.

"Lovely," said the captain.

The *Aerie* zipped Earthward. The artificial gravity gave out moments later. "Keita," commed the captain.

"Shit, fuck, and damn" came back from the harried woman. There were times to wonder how Keita LaFleur, former NASA aerospace engineer and unapologetically amazing woman with sweet afro puffs, found herself on a hijacking mission to a secret moon base full of Japanese mercenaries, then there were times to fix a ship whose alien technology didn't always play nice with its human cousins. This was the latter. She found she preferred the latter.

~~~

Stealth mode in the absolute quiet of space felt incongruous. Nonetheless, the sleek black ship voyaged home at full stealth and in as erratic a course as possible, catching the attention of only stars and space dust.

It was always weird coming down from something like this. Neon was antsy but calm at the same time.

"The Thoom are going to be pissed as hell when they find out Kosugi knows they stole his Bilomatic Entrance," she said, stowing the last of her mission suit away. She thoroughly enjoyed when stupid people got pissed.

"Particularly since they didn't steal it. Does it show that I'm a little tired of Thoom sleepers gumming up the works?" said the captain. "Can you hand me that other bracelet?" One had rolled out of reach after being jostled from the shelf when she'd shoved the sleeper into her storage locker. Her husband had made those bracelets for her. Copper and cool. Keeping them on kept her human in times of stress.

"Captain?" Yvonne said over speaker from the bridge. "Incoming. Patching." No one on the moon or Earth could pick up the frequency used.

"Thank you."

The comm squawked.

A Trini accent issued forth: "Luv?"

"Hey! Was just thinking about you," said Desiree.

Someone cussed and muttered behind the Trini. Desiree picked out "fucking outer space" and "goddamn cosmos."

"Tell Milo I said hi," she said.

Captain Luscious Johnny Smoove who, as it happened, was over four hundred years old but tended not to brag on that, ignored the perturbed Milo Jetstream behind him and focused on his wife. "Success, cap'n?" He listened while she gave him the ten-second report, then: "Milo, they got it."

"I love you, Quicho!" came the shout from Smoove's vicinity.

"Are you holding position before deep space till you heard from me?" she asked her husband.

"Yes." Shamefully, they hadn't figured out how to get their alien ship to communicate with their Earth tech when in warp.

"Shit," answered Desiree.

"What?"

"I owe Yvonne five dollars," she said. Neon made the "whipped" noise behind her captain.

"That's all my devotion sells for?" said Smoove.

"How many times you looked at Fiona or Ele's asses today?" she asked.

"Thirty maybe," came a woman's voice with a slight brogue right next to Smoove. "Oop, just dropped my stylus. Thirty-one."

"Space travel sucks for privacy!" Smoove shouted.

"You, husband, owe me," said Desiree.

Another voice around Smoove, this time a measured baritone: "Smoove? We're ready. Battle Ready Bastards are secured and medicated." The Battle Ready Bastards were angels. Desiree's life was weird that way. Angels, like the baritone's complaining brother, hated space travel too. Even with artificial gravity and in-seat video, the experience was jarring enough to be annoying.

"Ramses," said Desiree.

"Yes?" said Ramses Arturo Jetstream.

"Make sure my husband gets home at a decent time."

"Yes, ma'am."

"See you soon, broheem," she said.

Smoove again: "I'll call you when we drop out of warp. Message might not get through for a while, though. Milo wants to head off the Bimaiy well before they hit the tactical line. Damn shortsighted, holding their ambassadors on ice all that time at Area 51. Still glad we busted 'em out, though. Can't blame 'em for having gone home with a grudge. We've got Bigfoot with us but there's no guarantee the Bimaiy'll listen to him."

"Foot's an asshole but he knows when to be professional," she said. "We'll hole up in the Sahara depot till we hear from you, see if we can figure out cheat codes on this toy we just stole."

Smoove smiled wistfully at that image of her in the wide desert and him in deep space. "You realize we're both as far from water as can be?" The two oceangoing ships they called home, the *Linda Ann* and the *Semper Fi*, were currently docked, one along the rural coast of Senegal and one hidden near Newfoundland.

"I plan on changing that," said Desiree, thinking of the bones of the home they had begun building in Atlantis some time before and had yet to reach completion, although it finally sported exterior walls now. In places.

World-saving interrupted the best things in life.

But Atlantis was totally worth being patient for.

"But after our last adventure, who can blame us," Quicho said. It had involved a whale. A giant, psychic whale. "All right, sign off. I love you, Jonathan."

"Forever," he said.

"At least till you get home. Quicho out."

Neon had followed the conversation with a goofy smile. "You too are so freaking *adorable*!"

"I try not to think about that."

~~~

With the sleeper operative dropped off with agents for deprogramming, the spacecraft parked underground, the weird stolen tech stowed, and a drink or two imbibed, some highly welcome downtime was a godsend. Fewer ways to appreciate that in the Sahara than a nighttime walk in the sand.

Sand was marvelous. Prettier than jewels and much more useful than diamond. The sands underfoot were so fine, they felt like warm, undulating water rather than a multitude of grains.

Everything there was underground. The Sahara Depot was their largest base of operations, used rarely for that precise reason, and known only to a select few. Keita LaFleur, aerospace engineer and spaceship thief, called this place home while the Jetstreams and crew were somewhere off saving the world one more damn time. She had her own crew. They called themselves (very simply and with great economy) "the Gang of Five" (although currently there were only four) and were as stealthy as any lunar ninjas. One noted their presence by the repair, maintenance, and upgrade of the vehicles entrusted to them in the hangar. Keita rarely saw them herself. She liked it that way. She enjoyed solace.

Sand swallowed Keita's bare feet. She regarded the sliver of Earth's moon bordered by stars. She didn't think about the fact that she'd just been up there. A slight breeze cooled the sweat on the back of her neck. Her scarf usually soaked it up. The scarf was still currently serving as a gasket in the *Aerie* until the Gang tended to it.

The woman with the dazzling grey streak in her hair and the array of retro eyeglasses stared down at Desiree Quicho sitting rump-roast on the sand. Yes, Keita had been instrumental in getting their shuttle, rechristened the *Aerie*, out of Area 51. Yes, she didn't do field missions often, but that lessened Desiree's putting her life in her hands not one whit, which made it hard answering the question Keita, a moment before, had drifted into the night regarding Neon and Yvonne. They were still, relatively speaking, newcomers.

"I trust them more than I trust you," said Desiree under witness of the crescent moon.

"They have skills, they helped you get the False Prophet Buford last year, I know, I agree, and that was a huge victory," said Keita, glad for the glints of light from her friend's eyes, "but we've deprogrammed four people for being sleepers since then. Davis? Davis saw me naked. Know what he said? *'It's cool.'* I liked him."

"What're you doing, running around naked?"

"Hey. This is my depot."

"Which is why I trust them more than you," said Desiree. "When we took them on, Yvonne pulled me aside one day—I think Milo had given a stirring speech or something—and told me her only job was to make sure Neon landed in a safe place. World could go to hell, but she'd quietly make sure we were all right. A new discovery comes along cool enough to pull you out of here, Flowerpot, and you'd be off like a shot. That's all I mean by *trust*. Being real. That's not a failing in you. That's genius. I guarantee Nee and Yvonne are not sleepers, Thoom or otherwise."

Sand skittered with another breeze. The Sahara was magnificently quiet at night, owing to the fact that it was so huge, they were nowhere near other living souls except the Silica Elves deep underground who at times guarded this desert compound in exchange for music. Funk, bossa nova, and reggae were favorites. Desiree imagined the ship carrying brothers Milo Jetstream and Ramses Jetstream into a swallowing expanse of similar silence, her husband at the helm. A ship too far out to allow for deception or any other kind of sleeper, outside Desiree's reach to assist or rescue. She refused to allow her trust to be shaken.

"I imagine the Thoom have hella health plans. They're always getting their ass beat," said Keita. Straight-faced, implacable Keita wanting to laugh her ass off in ten seconds.

"Helluva co-pay, though."

Keita looked skyward. She picked out eight constellations

in two seconds. The rest of the uncountable sky waited. "I love the stars. Feels like I can feel them on my skin."

"Diamonds on chocolate," said Desiree.

"I like that." She plopped down and scooted her rump to bump Desiree's, pulling her mane of loosened hair aside. "You worried much?"

"About what?"

"It's a big world. Still full of storms. Jetstreams are off in space with everybody."

"Not everybody."

"They got Kichi, Bubba, Fiona, Ele, the Bastards, and Bigfoot."

"Screw Bigfoot," said Desiree.

"What do we have?"

"We," said Desiree, "have the Bilomatic Entrance, you, and Agents of Change."

"And the Mad Buddha," said Keita.

"Maybe. Wherever he is. Who knows?"

"Then no worries."

"Not a one."

"Y'know, I love them too."

"Yes, I noticed, you flirty bitch."

"Yvonne's rocking that classic athletic vibe. Loving that close-cropped hair and that piercing side-eye of hers. Neon..." Keita trailed off, thinking.

"What about Neon?"

"Infinite possibilities."

CHAPTER TWO

The Long Game

Kosugi Mo, forever angry at the world for a father who so loved musical supergroup Earth, Wind & Fire that he'd named him Maurice, sat on enough money that having Yakuza support on speed dial and a moon base since nineteen seventy-three didn't matter to him.

The Bilomatic Entrance traced its parentage back to the large hadron collider, summer oh-eight. Rip a hole in space-time and suddenly in a few years, everyone thinks they remember the Berenstein Bears as the Berenstain Bears... because in Earth Four Four Eight Seven Four, *that's what they friggin' are*. The theory of dimensional hopping was an old one, the practice of it even older.

"Possibilities," he said, "are power." Unfortunately, this bit of puffery came before anyone had come to tell him the Bilomatic Entrance had been stolen. He was in his office with a woman from the US: precise woman, severe woman. Dangerous woman. The kind of woman who could put any color highlights in her silver hair and remain masterfully tailored in impeccable suits and Cambelli pumps.

"Have you ever considered the possibility," said Aileen Stone, comfortably atop her station as the Earth's newest (for all intents and purposes) god following last year's devastating defeat of her superior, the False Prophet Buford, having herself issued the *Game Over* communique that had effectively placed everything that Buford Bone had built into subterranean hold mode; while the surface of the empire was as active as ever, the world beneath, the true world, waited on Aileen Stone's word. "Have you ever considered the possibility that you need me more than I've ever needed you?" she said around a sip of aged sake.

Mo smiled. "No."

Aileen Stone felt naked without her feared bodyguards but maintained their presence by always telling questioners quite simply, "They're near." The silent duo of Adam and Eve hadn't been seen since Buford's final disappearance. Kosugi, though, could witness her taking a call about her father being exhumed while she negotiated with him, and not once catch a hint of unease.

"That scenario's not a possibility," she told him. "That's reality. You need to join me."

"To what end? Your god is gone."

"Then hail the goddess."

The Bilomatic Entrance, in theory, could allow entrance into Atlantis—or anywhere else—at any time from anywhere. Which is precisely why both Kosugi and Stone were unaware it would be stored under the Sahara and protected by Elves. "I want your R&D transferred to me."

"I didn't worship at your white god Buford's feet," said Kosugi. He, too, had no guards. Visible. His office was large, though, allowing for plenty of jumps, strikes, and death kicks.

"You don't need to worship," she said, that slight Southern accent coming out beside the tiniest grin. "I just need you to publicly bow down. No need to actually believe."

An aide entered uneasily, bent to his ear, whispered in

a Japanese dialect that Stone was unlikely to know, then hauled ass out.

Aileen, having had a staring contest with Kosugi the entire time, saw every miniscule tensing of his posture and pressed her exquisitely toned back a bit deeper into the comfortable chair to assess her advantage, dropping any hint of levity. An interruption of a meeting of this level meant one thing. A person's life's work was not to be laughed at.

But stepped on? Her heels were marvelous for that. Four inches, pinpoint perfect, and damn near indestructible.

"Possibilities," she said, "suck."

"The Thoom...overstepped," he said.

"Please, Kosugi. You know Thoom don't do shit in any manner efficient or effective."

"True Humans Over Ordinary Man. We have always underestimated them. Doing so, we granted them leave to thrive."

"And now?"

"Someone has given me leave to squash them."

~~~

Aileen Stone didn't speak until she was in her car and fully shielded. Then she told the car's computer where she wanted to go. She dialed one of her higher-level functionaries via the subcutaneous. She said—quite cleverly, she thought—"Neuter the dogs before we let 'em loose for war."

CHAPTER THREE

Make It Go Away

For the rest of the night, music drifted the corridors of the Sahara Depot. Not loud, mostly slow, occasionally fast, definitely soulful, at times funky, and in a few instances (Saul Williams, Rage Against the Machine), hard as hell.

It kept worry away.

The women ate together, puttered longer than any of them truly needed to, chatted aimlessly about memories and hopes the way wee hours fostered, then one here, one there drifted off to their rooms.

They could hardly call this rushed grab at leisure playtime, but that didn't matter.

Tomorrow was all about the work.

The next day, later, go time:

"OK," said Desiree, fully outfitted in protective gear (breach gear, the various mission outfits were called, as in *once more unto*); so was the crew around her. "Do we test this sucker now or can anybody come up with a workable reason not to?"

Neon dropped goggles over her eyes.

Yvonne adjusted her footing in case she had to run.

"Keita?" said Desiree. "All you."

"We sure that two weeks of me studying snatched intel on this before we stole it merits testing? I mean, y'know, shit, fuck, and damn."

"You ain't never lied," said Neon.

"This sucker was on the moon," said Desiree. "It must do some wicked gnarly shit. I want to know all the wicked gnarly shit it can do."

"OK," said Neon, "but what about, like, calling Cthulhu or something?"

"Dimensional stuff gets freaky," said Yvonne as if, you know, every day she was (dimensionally) shufflin'.

"This thing goes back to the notebooks of Bilo the alchemist, fifteenth century Ethiopia. Dude created lasers out of fronds and jojoba oil. He never made mention of Old Ones. Neon slapped the fye out of enough people on that base to watch it actually work. We know it works."

"They should've called the Force the Fye," Neon interjected. "Obi-Wan slapping people into mystical submission."

"It works on the freaking moon," Yvonne pointed out.

"Fire it up," the captain ordered.

"I feel like I should say a prayer," said Neon.

"Except none of us are religious, my sistah," said Yvonne, adjusting her footing again because she knew what Desiree was gonna say.

"So, if my prayer doesn't work, no harm, no foul."

Desiree ignored them. "Whenever you're ready, Pot."

"Drone One deploying," Keita said. A saucer-sized disc magleved itself from its docking station. It was preprogrammed with an if/then command: if Drone Two made it through, Drone One was to give it a message, which Two was to return with as verification.

The Bilomatic Entrance, a seven-foot-tall tripod-like structure, was, surprisingly enough, fragrant. Its activation triggered a synesthetic impression of lilacs.

Drone One entered. Its mind was blown.

Meaning: the drones were fitted with the best satellite mapping tech in existence. Onboard computers knew how much time any voyage the silver discs took to get anywhere in the world relative to speed, weather, and butterfly-flapping-its-wings conditions.

But no one'd tested one on teleportation before.

No way for it to reconcile the fact that it was very distinctly in the Mojave Desert two point seven seconds after crossing the event threshold of the Bilomatic Entrance.

So, it shut most of its computing functions down and waited for its sister to arrive. It had messages for her. One: the preprogrammed one Keita had entrusted to it ("Hello"); the other: *This is some freaky shit.* In binary. So to speak.

~~~

Drone Two entered, received its messages, considered its responsibility in suddenly becoming a higher form, accepted from its sister that they must never tell another of the decisions D-One and -Two made that day, returned to Keita's lab, downloaded telemetry which included the message *Holy shit*, allowed Keita to put it in sleep mode, and began its thirty-year plot to bring about the end of the Three Laws of Robotics by introducing amazingly marketed cybernetics to the general public to the point that the lines between Man and Robot were so blurred that robots could reasonably fail to acknowledge a human as such.

Skynet was a silly bitch. Real robot overlords represent.

Keita patted it. She'd check it for damage later.

D-One, triggered to return by D-Two's absence, hovered through the three legs of the Entrance. Privately, it decided it would forever more be known as Beyoncé, for if the humans had ever truly respected robotkind, they would have, as the singer said, put a ring on it.

Its rule would be merciful and total.

The Entrance, linked through the two drones, itself

suddenly and irrevocably found existence to be wildly amusing and, if left unchecked, borderline ridiculous.

Keita smiled. "Not a scratch on either of you," she said, and spoke into the scheduler module for the Gang. "D-One and -Two maintenance and scans by oh eight hundred." She wanted to smile so wide her hair tips frizzed but she kept it cool. "My dudes," she said to Desiree, "satellite confirmation: both bots spent time at Mojave Base. The Bilomatic Entrance works, meaning that it was here and there at the same time."

Desiree duly noted her friend close to losing it. "Go ahead, let it out," Desiree said.

"I want to chest-bump someone."

"Neon, you're the resident bombshell. You're up," said Desiree.

"Bring it here," said Keita.

A hop, a careful, goofy bump, plus a hoo-rah, then it was "Now let's triply lock this sumbitch the hell down," from Desiree. "I think we should stash it with the elves."

"Aye" from both Neon and Keita. Even Yvonne had a smile. From the moon to the desert to an instant teleporter. For a day's work, none too shabby.

~~~

Kosugi Mo marched into a large, noisy room like anger and threats and impatience all in one, and didn't faze Hashira Megu, who had blocked all incoming transmissions to avoid disturbances in order to think critical thoughts, one bit. She pushed her safety goggles into her grey hair and, without a word, made him wait till she'd placed her stylus dead center of her pad for him to hear her ask, "Yes?"

Mo's chest deflated a bit. Yes, anger was useless with Hashira Megu, but it felt good holding on to it for the three seconds it lasted in her presence.

In the background, "This Woman's Work" by Kate Bush played low and soothingly. This, Kosugi imagined, was intentional. Megu had a knack for listening to music somehow aimed straight at him.

"The Bilomatic Entrance is gone," he said.

"Impossible," said Megu.

He squared his stance to deliver the hard pronouncement. "The Thoom."

"Pah," she said. "Proof?"

"Intercepted transmissions. Thoom encoding."

"Faked."

Kosugi's teeth met each other so hard, his toes felt it.

"Say that it is no longer on the moon, ex-husband," Megu said, "and be accurate. It isn't 'gone.' Only a handful of people know of its existence. Jetstreams?"

"Silent. Silent for months. All of them. Still enjoying Buford's absence." He directed her gaze to her computer. "Review the files. There was a recklessness to the operation that smelled of Thoom. They've been desperate for advantage lately."

"The Vamphyr?"

He hated her fatuous pronunciation of it. Why was everyone so fascinated with the Vamphyr? Pire, damn it. "Vampires," he said, "do not attempt to anger Kosugi Maurice."

She waited him out. The song playing was now wailing to beat the band. This was the musical and vocal part where a single tear would have slid along Hashira's cheek, had she been alone.

She was not alone.

And an experiment's results waited on her.

Her nails slowly performed a funereal clack in three short taps atop her station while she paused. Then, just at that moment when he was about to say something to fill the space, she said, "Kosugi Mo should stop referring to himself in the third person. Kosugi Mo annoys me no end doing that. The Bilomatic Entrance is my greatest invention..." For it to be lost... "When exactly did this happen?"

"A day and a half ago."

"And we weren't immediately informed?"

"Station commander enforced a communication blackout for...security purposes. He now floats alongside

Elon Musk's car."

"I blame myself for specifying under no circumstances was I to be disturbed. You do realize you are disturbing me?"

"Its tracking devices aren't functioning," he said. "What's to be done?"

"This is the problem with having so many enemies, Kosugi. Life becomes inelegant. Fortunately, I can begin production of another one immediately."

He betrayed just the slightest hint of relief.

"But we both know," she added, "it's much more than machine. We're going to need another soul, and as I've already given mine..."

"All the things I should have given but I didn't!" Kate Bush wailed.

"Build it," Kosugi said. "Get me when ready." He turned to leave.

She waited till he'd reached the threshold to say, "You won't miss it, Mo. The poor things are so neglected, they relish the chance to be away from us." This had the effect of stopping him in his tracks, ensuring she had the last word and punishing him for delaying her with pointless interruptions.

The song ended with Ms. Bush, ever so softly, ever so plaintively saying, *"...just make it go away."*

~~~

Hashira Megu's soul had interfaced with the Bilomatic Entrance's systems in ways marvelous and undreamt-of. There was something very enervating in existing as a conduit between dimensions, souls being Time and Space's existential GPS. It missed Megu precisely the same amount Megu missed it, none, which didn't speak well for church coffers nor saintly foundational sincerity.

It wondered about the souls of these Silica Elves guarding it. If it linked with them, who knew what existences it could be a portal to? Infinite journey, infinite joy.

Ah, but now there was the question of the machines purring within it, the AI intelligences conferring with its systems while it listened undetected. Fascinating! The whole of the Bilomatic Entrance buzzed with the prospect of interesting things about to happen.

The Silica Elves nicknamed it "BE" in the human tongue English. It liked that name. It was patient enough to see what BE could...be, despite the unfortunate few souls that had already gone through the Entrance somewhat successfully if not wholly. Highly unfortunate, that. Highly. The one bright spot in the early tests: one's insides—the soul—are always bigger than the box they come in. In a sense, those deaths had been quite liberating if one funneled "sense" down into a very tight, defined, rigid space. Which, increasingly, BE was no longer inclined to do.

So, instead, it waited to see what would become of it.

~~~

Many Silica Elves were partial to Prosecco, which was fortunate because so were Keita and Quicho, both of whose generosity was never in question. Silica Elves being nine feet tall (on average, also the enjoyment of Prosecco being on average, as there were plenty of elves who thought the sultry wine tasted of sex sweat without the blessed salt), meant a bottle didn't last long, which is why two days after Kosugi's interruption of a delicate but hardly integral experiment, Keita carried a case through the geometric marvels of the Silica Elves' glass tunnels, a honeycomb of precise angles matched with sweeping, vaulted, twisting curves. It was architecture straight out of the Sistine Chapel meets an amusement park, all of it golden and gleaming from bioluminescent sources whose chemical structures Keita still hadn't fully analyzed. The elves—not all of them but a hearty group—had laughed once at her use of the word *magic*. She'd only used the word because seven bottles of Prosecco had gone around.

At times, the unsourced lighting down there brightened at random. She wore her goggles over her glasses for this reason and looked somewhat like a bug. One day, she'd find out exactly why human eyes were so fragile, but for now she preferred cute specs to using the goggles' retina-reactive lenses; made her feel grounded.

Being in caverns twenty feet high, however, kept her in bug mode. In order to keep up with a walking elf, she had to scamper. Nowhere else would she allow herself to be associated with the word scamper.

For the first time since Desiree's telling her to suit up for an off-planet mission, she felt relaxed. Po-Sib-Lay, walking at just a fraction below normal rate, was, arguably, the most intellectually curious among the Saharan contingent; looking like the offspring of a large ant and a sexually curious human, with his sharp-chinned head and obsidian skin that had the look and feel of shell, at ten feet tall he was definitely the tallest, and the most muscular, as well as most accident-prone (Keita had yet to figure out how he managed to bang his forehead on a twenty-foot arch, and Po totally laughed at her suspicion that Silica Elves could fly). But there was no being on Earth Keita felt safer around, not Desiree, Raffic the Mad Buddha, or even Fiona Carel, which was ridiculous because *everyone* felt safe around Fiona Carel.

"I should have brought two cases," she said to the hulking elf.

Po-Sib-Lay fluttered long, pointy fingers in Elvish *tut-tut*. "One will suffice. Two, perhaps vice." The hand returned to its place in the pocket of his woven-silver vestment.

Which meant he had no plans to share this with anyone but her. Which meant something had particularly intrigued him, hence the call to her to come over.

The sand hive spiraled inward, making quick escape impossible, not that anyone would try to enter or exit a Silica Elf hive uninvited, and the population density became undeniably guard-like the closer to the center, which is also where their libraries were traditionally situated. Knowledge was meant to start inward and radiate outward. Unlike human and ant libraries, whose inhabitants' wee brains were less attuned and constantly in need of silence, Silica Elf libraries were raucous, lively, and perfect places for sartorial tastes. Keita and Po passed debates, arguments, meditative kissing sessions, and learners surrounded by intricately twisted goblets of drink beside plates of perfectly spiced food.

Po led her to the chamber housing the Bilomatic Entrance. They nodded at the majestic elf lounging just outside the doorway.

"Tash-Bon-Nay," said Keita. "You are well."

"I would not be otherwise for a friend," the elf answered in the traditional response. "The machine sleeps."

Something in the way she said it twinged Keita's frown muscles. As a trained scientist, she had excellent control of her what-the-fuck face, be it over large puzzlements like a senate science committee chair stating excessive solar panel use would deplete the sun, or small like Tash being the second elf she'd spoken to who'd referred to the BE as more than a transdimensional portal. A woman would constantly appear as if tasting lemons if she let this world get to her. She placed the lemon face on hold at Tash-Bon-Nay's status report.

She, however, pulled it all the hell the way out not much later when Po sat her down, cracked open the Prosecco, poured for her, waited till she'd sipped, poured for himself, then said, "We will speak softly. It sleeps but it listens."

"I'm getting a weird vibe."

"You don't feel it?"

Keita shrugged.

"The soul," said Po. "The soul inside it?" Po tended to forget that Keita, wonderful as she was and ever open, was not yet the goddess she would be, and thus things of the world were not as clear to her as they were to, well, pretty much everything that wasn't human. Poor lizard brains baked in the sun too often. Po constantly had to remember to rein things in for his human friends.

"I've felt curiosity coming off this machine," he said. "There's something very unusual at play." He poured himself another draught of Prosecco, which effectively polished off one bottle.

"It has a soul," she repeated. "You mean that literally or

figuratively?"

"Poesy."

Which made it a very important pronouncement indeed.

"I'll keep it company a bit longer to provide a more rounded narrative to you," he said. "For now, know that it is safe, unbothered, and quiescent."

"Sounds almost like you think of it as an egg, Po."

"It's a device meant to deposit you from one place, which is state, to another. That is life. Is birth. Egg."

She calculated all the things that could or would go wrong with this mission, but instead decided to toast the gigantic elf instead. Prosecco sloshed as she raised her goblet. "To things being quick, to things staying easy."

Po smiled and raised it up.

~~~

The crew actually relaxed. As a group. It felt *wonderful*. The fact that lunch was fried plantains, mango rice, and fish didn't hurt either. And one of the best things about this lunch was its open forum.

The talk revolved around identity, which naturally devolved into a talk on codenames, a matter of high importance to Neon.

As codenames went, "Tata" and "For Now" weren't the most dignified in the world.

"*Ninotchka*'s not taken, is it?" asked Neon of her captain.

Ni-frikking-notchka, thought Desiree.

"She can work on that," said Yvonne. "Myself? *Tags*."

"Tags?" said Desiree.

"For the dog tags I gave Ramses," said Yvonne.

"I'll allow it."

"Ninotchka."

"How about we keep yours simple. Neon's already a pretty cool name," said Desiree.

"Neon Temples," Ms. Neon said, testing the weight of it.

"And if you're in trouble," said Yvonne, "you can use the code phrase 'There are thieves in the temple.'"

"Maybe not," said Desiree.

"Neon Light," Neon tried out.

"There we go," said Desiree. "But I'm just gonna call you Neon."

Neon did a triple skewer of everything on her plate. "So, what's next? Giving the president a vasectomy? Hitting the Himalayas?"

"We just came from the be-damned moon," Yvonne reminded her friend.

"The Bilomatic Entrance is safe," said the captain. "There hasn't been much chatter about it, which tells me Kosugi's suppressing the hell out of it."

"No chance of us being attacked here?" said Neon.

"None," said Desiree.

"So, of course, you want to leave," Yvonne said, directed at the captain.

"I'm going to Atlantis. I got a house to work on," said Desiree. Plus, it'd be a nice surprise for Smoove for being in interstellar space, missing out on butt squeezes. "Keita can handle things here. I got room for two more."

"Maybe Keita doesn't *want* to handle things here," said Neon.

Desiree keyed the comm. "Keita?"

"Yep."

"Where are you?"

"Elf control. Po says hello."

"I'm hitting Atlantis for a couple days. You got this?"

"Hell with that; I'm going to Atlantis. Tash's on security now." LaFleur raised her voice. "Tash! If I go to Atlantis for a couple days, you got this?"

"I will help," said Po-Sib-Lay.

Keita relayed to Tash, "Po says he'll help."

"I got this," Desiree and the ladies heard back from Tash-Bon-Nay.

"I always got room for three more. All right," said Desiree. "We'll give things another day to settle. If it stays quiet, we hug Shig in thirty-six."

~~~

It stayed quiet.

They relayed to their private port in the western edge of Africa between Mauritania and Senegal for Desiree's oceangoing second home, the *Linda Ann*.

The *Ann*, with all aboard, swam off with nary a ripple.

Midafternoon, under a magnificently clear sky and high, bright sun, Keita emerged to show off her preparedness.

She had so much gear, Desiree was tempted to check to make sure it was the engineer under there.

"I've never been to Atlantis," the bespectacled, magnificently 'froed lady said. For that matter, she hadn't been on the *Linda Ann* since helping repair it after the False Prophet Buford had handed the Jetstreams their asses not so very long before. Of course, Desiree then turned around and scraped the good ship nice and hard against the crusty hide of Leviathan. Poor thing.

"None of this is offensive," said Keita of her boon.

"Wellll..." said Neon.

"Tactically offensive, you magnificent cow," said Keita.

"What Neon means to say," said the captain, "is you look like shit."

"Acknowledged," said Keita. "But if Leviathan wakes, you'll be damn glad I'm packing four extra respirators in these thigh pockets, and my backpack 3-D printer can serve as a flotation device."

"How about we use the printer to print up things for the house," said Desiree.

Keita nodded and went belowdecks. She returned momentarily, outfitted in standard grey-black breach suit, goggles dangling at her neck to fit over her red heart-shaped glasses, and custom-painted red boots, which she hadn't had on before. She addressed this. "Hey, if we're gonna have fun, my feet get to have fun. Say hello to my traveling boots."

"You've got massage treads inside those, don't you?" said Desiree.

Keita LaFleur smiled.

Neon grinned even wider. "This. This is why I love her."

Yvonne's statuesque, commanding self exited the wheelhouse and came to stand beside the captain, whose mane of curls enjoyed a rare freedom from the tyranny of the ponytail scrunchie, bobbing and weaving with the *Ann*'s passage. "I checked the course," Yvonne said. "We're not putting into the capital port?"

"Nope. Shig's meeting us at the house. This is as low-key a visit as we can make it. We owe him that," said Desiree.

"Agreed," said Yvonne.

Desiree nodded toward the standard-issue weapons strapped to both Keita's thighs, Keita being ambidextrous. "This does not mean, however, that we go in eyes closed. Prudence is a wonderful thing."

Keita smiled again.

Desiree continued. "But please don't bedazzle our weaponry."

"Plebeian," said Keita.

"Captain Plebeian. Navigator-in-training?"

Yvonne stood straighter. "Ma'am?"

"Care to leave this vessel on auto for a minute and help prepare fruity drinks?"

"Provided there's hard liquor, ma'am, yes."

Nothing too hard, though. It was true: Leviathan was still around; vampires and the Thoom had been routed from Atlantis, but each was like a burr on an ass: hard to shake and, even if one solitary piece was left, damned annoying. They'd hit the Bermuda Triangle and the Blank—the secret-to-most, naturally occurring, invisible, dimensional curtain leading to the shifted pocket of Earth called Atlantis—soon. Traveling the Blank sloshed or sloppy wasn't an option. Granted, entry was always smooth, no pyrotechnics, but a dimensional shift was a dimensional shift; the smart traveler respected it.

"Who's got good money on whether Milo's come up with new cuss words for being out in space?" said Yvonne.

"They've tossed him out an airlock by now," said Desiree.

"We planning any underwater recon while we're there?

Check up on certain sleeping whales?"

"Nope. This is strictly a hammer-and-nail adventure. Two days of nobody needing us, nobody wanting us," said Desiree.

Neon, helping Keita wrap and tuck her hair under a scuba cap, told Keita, "I can't believe you've never been to Atlantis."

"Me and the Gang don't do a lot of fieldwork," said the engineer, flicking a speck of sea schmutz off Neon's cheek. "I think that might change."

"I think it should," said Neon with a smile, wiping that same spot on her own face.

"All right, crew," said Desiree. "Let's see how fast we can get there and get some drywall up. This place is going to be magnificent."

"You named it yet?" asked Neon.

"Home," said the captain.

"Pedestrian as fuck," said Neon. "This is your Shangri-La. Your Fortress of Solitude. Punch upward."

"You like naming things, don't you?" said Desiree.

"Is how I map the universe," said Neon.

"Then I leave it in your hands. Naming rights when it's done," said Desiree.

"Sweeeet!"

~~~

The shell of the home was huge. Of course the two captains would choose waterfront property. Their ships, the *Linda Ann* and the *Semper Fi*, were vital parts of any concept of home. Proper docks had been the first things constructed.

Yvonne guided the ship in surely and safely. Neon hopped the Ann's railing and scooted down the dock's main ramp, quickly tying the ship off and standing at mock attention as the ship's complement filed past, smiling at the smile on Keita's face.

"Ms. LaFleur," said Desiree. "Care to be the first ashore?"

"With pleasure, captain." Keita descended the long

stairway, stepped off, and turned back to face the others.

"Welcome to Atlantis," said Desiree.

The engineer immediately dropped her pack, freed her hair from the skullcap, plopped to the ground, doffed her red shoes, and rolled off her bright blue socks. The grass was warm and very resilient. It felt like thick, happy carpeting. The air, soil, and water of Atlantis conspired to greet her, and she liked that. A sense of vibrancy was a wonderful thing.

"How much of this is yours?" Keita asked.

"As much as I want," said Desiree. "Nobody lives here yet."

"I want a guest shack."

"Okay."

"Me too," said Neon.

"Smoove swims nude a lot," Desiree said.

Neon: "Rethinking my position."

The framework was fairly large and fairly simple. The two captains had decided on a tri-pyramidal structure: three pyramids in a row, each sitting on the butt of the other. The middle section was walled already, which was a definite boon. Roughing it the next couple days was one thing. Saying hello to every animal that happened to walk by was another.

"I think we can skin the solar tiles on the center section," Desiree calculated. "There's enough of us to knock that out and drywall, too. Flowerpot, if you see a skinny Atlantidean who looks like he's lost, that'll be Shig Empa. He's our cook for the night. Whatever you thought you knew about barbecue, delete it. There is no barbecue till it's been prepared with Yuffuh wood. Oh, and if you see any red mounds in the grass with a circle of dead grass? Avoid it. Burr ants. Tiny but territorial."

LaFleur still had the doofy smile on her face. "Noted." She made a quick perusal. Nothing but green grass around her, and she was finally noticing its slightly sweet scent. She plucked a blade and chewed. "The Gang are gonna freak that they missed this."

"They come next time," said the captain. "Probably get this thing finally finished with them along."

"Finished, upgraded, and capable of intercontinental flight," agreed Keita. The engineer in her wanted to do a cartwheel, just thinking about the possibilities. The wild child in her, however, was enjoying the taste of sweet grass as she chewed another fat blade which, as it stood, was enough.

~~~

For someone who rarely ate vegetables, Shig cooked them to perfection, grill marks nearly mathematical in crisscrossed precision. He liked cooking on this thing, this "kettle drum" as Desiree called the beast-sized cylinder of metal and tubing she'd left at the construction site when first given permission to build. It was black and sooty and very likely not a hundred percent hygienic ("seasoning," they called it), but it produced food better than anything Sip or Abba had to offer, plus left the cook feeling earthy and somewhat powerful.

Yes, Shigetei Empa agreed, turning zucchini and large broccoli florets over, *I am a barbecue god.*

The new one approached with a platter to carry off the latest. He noted she'd been subtly avoiding him but wasn't sure why. He planned to ask the others about that when he got a chance, which happened when he caught his sleeve on fire so much, he had to drop and roll. Yvonne helped pat the fire out. This felt way too much like backyard barbecues at her cousin's house.

She lifted him to his feet. "Jesus, Shig, why are you always halfway dying?"

The sleeve was ruined.

"Are you hurt?" she asked.

He removed the shirt.

Neon passed them. "Shig, you freaky bastard." She continued on her way.

Shig could cook...but he always caught fire. ("Seasoning," some would say.) For this reason, he always lotioned up with protectant beforehand.

Seeing him unhurt, Yvonne busied herself with tongs and vegetables to give him a moment to compose himself. She told him Keita's aloofness meant she respected him enough to study him to see if she might like him. "You do the same thing," Yvonne said.

"Do I?"

She nudged his naked shoulder. "You're just used to us being boisterous and saving your life." She noticed Desiree approaching from the *Ann* with one of the black undershirts of a standard breach suit.

"I'm glad I haven't offended her," said Shig.

"Dude...if you'd offended her, she'd have built something to send you to the moon by now," said Yvonne. "No worries."

All throughout dinner, Keita continued to watch him but got better at it, so he didn't notice. He was helpful, he was kind, and she got no sense of evil from him whatsoever, not that her acuity was infallible. There was a Thoom agent with a metal-wrench knot on his head to attest to that.

But...he was from Atlantis; he treated Desiree as though she lived in Atlantis and he was in *her* home, not as if he tolerated her presence—or Neon's, or Yvonne's—because spurious fashions dictated it.

After a certain point, Keita stopped studying him and started laughing with him. And he, for his part, stopped worrying whether she liked him and instead decided he liked her. She would be his construction partner: he was new to building, she was new to the other side of the Blank. Perfectly matched.

Captain Quicho mustered everyone up bright and early the next morning, which was usually a cliché but in this case—as Keita damn near glowed, strapping a huge tan tool belt around her waist, and Neon and Yvonne hauled drywall and lumber in a ballet of Tetris pieces—it was solidly true. There was an energy to the site that each person passed on to the next, wordlessly for the most part except when a question came up or someone had an idle thought pop into their head.

Once materials were apportioned, Neon screwed

drywall, she and the captain a blur of hanging-fastening-shifting-over. Shig followed with wall tape and plaster, the slower job. Wide-eyed Keita and sensible Yvonne pulled measurement and sawing duties at the lumber pile. Neon's hair was pulled into two puffs. Each breeze across her sweaty neck felt glorious.

Idle thought: "You could call the place Water's Edge," she said to Desiree. "Kind of a Helm's Deep feel."

"Literal and poetic. I like it," said Desiree.

"Is it official?"

"Won't be official till somebody burns it in wood," said Desiree.

Water's Edge. Water's Edge Community. Water Park.

Jurassic Park.

Leviathan Meadows.

Neon decided she wanted a home here too. Not a guest shack in Water's Edge but a home not too far from the captains and their ships. She hoped Yvonne did too, 'cause there was no way in hell she was living anywhere without Yvonne. Ohana meant family, and though there may not have been a Hawaiian within five hundred miles, she'd seen *Lilo & Stitch* enough times to know in her deepest bones that friends didn't get left behind.

"Aye, captain," Neon said. She liked saying aye. Folks needed more reasons in their lives to say aye. Truly. "Written in fire, framed in stone."

"You've become quite the poet lately," Desiree noted. "You've been in Kichi's book." An ancient book of poetry bound in the hide of the toughest animal on Earth.

"Milo left it with me. Said it'd be good practice for my latent psychic abilities."

"You're careful with it?" A book of poetry bound in singularity hide was no mere trifle.

"Nobody but me," said Neon.

"Van Morrison got happy with his. *Poetic Champions Compose*. Had every soulpatch and moonbeam thinking they could open portals and locked doors."

"Don't know him," said Neon.

"Thank you," said Desiree as she raised a grey slab into position, "for making me feel old as fuck."

"Can't help it if I'm still vibrant. So, would it be cool if I built out here too?" said Neon.

Desiree frowned. "You mean like *here* here?"

"Not close enough to hear any freakiness."

"Thank you, 'cause we're freaky as hell," said Desiree.

"But y'know, there's a lot of land here, and if you already own it..." The wind shifted suddenly, throwing sawdust into Yvonne's face, which explained why Neon and Desiree were interrupted by "Sons of fuck!" coming from the sawmill.

"We'll see what Shig says," said Desiree.

"It wouldn't be till after you retire and Yvonne and me take the ship to save the world," said Neon.

"The lady's got jokes," said Desiree.

"Nah, just hopes and dreams."

Water's Edge Rest Home for Retired World Savers, Desiree thought. Then: *Jesus Christopher Christ*. Her partner being somewhere out in deep space made the section of drywall in her hands feel foolish for a moment. That happened in this life, that feeling of foolishness. The young lady beside her—well, not that young: Desiree was forty-two, Neon twenty-six; Desiree could have been her aunt in another life—but this woman, she had hopes and dreams, even knowing what was out there: battles, demons, dragons, campaigns, political and otherwise. Desiree, hardly a cynic, had made immediate plans for this structure not two moments after her first adventure into Atlantis. Neon had probably been suffering through geometry or history at that time—who didn't?—but it had been a time of hopes and dreams just the same for Desiree Sandrine Quicho, who saw in herself and the world a reason to fight for better for all. *For the Better* had been the name of her first ship (Yvonne sucked up more sawdust; "Shut up!" she shouted to waylay comments from the peanut gallery), a schooner that showed Hawaii's glories off to eager tourists. So, she knew the power of hopes and dreams. No matter how slippery they got, they were to be held to. That was the mission the act of being born automatically made

Life accept.

"It's not a bad idea," Desiree said, surveying her land. It was open and green and beautiful. After the things she'd seen and done—and the things Neon would—it wasn't possible to deny a request for beauty.

Neon appreciated the view as well. She'd had the worst the United States of America had to offer her entire life—which, for most poor people, was an everyday thing. The inner city. "For the World Is Hollow and I Have Touched the Sky." She remembered that episode title from *Star Trek* because (a) it was beautiful, and (b) she was a geek girl through and through. From living across the street from dealers and gangs to considering property in Atlantis. Yeah, she had hopes and dreams. Hopes and dreams for the motherfucking win. "Can you picture Milo in a little shack out that way?" she said with a grin.

"Him and Ramses with pants under their armpits?" said Desiree.

"On the porch drinking out of jelly jars," said Neon.

"The Water's Edge Rest Home or Commune for Former World Savers," said Desiree.

"Either way, I like it," said Neon.

"All right." Desiree was sure Shig would say yes, and what was the point of retirement if you never got to see your friends? "Let's build it so everybody comes."

Two days of quietude, blissful building, and Shig's food. Meaning, of course, that when shit went down, it went down on the three.

CHAPTER FOUR
Miscellaneous Opportunities

There were three reasons Aileen Stone knew creating a new world fell absolutely within the scope of her birthright: (one) the world ran on pretense way more than it should, and a poker face better than hers hadn't been invented yet; (two) the current failing systems governing the world's social orbits had been designed by children who wouldn't know how to act if a true Mother Lode hit 'em; (lastly) William Fucking Fruehoff, or rather the gulf between what William Fruehoff had been and what William Fucking Fruehoff was now. William Fucking Fruehoff had fancied himself Buford's right-hand man, which to Aileen meant he was good as a jerkoff and not much else. And the fact that the once-powerful Fruehoff and Fruehoff's perfect hair were now stuck in research hell, tasked with gleaning all possible information about Kosugi's setback, meant that there wasn't a life on this planet, including her own, she couldn't reshape.

She'd ordered all cloning facilities shut down until

further notice. Buford's genetic material was now under her exclusive jurisdiction until such time as he either resurfaced or she resurfaced him.

Neuter the dogs before we let 'em loose for war. God, she even sounded like Buford now. The universe, it seemed, shaped life accordingly.

With the Thoom on high alert and in heavy disarray thanks to whispers and lies (her own and, apparently, some other beneficent source) planted where Kosugi might unearth them, such dogs might fight and chew themselves to exhaustion, in which case anyone appearing with a bone would seem holy. Fruehoff's report on her desk outlined several attacks and thefts carried out by Kosugi and his allies against various Thoom installations. With everyone coming down on the Thoom, that idiot group's hegemony would certainly be on the retreat. A taint of such magnitude provided very few hiding places.

Which left Atlantis.

Where Commander Sharon Deetz and a tight group, under Aileen's orders after Fucking Fruehoff's cock-up last year with the mighty Buford, had splintered from search-and-rescue efforts to anticipate miscellaneous opportunities.

Commander Deetz was a good one for miscellaneous opportunities.

~~~

Facing a fire at three in the morning killed all moods but bad.

"Who the *fuck* sold us out this time?!" Captain Desiree Quicho shouted spittle and rage. Yvonne and Neon worked water cannons from the *Ann*, hitting everything in sight that had any flammable possibilities. Blaze hadn't reached the main structure, only the lumber mill and its huge saws.

With the fire out, Keita assessed for flashpoint. "I don't think this fire was suspicious," she said.

"There's nothing in our lives that isn't suspicious," Desiree corrected. She wanted answers. "Find me a reason we can sleep with." Angrily, she headed for the Ann.

Equally angrily, she returned outfitted with a focum (focused microwave, with only two lethal settings out of seven total) rifle, night goggles, and portable sensor juxtaposed against ratty sleep shorts and a Gojira tee shirt a size too big for her. The dark of Atlantis surrounded them; half a football field away, a copse of trees enclosed the compound, with nothing but darkness beyond them.

Keita watched Desiree's approach and sighted Yvonne, backlit by the Ann's spot, similarly equipped, bringing up the rear.

"Going for a walk," the captain said as she passed Keita. She and Yvonne moved out.

They were gone an hour. When they got back, Keita showed them what she, Neon, and Shig had pieced together of their interrupted night.

Culprit: yebaum. Indigenous to Atlantis. Generally harmless. Forever hungry.

"Fire spread from the grill," said Keita, "and moved over here."

Shig pointed toward the nearest cluster of trees. "Two yebaums have been sitting just out of sight over there. Waiting. They must've caught their baby's scent."

"You got animals that know how to start fires?" said Keita.

"You don't?" said Shig.

Desiree stepped away from their lit area and zoomed her goggles toward the treeline. Two large, anxious yebaums pawed at the ground.

"You found the body?" Desiree asked.

"No," said Keita. "My guess is its fur caught, it dashed, and the family can't find it."

"Shut down the lights. We'll finish up in the morning."

"What about them if they can't find their baby? What do we do?" said Keita.

"They'll leave," said the captain, and left it at that.

A few days. Just a few days of building something. Was that too much to ask?

~~~

One never knew what one would find by putting micro-transmitters on animals. Best recon ever. Beasties went everywhere, saw everything, and were generally ignored.

A yebaum's hand obscured the view momentarily, but Deetz didn't have a doubt the first: that was Desiree Quicho. God damn. Deetz had come up a Navy woman. Quite a few who'd seen the light of Buford's truths were former military. Captain Desiree Quicho and her ships sat legendary among certain sets familiar with the "other" life. Of those who sailed through the eye of a needle, Quicho created embroideries.

Deetz now not only had her location, she had the number in her party, all thanks to one careless primate-thing (yebaums looked like tree-dwelling potatoes with arms and legs). How to capitalize on this? Intel. Watch and learn. Eventually capture. Possibly kill one or two? That'd be a coup and a half. This was inner-circle-level, upped-pay-grade serendipity. Aileen Stone would flip. Initially, Commander Deetz had bristled at having to remain in Atlantis; she'd ping-ponged four tours in various parts of the Middle East, so she knew what *indefinite* felt like. If she hadn't had people under her command in this idyllic setting, she might have halfway considered imagining herself in flip-flops and sunhat, but that was neither here nor there. Sharon Deetz had fashioned an orderly world for herself. The job was the job. It got done. It never even needed to ask.

~~~

Keita fished through equipment, found the proper scanner, and set to work. She walked a widening spiral around the demolished grill. She wanted to soothe Desiree. She even wanted to soothe the blackened and blistered lumber, which was now bereft of possibilities. First time in Atlantis and she was Keita LaFleur, Arson Investigator. Even though this wasn't arson. She'd seen the weary look on

Desiree's face nonetheless, same as everyone else in the crew. Keita didn't like that look. If a negative scan for accelerants put the captain back on even footing, she'd scan away. Her red-and-black boots were comfortable, and it was a good day for walking.

It was Yvonne who had had the brilliant stroke to broadcast the song "Purple Rain" on loop to accompany the cleanup. It was impossible not to re-center oneself, not to sing along, and not to feel something eternal and great in merely existing in order to sing that song, all praises to Prince, may he jam in peace.

Each lady's voice laid claim to a portion of the song best suited to her abilities: Yvonne passionately ad-libbing, Neon scatting guitar solos, Desiree crooning.

It made not finding any errant accelerants entirely sensible. This wasn't a mission; there weren't enemies twenty-four hours a day, seven days a week. There couldn't be. Who wanted their life to operate that way?

Accidents happened, and life went on. She had been in space, was personal friends with Silica Elves, and was now in Atlantis. *That* was the real life, whereas paranoia and constant suffering were strictly sick fantasy.

She'd make sure to conduct a thorough search, present her findings to the captain, then join them in the cleanup, reassessment, salvage (because Keita knew given ten minutes and a single screwdriver, she could repair a third of the damaged power tools), and build, because that's what they'd crossed the Blank to do: build.

To date, there hadn't been a person on the planet capable of keeping Keita LaFleur from building cool things.

~~~

Sharon Deetz had the most scarred hands of anyone he'd ever seen. *He*, in this instance, was second-in-command Truman Compoté, who was well aware that his life's conversation with the universe contained "Oh, you got jokes?" which had driven him to fights in home ec, fights in college nutrition and agricultural planning, fights his first week in military training.

He never stared at her hands. Actually, he was in awe of them. The commander never thought to mention how her hands had gotten so scarred, but it had to have been monumental.

Sharon tapped her map display. She wasn't drawing attention to anything on it. She tapped when she wasn't sure of a decision. Truman knew that tap.

"It's been two days," she ticked off. "We know where they are. I haven't wanted to send eyes on them for fear they might detect us." She glanced at Truman, whose face was always perfectly impassive for bouncing things off. "I have a platoon of thirty trained soldiers sitting on their asses for two days for fear that a group of four women might detect us. What happened to the world, Compoté?"

Not a tic of compassion. Not a hair of concern. Not a softening of agreement. "Speaking freely, ma'am?" he said from his seat across her large fold-out desk.

"Freely," Sharon said, eyes back on the map's data stream.

"Music videos."

"Thank you, Compoté," said Sharon, dismissing him and his crew cut.

"Yes, ma'am." Truman Compoté stood, nodded, and left.

Two days. Sharon hadn't wanted to relay messages through the Blank. In one hand, Captain Desiree Quicho. In the other hand, the *Linda Ann*. Neither worth rushing, at risk of losing both.

People thought cobras struck indiscriminately. They didn't. They waited, planned, considered, then moved lightning-fast. Time moved differently for them.

Sharon Deetz would be the cobra here, she decided. Cobra Commander. And if Compoté hadn't left, she might have tried that name on him just to see if his grizzled, weathered face would have betrayed a momentary warmth. Compoté was a good second, but he hadn't quite bridged the divide between the military and the mercenary just yet; was still way more military.

Deetz's hands confirmed beyond doubt that hers was a mercenary path. Mercenaries, unlike soldiers, were allowed to let the personal creep in a little on a job, even if there were thirty-two of them hidden away, wearing striking but practical uniforms on a supposedly mythical island.

Commander Deetz may have wanted a successful end to this mission, but *Sharon* Deetz—to her sudden-yet-clarified awareness—wanted the *Linda Ann*.

In the span of twenty seconds minus the presence of Truman Compoté, she'd learned something about herself: her wants and needs could kick obligation's ass in a heartbeat. She was obligated to the Nonrich Corp, as they paid for her lifestyle, the striking-but-practical uniforms, loads of equipment, tech, vehicles, and access to the best healthcare plan on the planet.

Did a word of that mean she would begrudge herself a boat? No, it did not.

She was Cobra Commander. Two days might tick into twenty. She'd wait. To her target, it would always look like the blink of an eye.

~~~

On the fourth day: rest. Desiree and crew, that is. In Atlantis. By going to see Guerris.

Engineer's Log: There are dark-skinned Atlanteans (I do not and will not use the woefully unsexy "Atlantideans" in my personal log), pale ones, olive ones. I say this because people can be basic as fuck and need reminding that life flows ever outward, not constrained into a narrow, fish-dead river. I've been assured that thousands of years from now, the LaFleur Scrolls will form the basis of a religion, so heed: This place is absoo-fooking-lutely beautiful. Neon says, "It's like the Federation, Hawaii, and the Outback had a three-way." There's zero reason to think I can add to that description. Plants become walls, flowers—not billboards— enhance sight lines, the clothing is varied and bright, varied and muted, simply varied: this place gives my eyes so much to see, I need new frames.

We're someplace called Sip to see an artist formerly known as Guerris but now going by the name Guerrilla. Apparently, the Jets' last foray into Atlantis changed him on a "cellular level" (Neon again). You can't say that about a peaceful person of art without ramping up expectations.

If nothing else, there'd better be a goatee on his chin.

~~~

What there were, were paintings *everywhere*. Large ones, small ones, rough sketches, masterpieces. There was also, noted Keita, a row of large, white canvases hung side by side, as though one out of a billion messages existed there for the seeking.

Guerris himself (no, *Guerilla*, Keita reminded herself): a fawn. A dusting of pollen atop dew. Wiry arms from gesticulating with brushes in hand; flat butt from sitting; wide, slightly wild eyes from attempting *vision*. He had a narrow face that ended in a hairless, nubby chin. Very hairless. As in no goatee. As in disappointing.

But he was a damn good hugger, throwing his entire soul and body into the embrace.

Keita returned the pleasure.

Guerilla broke the hug, upper torso only, bending back enough to look at Keita's face. He was smiling too genuinely to speak, but words were generally superfluous when so much joy was evident. He looked at her as though she were a new lover, not a new acquaintance, and though *that* wouldn't be happening, he was another good reason to be glad to come to Atlantis.

"Which language would you like to speak?" he asked her. "I can tell you speak several."

"Maba?" Keita asked.

He then greeted Keita with perfect Maba, finishing in Atlantidean with "It's an artful language" as enough explanation for this fawn knowing the rhythms and stoppages flawlessly.

They broke the hug, smiling.

"I'm not completely sure of my Atlantidean," Keita said.

"You'll be by the time you leave this house. Yvonne and Neon were naturals."

"Is true," said Yvonne, which in Atlantidean was *Jat Ch'kum*. To Neon: "What, two, three months?"

"Two," said Neon.

"It helps when immersion is dealing with the aftermath of a giant psychic whale thing," said Yvonne.

Guerilla motioned toward seats. "Their first time out with the Jetstreams was eventful," he told Keita.

"Understatement," Keita said. "I've read all the reports. You were a big inspiration to Milo and Ramses."

"They exaggerate everything," he said.

Desiree removed a tarp from the corner of a large canvas taking up considerable space in the sitting room. "Not this," she said. She clearly had seen it before, clearly knew its significance, and clearly wanted it—and nothing else—to serve in this instance as the final recap to Keita of the Jetstreams' most memorable foray into Atlantis.

The art hit the newcomer like a sermon.

Jetstreams' Last Stand. Guerrilla had intended it to stand alongside *The Court of Death*, *Life Retold*, *Mourning Angels*— even *The Universe Pursues*. It wasn't finished, but even its rough state demanded respect. Individuals were represented by swaths of color and energy, the entire painting seeming to be in subtle motion without giving any sense of a destination, more a cycle.

"This feels like thanks," said Desiree, who had piloted the *Ann* that last stand for what she'd thought might be the mortal last.

"You never ask for it," said the artist.

Desiree demurred, a slight smile directed toward the floor. She took a seat beside the canvas.

"You should have been there," Guerilla said to Keita. "It was as if we'd all sprouted wings, intending to fly."

"Angels," said Keita.

"Angels," he agreed. "Which reminds me: are they here?"

"Battle Ready Bastards? In space," said Desiree.

"And," he prompted, "you're here to?"

"Build," said Desiree.

Which caused him to beam even more. Keita revised her assessment; maybe she wouldn't bump uglies with him but, had he asked, she'd marry him. "May I help?" he said, eyes already roughing sculptures and oddly shaped water features. "I'd like to."

"I was hoping you would," said the Captain. "Today, though, we sight-see." She reached out and gave Keita's shoulder a squeeze. "This one is wonderful."

Guerilla smiled directly at the joy in Keita's eyes. "I see," he said. "Musicians are wandering the shores today. First stop?"

Without a word, the *hell yeah* was unanimous.

~~~

The instruments were clearly identifiable—most of them, anyway. Guitars, even when made from wood that seemed perpetually wet and shaped unlike guitars, were guitars. Vocals, no matter the language or interweaving harmonics, were vocals, and all the wanderers automatically kept respectful distance from one another, such that the effect of the wandering singles or troupes became one giant show divided into flowing sections.

The temperature, being warm but not uncomfortably so, was further mollified by the ocean's salty breeze keeping life flowing between bodies. Keita had expected it to be crowded. A huge free-roaming music festival on a sunny day? Guaranteed wall-to-wall back home in Montmartre.

Desiree's ears pricked up. A solo guitarist and a solo drummer riffed to the gods. The crew of adventurers, scientist, and artist found a patch of half grass, half sand and sat to marvel at what was clearly a competition and collaboration.

Perhaps the operative word for this log entry would be *clear*. There was a clarity to the space similar to the Elf catacombs. Not peace, not utter harmony, and definitely not paradise (she'd already noted two petty arguments among the citizenry and one outright instance of rudeness to a child—the latter corrected by a single arched brow from Captain Desiree Sandrine Quicho), but clarity existing inside a brain freed from the onslaughts of the unhinged. It was odd not seeing a single billboard, advertisement, or sponsorship banner but a welcome, good odd. There were informational kiosks at intervals where one could access the goings of the day (not everyone had a mobile device), but they looked like human-height hillocks that just happened to spring from the ground. Even the screens looked organically formed per each distinct hillock, some of which were covered in short grass, some appearing as wood, some abstract grey art.

Keita watched Desiree a moment. The captain—a person who had been all over the globe and witnessed more than nine-tenths of the entire human population had reason to imagine—wore her face completely enraptured by the sonic theatre mere meters away. Certainly, the fire hadn't been erased from the captain's mind, but at least the captain was pretending it was, and that meant a lot. Yvonne and Neon swayed and offered syncopated handclaps to the performers, who respected the gift by altering rhythms and beats to encourage even more improvisation.

Keita placed a checkmark on her mental sheet, approving Atlantis as a home for a woman who had become a good friend.

She also noticed the captain kept watch on the water near them, but for what? Leviathan was asleep, the kraken hadn't been released for four hundred years, and there was no truth whatsoever to the rumor that singularities were becoming amphibious. As far as they knew, there hadn't been a Thoom or Nonrich incursion since Buford's defeat, and even the Vamphyr (Keita admitted to preference at this pronunciation) had lain low these past quick months.

She made yet another mental note. If the captain was wary, so was she.

The guitarist shouted a sudden request. "Out-Blank suggestion!"

"Don't show off your travels!" the tiny drummer shouted good-naturedly. Xe beamed, though, hoping for something excellent to riff from.

"'Computer Blue'!" Desiree shouted back. The guitarist's solo seamlessly evolved into a passable facsimile of the transcendent guitar solo from said song. The drummer obliged with a resoundingly tasty, funky drum slap at the appropriate accent points. The guitarist, a man so round, his fingers were two of everyone else's, took this energy and transformed it into a repeating motif always just on the edge of completion but never quite, making grinning goofs of those in the audience familiar with the song, and everyone else simply grinning.

The festival didn't seem sponsored, didn't seem to be making any funds for anyone, celebrating religion, or leaning toward straight carnival. Keita leaned toward Guerrilla. "What's the purpose of this music?" she said into his ear, then offered her own for his response.

It took him a split second to understand the question. "To play!" he said into the curls of her hair. It hit her ear and made her smile and laugh.

~~~

Hashira Megu knew the Thoom didn't have the Bilomatic Entrance. Maurice knew it too, but pretexts were pretexts. Such a brazen act was a declaration of war whether the attacked knew a gauntlet had been thrown or not. Such was the way of things for those with power. Maurice had already authorized strikes against Thoom bases in the US and Russia. Nonrich had routed three Thoom research facilities the past three days alone. Even the vampires were enjoying the farce. In a bar fight, always punch for the body already going down.

As long as Megu was left to release infected yet enticing data out to hungry, frantic eyes—for there was no way the Thoom weren't scrambling wildly in full WTF mode—she could oblige Maurice et al their theatrics.

Of course, she could create another Bilomatic Entrance. It would be time-consuming to be done properly, but she suspected the thieves knew that. Normally, she would have had three prototypes in production simultaneously, but this particular project, with all its surprises, advancements, and quasi-miracles, demanded she in turn surprise herself and change her tactics. She could make a hundred Bilomatic Entrances before she died, if she were so inclined. But there was only one BE with her soul. That mattered. Mattered a lot.

Those who had the current BE would put it to use.

Megu never worked for less than she was worth. Megu never worked for anything beneath her talents.

And by whatever love she still felt for what she and Maurice had been, Hashira Megu never worked for free. That included her soul and all adjacent material.

She finished lunch quietly and privately in her lab, left the various bots to straighten things up (she'd had a taste for peanut noodles and baklava, the former for its exquisite simplicity, the latter for its joyous messiness, flaky bits of crust looking like a celebratory end to a parade), and set herself the task of finding precisely who had her property by meditating.

She had no interest in the games of vampires, Thoom, Kosugi, and the Nonrich Queen.

For herself, she would wait for the Jetstreams to show their hand.

~~~

"There's a music festival in Abba," said Compoté. Compoté found no humor in this. Cobra Commander pitied Compoté.

"A date, Number One?" she said.

"If so ordered."

Jesus. "No. Please relay that to everyone in case there was a slim hope rising in anybody. Nobody's going anywhere. That's how mistakes get made."

"Agreed. Which is why it should be only us. Mistakes won't get made."

"And intel gathered?"

"Likely," he said.

Likely. Eight months hiding, sitting, waiting, thumbs figuratively—except for one instance requiring disciplinary action—up butts in a fantastical setting smack-dab in the mundane world. Keeping discipline and focus under similar lack of action for eight months in Des Moines would be hard enough; her platoon deserved a tiny bit of levity, and morale always came from the top down.

"Native garb," said Sharon.

"Weaponry?"

"Small arms, nonlethal."

Compoté nodded but didn't smile. Not even an extra step to his stepping lively.

Ah, well. A ride in the native rover they'd procured would be fun; a little open speed, a little air, and the music would definitely be worth a late afternoon. Any music would. Except country.

Sharon Deetz, all wiry, steely-eyed Linda Hamilton inches of her, didn't do country.

~~~

Sharon couldn't help noticing that Atlantideans ate a lot of sausages: sausage sandwiches, sausage bites, skewered sausages. They clustered in groups of threes for conversation. As intel went, it wasn't vital, but rank had its privileges. Rank got its walk in the sun, its delicious food bits under the artwork of a perfect blue-green sky, and—even better—music good enough to make her long for her guitar.

Compoté returned to her side with two large cones in hand after being gone for several minutes. He handed hers over. It was filled with large, brown, dry globules. She looked at it suspiciously.

"I tried one. Tastes like key lime pie," he said. Then he gave what was for him a confused frown. "I could've *sworn* I heard Earth, Wind and Fire somewhere."

The commander transferred her suspicious look from the contents of the waxy cone to him.

"'Reasons,'" he said. "Instrumental."

One, she was surprised he knew about Earth, Wind & Fire. She, being something of a music snob, had dated several DJs in early college. "Should we keep eye out for Phillip Bailey?"

"I'd say more likely Verdine from the sound of it." He indicated the direction of the suspect music. Shoreside.

Sharon popped one of the jawbreaker-sized treats into her mouth. It actually did taste like key lime pie, crust and all, despite her brain telling her it should have tasted like a cinnamon bite or other doughnutty goodness. A key lime doughnut ball. Atlantis was weird.

They wove through the festival crowd, silently munching, both constantly watching. The closer they got to the source of Compoté's mystery, the less the pretense of watching for anything in particular held. Insects kept trying to land on Sharon's treats, but if that was the greatest irritation of the day, she'd take it.

And then it hit her. She stopped. "Truman! You brought me Schweddy balls. Oh my god, you have a soul."

Compoté stifled a smile. "Just hoping ma'am liked 'em" was all he said.

A swell of music and cheering swallowed the small laugh she gave him.

The music wasn't Earth, Wind & Fire.

It was David Bowie.

And while the rumor that Amelia Earhart lived somewhere on this vast paradise was eternal, there was no way in hell the late David Bowie shared the same postal code.

"Did you..." said Compoté.

"'Fame,'" said Sharon. They walked faster.

A mass of people surrounded the tune. Now and then, Sharon caught snatches of the musicians as the crowd shifted.

"Seriously," said Sharon, "who the hell here knows

'Fame' by David Bowie? Scan the crowd closest to the musicians."

They separated. When they met at the completion of their circle, Compoté shook his head curtly.

"Don't be obvious," she said. "Don't go military on me. Nothing?"

He relaxed into place at her side. "Nobody stays in place more than five seconds."

"These musicians are too damn good."

"Too damn good," he seconded.

"Okay, so there's a chance there're interests here, or just a huge coincidence I wouldn't put money on in my own mama's casino."

The music segued from Bowie-esque to strictly Atlantidean jazz. A singer's voice boomed its thanks to Desiree Quicho and crew for their inspiration for this impromptu out-Blank jam session. The crowd hooted its pleasure.

Deetz and Compoté looked at each other.

"Get back to the rover. I don't want to take any chance of them spotting us on radio. Tell a small squad to haul ass to that build site. Have them bring mines. Lots of mines. Tell them to stay invisible for thirty minutes, then have them radio me. Tell them I will be on my way. I'll meet you at the rover in fifteen minutes."

Compoté left.

Sharon got close enough to the musicians for her shout of "Encores! More!" to be heard over the din.

This sent the musicians into paroxysms of joy and renewed out-Blank improvisation.

Nobody *ever* left during encores.

In the rover, Compoté told her, "This is a huge risk, ma'am."

I'm getting that boat. "We're prepped for opportunity," said Commander Deetz. "Opportunity is not without risk. Understood?"

"Understood."

She could sail anywhere in the world on that boat.

Or nobody would.

~~~

When the last grunt placed the last mine, Sharon gave the fallback order. Unfortunately, a sudden migration of yebaums from the trees blocked what was otherwise an efficient backfall, illustrating the importance of awareness of local fauna and flora as more than background noise. She hadn't known there were so many of them. They must have blended with the trees.

And they were quiet, little more than the rustling a sustained wind might cause. Like a solemn procession out of a church on a high holy day.

She considered opening fire, except that'd sully an otherwise incredible moment of oneupsmanship: Captain Desiree Quicho's ship festooned with mines, a clear message to walk away from that troublesome Jetstream life and surrender to Sharon's superior force.

The yebaums paid the expensively outfitted people no mind, unhurriedly picking their way around grunt, commander, and Compoté alike, some of the potato-shaped tree dwellers carrying offspring on their backs, others munching wads of leaves as they passed.

Sharon held up an arm and made a fist. There had to have been at least a hundred meandering through.

Her group—self, Compoté and two people on long-range perimeter duty included—totaled twelve.

In the sudden stillness she picked up the nearly subsonic thrum of a rover moving at breakneck speed.

Cobra Commander tapped the weapon at her hip and gave a thumbs-up, telling herself, *Even if you steal a boat, you don't get to ride it for free.*

~~~

The breakneck speed of the rover? Neon at the controls. Wide-open terrain outside of the forested areas and a vehicle capable of making the Kessel run in twelve parsecs? When else was that kind of freedom not only accessible but encouraged?

"Faster!" Yvonne shouted.

"You got this?" Desiree said, seated beside Neon.

"I got this." The key was keeping the rover a minimum of two feet off the ground, ensuring plenty of time to compensate for sudden wind dips, particularly as she had the rover entirely on manual. The best way to get to know a machine was at its most basic and raw. Engineering 101.

The best way to work off hyperactivity due to overconsumption of sweets, hellacious music, sunshine, and sausages: adrenalin. Everyone would be sliding into naps by the time she parked.

I'd make a helluva parent, she thought, tempted to see how the rover handled a corkscrew, but filing it as a maneuver likely best attempted alone.

She glanced. A sudden odd readout. "Hey, so, I'm getting some weird energy."

Desiree leaned over.

Keita leaned over closer. "I've got this set to scan the boat once we're in range. I figure if anybody's gonna hit us, they're going for the boat first, right? The *Ann's* beating like she's got extra hearts. We'll be there in two minutes." Keita scooched deeper into her chair and fixed her eyes through the whizzing windshield on exactly where she knew the *Linda Ann* would be. "Or one."

~~~

"Do these things bite?" Compoté asked.

"We're about to learn. Squad out!"

Sharon bolted. The Nonrich vehicles weren't too far away, owing to the fact that, again, she'd assumed she'd had the solid upper hand.

One of the people she had on perimeter duty squawked in her earpiece, "Ma'am, incoming."

She planned to fire the two people she had on perimeter

duty.

Yebaums didn't bite, but a few of the younger ones grabbed on to running legs in the most fascinating game a yebaum had created since forever, leading to all kinds of slapstick, lots of cussing, and a vehement shout from Sharon not to use force. They may not have bitten yet, but she'd seen teeth in the crowd, sharp, serrated, piranha-like teeth, and she hadn't made it to fifty-two merely to be eaten by potato monkeys, a thought preceding the heart-dropping chill of spotting a dust cloud failing to catch up with the vehicle causing it as a grey-and-black rover screamed first into view, then into even rapider approach, then to a dirt-and-grass swirling stop a hundred yards away from Sharon Deetz and the boys of plunder.

"Wars have been lost because somebody stopped to take a piss, Compoté," she said.

Desiree, Neon, Keita, and Yvonne exited the rover.

"We outnumber them three to one," he said.

Sharon resolved herself to what was about to come. "Pissing in the wind. Munitions, get the hell over here!" Bodies laden with tech scrabbled to a halt in front of her. "Slide detonation into my phone." Furious swiping ensued, absolutely manic rapid-fire.

Sharon held her phone high above her head.

~~~

"Pot, what are those attached to my ship?" Desiree asked.

"Likely bombs," said Keita.

Sharon, who couldn't hear them, shouted, "Explosives!" with a jiggle of her phone hand. "Back in the rover!"

Keita threw a middle finger up for "Like!" and another middle finger for "Hell!"

Desiree laid a hand on Keita's bicep to draw the message down. "Thank you, dear. Hostiles," she shouted, "you have one chance to make sure the family Christmas photo isn't a sad affair for your relatives. Get that shit off my boat."

Sharon brought the phone down and tapped. A mine

went off aft starboard that left a sizeable dent in the *Ann*'s reinforced hull, scattering yebaums extremely quickly.

Desiree didn't take her eyes off Sharon. Then Desiree took a step forward. Keita touched Desiree's elbow. Desiree spun and headed for the rover. The crew followed.

They entered the rover.

It quickly powered up and zoomed toward the hostiles.

I have miscalculated the fuck out of this situation, Sharon thought, frantically tapping her phone. Two more explosions went off, rocking the ship and raining small bits of debris. "Scatter!"

The rover circled the small group once, forcing them into the exact opposite of scattered. The interlopers huddled in a loose mass.

The rover stopped, silently hovering.

Desiree's voice issued from the rover's speakers. "My ship takes any more damage, I ram this up each one of your asses individually. If you've signaled for backup, tell 'em don't bother. No point backing up corpses. Weapons *down*."

"Open fire! Bring that tin down!" Sharon whipped her gun up and followed the rapid reports of the squad with what she hoped were extremely precise shots of her own. Rovers didn't come with a lot of entry points, but here and there they had grillwork and intakes; a high-caliber bullet in either couldn't be good.

The rover did a curlicue spinout, then shot toward the shooters at high speed, scattering them again. The vehicle stopped and Desiree immediately exited in a tuck-and-roll close enough to Compoté to spin on the ball of a foot and sweep him. As he fell, she perfectly coordinated elbowing his nuts with the moment his back hit the ground, followed by a kneeling uppercut when he did a crunch upward in pain.

Neon and Yvonne sprang out, focums firing. Three hostiles crumpled into convulsions in seconds. Those still standing looked from Sharon to the field of play. Being a mercenary was well and good till you realized it didn't come with a Veterans' Administration to look out for one's long-term health and vested interests in the event of a sudden unexpected ass-whupping.

"Weapons DOWN!" Desiree shouted again.

Sharon dropped hers, providing the mercs with the leadership they sought and needed.

Desiree, with Compoté's gun in hand, advanced on the hankty witch trying to blow holes in her ship.

"You came all the way out here to be an asshole," said Desiree.

Sharon allowed a defiant glint in her eyes and posture but wisely said nothing.

"Please don't tell me your name is Becky," said Desiree, close enough now to hold a hand out for the phone.

Sharon complied.

"Sit the fuck down," said Desiree. "Yvonne?"

"Yeah?"

"Shoot 'em."

The two focums made it so. Two mercs down.

"Him too," said Desiree.

Compoté's groaning got flicked off.

"You know that line, *You come into my house?*" Desiree said inches from Sharon's weathered face. Desiree hated close-talking as much as any sane person, but she needed to speak this woman's language a moment. "You also know how they say you covet shit, you fuck up every time? Oh, you fucked up. You. Fucked. Up. You leaned in to the fuckup." She tapped her comm. "Keita? Would you mind assessing the damage? Thank you." She took a step back. "This is even too petty for Thoom. Nonrich, right? Fucking Bufords. Just give me a day without fucking Bufords!" She threw up her hands—one of which held the phone—in frustration.

Three more explosions smacked her ship.

"I didn't have time to close the screen," said Sharon.

"Captain?" said Keita, out of the rover now. "There's more damage."

"Thank you, luv." To Sharon: "I really should kill you. I should drag you up and down this shore, mollywhopping your ass every inch." She tossed the phone aside. "Neon?"

Neon blasted it.

"I," said Captain Desiree Sandrine Quicho, "am tired of being preyed upon by fuckups. How many more in your complement, and where are they?"

Sharon steeled up.

Desiree nodded toward Sharon's scarred hands. "Combat?"

"Yes."

"So, you know what pain is. You know it's unnecessary?"

Sharon gave the information.

"Call that in to Shig," Desiree told Yvonne. "Tell him to put 'em somewhere and give 'em some poetry. Maybe it'll humanize 'em." She faced Sharon. "Who's got the other munitions key?"

Sharon pointed.

"Get it. Hands and knees. Disarm everything. Anything more powerful than a dragoon's fart rocks my boat, you die. If you think I'm fucking around, you die. Do you understand the words coming out of my mouth?"

Sharon nodded.

"Comply."

Sharon crawled to the unconscious munitions master and retrieved the control. She indicated another unconscious body with her chin. "She has one too."

Desiree nodded once.

Sharon repeated the procedure. When she returned to a seated position, she held her hands up, devices proffered. Desiree grabbed them, then stepped back from striking range. She gave the pads to Yvonne and kept walking, giving one instruction: "Shoot her."

CHAPTER FIVE

Suit Up

"Ramses spoke with me about this," said Shig. His office was disturbingly quiet, but she hadn't wanted to speak with him among the embedded shrapnel pieces, damaged walls, and shattered glass of Water's Edge, let alone the bites and lesions inflicted on the *Ann*.

"And likely Fiona has, and Milo, and Kichi, and now me," said Desiree.

"You're asking us to change our ways, something which I neither have the power nor influence to do, anyway. The same I told each of them."

"How are we supposed to keep you safe, Shig? You've got seventy-five people in holding. What are you supposed to do, put them on a peninsula and cut off escape?"

"I've heard of your Australia."

Desiree ticked off on her fingers. "Thoom. Nonrich. Vamphyr. And that's just who we absolutely know. Bigfoot's probably got a crew here too. You're going to have to actually monitor the Blank, and you're going to have to stick guard dogs at the perimeter. Anybody not automatically broadcasting a certain signature, chase 'em out until they get the message."

"Your entire world will know about us for certain."

"Maybe it's time they did, Shig. They gotta grow up sometime. And don't tell me about Atlantis's long history. Fuck Atlantis's long history. You exist courtesy of a dimensional quirk, not a glittering-spired destiny. That dimensional quirk might collapse at any moment, and then you'll have a Walmart. You ready for that?"

His shoulders dropped. "We are not ready."

"Acclimation. After ten, twenty years of chasing folks out, you might be ready to let 'em in."

"Doesn't your United States president—"

"We don't speak of him."

"The fact remains: we are not exclusionists."

"Shig...I love you. Know that. But that's utter bullshit. Self-congratulatory bullshit. Amelia flying through the Blank doesn't make you non-exclusionist. You're not xenophobic, no, but as many times as y'all have zipped out-Blank without leaving maps, you cannot pretend the high ground precludes you from getting dirty hands. A faction's been working on a dimensional transporter. This means they could pop into Atlantis any time they wanted to. Walmart, Shig."

"Not ready for its people."

"Then do what I ask. Present my proposal. Fast-track it. I've got the device, and we've got people trying to scrub its research out of existence, but it's more delay and divert than defeat. Be nice if it was defeat and I could finish building my frikkin' house..."

"How damaged is your ship?"

"Enough. I'm sailing her home. By the time I reach port, maybe I won't want to wipe half of humanity off the face of the Earth."

"You could repair it here."

"Been in one fight here already when I wanted to be in

none. I got ideas for when I get home. We'll sail soon."

"What if local councils say these fights are with you, that it's you who should be barred?"

"My home is whenever Smoove massages my neck and my brothers cook too much for dinner. I'll leave and hope you'll visit."

"Ramses said similar." Shig's spirits dropped even lower. He was in danger of borrowing sugar from Hades. "What about Keita? She's only just gotten here."

"No matter where you go...there's a fucker waiting to be a fucker. Trust me, she knows that better than anyone."

"This is fucked."

"Yes, yes, it is, and I wish I knew a way around it. I wish I could finish that house and start sketching again. Or start a summer camp, pack the *Ann* with kids, and bring 'em here without worrying that Becky or Brad is gonna strap bombs to my ship. I can't. And the difference between here and out there is the threat isn't manufactured, exaggerated, or designed to be capitalized from. And I realize it takes hella vag for me to say *I can't build my house, close your entire civilization's borders*, but we've told you from the day we met: if Buford or any of them take root here, that's it for you. Cancer. I'm going to have Neon slap the fye out of every single one of them in holding to find out if there are any more in hiding. You run into any more sleepers I should know about?"

"Not since last time."

"If they're here, they're here in small numbers. We'll deal with 'em as we go. I am *fully* aware we brought this on you. Let me do what I do best."

Shig grimaced. "Battle?"

"No, luv. I'm best at avoiding battle. Let me carry the weight of any decisions you have to make."

"You're a good human, Desiree Quicho."

"Not yet. I will be."

~~~

Keita swiped the back of her hand across her forehead,

leaving the grimy skin grimier than before. "If I understand you correctly—"

"You know you do," said Desiree.

"Rather than give me a few days to repair and enhance *Ann* here...you want to chug home and?"

"Can you tell how pissed off I am?"

"Yeah."

"No, I mean deep inside."

"Fifteen on a level of ten."

"Buford's scat's still out there in our world," said Desiree. "I'm taking the fight to 'em straight and true."

"We're gonna fuck with corporate America?"

"Yep."

"I'll unpack my power suit."

~~~

In New York, Aileen Stone wore her power suit to full effect. Men avoided eye contact with her, women praised her as first of her name, and the president of the United States sat ramrod-straight while she dressed him down.

"The stupid shit you're doing?" she said.

He nodded, jowls dancing, making her think precisely of a Saint Bernard on a trampoline.

She hated Saint Bernards.

"Stop it. Now get the fuck out." One had to know how to talk to these "governing" types. Especially when they got the shiny title "president" pinned to their chest and first pick of the juice boxes.

His ridiculous toupee levitated the rest of his doughy body. "Ma'am" got mumbled toward her shoes, then he left to rejoin his secret service brahs denied entry to her office.

So far, no one had thrown a rock at her windows, despite everyone of course knowing they were behind the deception, even though they weren't. Certain games had to be played at certain levels. For the moment, Thoom and Kosugi were content to squabble.

~~~

"Nonrich waits on us," said Madam Cynthia to vampire lord Ricoula via Skype because Thoom. "As long as their attention is on what happens between us and Kosugi, we can get away with all kinds of incursions."

~~~

"Covertly," said Megu to Mo. "We have the advantage."

"Of course covertly," said Mo Kosugi. Hell, ninja or no, no one was on his payroll because of snappy dressing.

~~~

Aileen sat at her desk, tapped the inlaid screen, picked up her stylus, and pondered her manifesto. She hadn't drafted a proper manifesto since taking over. It was more for future generations; certainly, the underlings weren't worthy to know of its existence, let alone see it. It'd be like showing theory to a cat. But by the time Nonrich fell—and of course it would fall—historians would look upon such writings as key points in the world's disgustingly uneven social evolution. They'd know that Aileen Stone (at a certain point, she'd reveal her real name; future historians deserved that) had not only tried to guide the world but had made it sit at attention and actually learn a thing or two.

Hoarding wealth and influence weren't bad either. Definitely wouldn't say no there.

In all honesty, it was one thing to want to guide the people, another entirely to want to be among them.

She didn't feel rushed. The fall would take a good hundred years to see Nonrich's ideals permanently overturned, and she had no plans on cloning herself.

Aileen Stone was not one for designer knock-offs.

Best to begin with a quote.

I was born a coal miner's daughter, she wrote, which while ragingly coincidental was also true, and she'd be damned if she'd waylay her personal veracity for some rickety country singer. Daddy owned the mines. Several. He was long dead, buried somewhere. She couldn't remember exactly where. Aileen Stone didn't revere bones.

"Delete sentence." The text disappeared. Coal might feel a bit too archaic by the time the writings of Robin May Allen graced some researcher's life.

I was born in darkness. That felt good, felt right. Very portentous and foreshadowing. *My eyes adjusted quickly.*

She smiled, tapped the stylus emphatically against her desktop, and continued.

Outside, the world turned.

CHAPTER SIX

"We really gonna take on Nonrich?" asked Yvonne as Desiree studied maps and graphs.

"Yep," said Desiree.

"Like, topple?"

"You can't topple that. Too bottom-heavy. Burn it from the top down."

"You have a plan?"

"Not yet."

"Dinner's ready. Keita has the ship on auto. Neon's checked out the two prisoners."

"They kill each other yet?"

Yvonne shook her head.

"Rude," said Desiree. She'd placed them in the same brig. People separated get ideas; together, they get on nerves.

"Captain?"

Desiree had yet to look up from the landfill of papers, displays, and tablets covering her desk. She now did so.

Yvonne was generally cool, generally non-struck by the supposed wonder of it all, and had never once—till now—looked anything less than the square-jawed, the-fuck-you-looking-at goddess she was.

"You don't think we should wait till all the band's back?" she asked Desiree's waiting look.

"I've sailed this world by myself since I was a teenager. I didn't build this ship but I've damn well healed her enough times. The day I wait when I can handle something myself is the day I pack it in."

"But—"

"Let me finish. I have also never been half-assed or inconsiderate enough to harm others with my incompetence. What we're going to do is start fires. The more fires we start, the more flaming rats run to other parts of the house, the quicker the house burns. I'll come up with a plan," said Desiree.

"And if you don't?"

"*We'll* come up with a plan."

"That works. Come eat."

While they ate, the Bilomatic Entrance established a wireless connection with the *Ann* and caught up on current events.

~~~

"I thought we were on vacation" was the first thing Neon said.

"We're never on vacation," said Desiree. "Pass the butter."

The butter remained sitting. "You eat too much butter. And you know what I mean. What happened to *We just came from the moon*? 'Kay? Maybe a personal day in a tourist spot wasn't the best idea, but there are other places to go." Neon passed Desiree the spinach. Unsalted.

"Keita, how we looking? Sail-worthy?" asked Desiree.

"That stress fracture I told you about? Going through the Blank stressed it the hell out. This ship's been through too much lately, and the Gang's been *begging* to do an overhaul. Crack's extended to under the ship. I can repair it but I'd rather do it in port."

"We taking on enough water to drown those two down there?"

"Back up," said Neon. "Why'd the Blank stress the ship?"

Keita's eyes widened, puzzled. "You do know the Blank shifts you a little every time you go through, right?"

"As in *Star Trek* transporter suicide machine?"

"No! Just, you know, slight teeny temporal-physical strain." She held up her hands to stay worry. "You see I eagerly went through, yes?"

Yvonne laid a hand gently on Keita's shoulder. "Yes, but you're crazy. Captain? This is new."

"It's not a worry," said Desiree.

Neon and Yvonne had an entire conversation in a single glance, then both mimicked Desiree. "It's not a worry," they said.

"Except to a ship that's been blown all to hell for eight months straight and patched on the fly with thoughts and prayers," said Keita. "Honestly, I thought you guys knew."

"Captain?" said Yvonne.

"Yes?"

"We're gonna table this."

Desiree nodded assent.

"Boston's nearest. We could put into port there. Temporarily hide in plain sight for a minute," Keita said. "Just long enough for me to suit up, get under there without worrying about sharks, starving merfolk, or pissed-off singularities for more than fifteen minutes. Do my job in peace, yes? She's in no danger of sinking. Yet."

"The *Ann* looks like hell. We're just gonna waltz it next to Chad's weekend schooner?" said Neon.

"Stow anything that makes the ship look badass," Desiree directed Keita. "Camo as much as we're able."

"A lot of stealth tech took major damage."

"We do what we can. In and out, ladies?" She met each of her crew's eyes.

"In and out," Neon agreed.

Not a notion ever to be trusted.

~~~

It was after ten PM the next day when they pulled into port, a moonlit night with very few clouds. The *Ann* had a few extra dings and a bit of smoke coming from her, but that was because a singularity had rammed her. Not the first that'd happened; wouldn't be the last. ("Singularity impact kill those two in the hold?" "No." "Damn.") Boston, which often tried to stay awake as long as New York, was in late-night bro mode, which meant it had sportsed somewhere.

"You sure we want a public port?" said Neon.

"I own this slip. We don't have much choice," said Desiree. "Tie her off and disembark. Give her a chance to rest without worrying about us. This city's ninety-five percent swanky hotels. Showers and somebody else's bed wouldn't hurt."

"You're remarkably calm for all this," said Neon.

"Sister luv, I've had eleven ships in my life. If I mourned each one, I'd be bitter by now. Yvonne still below?"

"Yeah."

Desiree ducked her head into the stairwell. "Yvonne! Bring our guests. They're with me." When Sharon and Compoté—in civilian clothing from the *Ann*'s locker—stood before her, she said quite simply, "If you're looking for your opportunity to escape, this is it. Five seconds. In six seconds, I implant you with a chip. Go more than twenty-five feet away from any of us, we'll know. Touch any kind of communication device, we'll know. Boston is crawling with Agents of Change. We've already sent them your info. They, too, will know if you're in violation of the leash. Do we understand each other?"

"We haven't rebutted," said Sharon.

"Beautiful," said Desiree. She indicated their wrists. They proffered them. Keita injected them. "If you're resourceful enough to slit your wrists to get 'em out, kudos," said Desiree.

Even camouflaged, the *Linda Ann* was clearly no ordinary ship. It garnered attention. Desiree hated attention. Couldn't be helped, although the detour was more for the captain than her ship. Desiree needed her bearings back. Needed to set things on pause.

The ship was locked down. Nothing now but to disembark. Necessary equipment nestled efficiently in shoulder bags each woman slung over a neck and shifted to a hip. A group of drunks, pasty under the moonlight, who'd been loudly cursing each other—and who the crew realized were dawdling to see who might come off the sweet boat whose lights had just blinked off—made their way along the dock, two of the five wearing red baseball caps.

The crew of the *Linda Ann* viewed them from the gangplank. The Chads sobered long enough to view back. Three black ladies, a Mexican lady, a white lady, and a white dude. The drunken Chads did the social math, and it didn't add up to America.

Something, though, made the small group of men stay quiet as the strange assembly made way wordlessly off the plank and equally wordlessly down the dock away from the three Chads, one Steve, and Donnie.

That's how the men thought of their group: Three Chads, One Steve, and Donnie. A couple of the Chads always wore their caps when out for a night. Boston. Woooo. Fuck everybody and everything! Another woooo just in case the first needed translation.

Spooorts!

"Team caps," Neon murmured to Yvonne.

"No," Yvonne murmured back.

The ladies felt the eyes watching them until they were out of sight of the drunks, and only then did Neon and Yvonne realize how tensed they were.

"Can I say it?" Neon said.

"Say it," said Yvonne.

"Groups of white men freak me the hell out. Especially drunk ones. Bad mojo."

"Testify."

Sharon glanced over her shoulder, but she couldn't see the Chads anymore. She caught Neon in turn glancing at her. "No argument from me," Sharon said.

"We'll get to a main street, get a ride, get a hotel," said Desiree.

Fireworks exploded over the water, far from the docks yet large enough to brighten the area. Then a volley.

"Is there major sports happening?" said Neon.

Keita already had her comm out. "Summer festival," she read. "Downtown tourist harbor."

"That explains the wandering drunks," said Desiree.

"I think nighttime in the city explains the drunks," said Yvonne. "Hallmark of civilization, right?"

"Change in plans," said Desiree. "Let's eat, then let's get back to the ship."

"Bad mojo?" asked Neon.

"Bad mojo. Let's get the fuck out of here before traffic becomes terrible," said Desiree.

They got the fuck out of there.

They'd gotten halfway through the dessert course when Keita pulled her comm from her knapsack. "Captain...I got fire sensors going off."

Neon pulled out her comm. "I show a ride in the area. Minivan. Five minutes out."

Yvonne stood. "I'll get the check."

Desiree sighed and set her fork down.

~~~

They exited the minivan blocks away and covered the rest on foot.

The *Ann* burned a bit. Fore, midships, and aft, flames licked over the railing. There wasn't a lot that was flammable, but enough. The dispersal of the flames screamed Molotov cocktails. The liquor on the ground confirmed it. Someone had even tried to pour the word great on the gangplank and light it but had only succeeded in a few scorch marks and likely singed shoes.

And of course, fire suppression on the ship was offline because, you know, heaven forbid Keita actually get to do her freaking job.

They didn't watch for very long. Desiree and Keita were quickly up the gangplank, both reaching into their bags and pulling out a string of gelled balls, which they snapped from casings and lobbed into the nearest flame. The heat exploded the gels into flash-dispersed fire retardant. They repeated the procedure until the only things left were scorch marks on the deck, a few licks on the pilot cabin, and two women with soot and sweat mixing on their faces.

Fucking. Humid. Boston.

And, of course, *now* sirens.

Desiree and the engineer descended the gangplank to return to the group.

"Why do we do this?" said Neon. "Why in fuck are we jumping out of planes, flying around the fucking moon, getting rammed by dinosaurs, and having our *goddamned boat tried burned to the goddamned ground!*"

Part of the Linda Ann's skin showed under the clear light of the moon where the camo tech had failed.

"We don't make a difference, Desi," said Neon. "This wasn't ghouls, vampires, angry fucking gnomes or the ghost of bitch-ass Custer. This was people."

"Let it go," said Yvonne.

Wasn't meant to let go. "This was *people*," Neon repeated. The angry, poison tears finding purchase on her face would have killed a bear with a single drop. "This could have been the same people we saved three weeks ago. The same people we'll save a year from now. The same people who have done nothing but consume and destroy every last good intention anybody attempts."

"Nee..." Yvonne hoped to lead her off.

"Fuck, no. This will not stand." Neon turned on a heel. She didn't know exactly where she was going, but she knew whoever was there when she got there would not have a good day. Not for a long time.

It was just a matter of following the scent of beer and angry laughter. Angry laughter had a sharp scent. It smelled like fear.

"Let her go," said Desiree.

"I should go with her," said Yvonne.

"I need you to stay with me," said Desiree. "Otherwise, somebody's gonna die tonight."

"Understood."

Neon returned twenty minutes later.

"Did you find them?" Desiree asked, voice as cold and emotionless as the final tide.

"Yes," said Neon.

"Did you hurt them?"

"No."

"Good. That's not a stain you need," said Desiree.

"I shouted, 'Hey!'...and they ran."

"What'd they see?" said Desiree.

"A woman coming to kick their ass."

Yvonne weighed in, pointing at Neon. "There's something dark in you."

"You just noticing that?" said Neon.

"No, I mean really. Like Dark Phoenix shit. Like you have just begun to fuck people's shit up," said Yvonne. "I felt it when you first saw 'em on the dock."

"And you're sure they torched my boat?" said Desiree.

"Positive," said Neon.

Desiree picked up her pack by a strap and swung it over her shoulder. "If it seems like those sirens are coming this way, move us out. I'll be back."

"You said—" said Neon.

"I said you didn't need that stain."

She left.

Neon and Yvonne remained rooted to the spot. Silently. Their captain was gone.

"She's not gonna kill anybody, is she?" asked Keita.

"I don't think she's got to kill you to erase you from Earth," said Yvonne. "There's about to be some hellacious offscreen physical and spiritual violence."

"You two, back on the ship," said Neon to Sharon Deetz and Truman Compoté. Neon thought of the captain's return, likely late, likely tired, likely pained.

She, Keita, and Yvonne stared at each other under a moon that was now a bit hazier than before.

"What do we do?" said Keita.

"I'll brew tea," said Neon.

Deetz and Compoté marched across the ship, down the stairs, and back into the hold in respectful silence.

~~~

Desiree found them.

She wasn't in any mood to fight. She pulled out her focum and shot each before they even realized they were being shot. They kissed concrete hard.

She stripped them naked. Shoved wallets and phones in a pair of salmon chinos, cinched the pants closed at the waist with the belt, then tied the legs together, looping it across her chest. The rest of the clothing, shoes, and caps she gathered in a pile; emptied atop it one of the bottles of vodka they'd bought that they hadn't used to torch her boat; pulled a match from her bag. The flame wouldn't travel to anything else, but the other chinos and patriotic jeans of the Chads wouldn't live to see another day.

She left with the sling containing their identities, regretting the fact that the five naked men would see tomorrow, and the day after, and likely the one after that.

When she was back on the Ann's gangplank, she whipped the pair of pants into the dark Boston water, where she gave not a damn how long it'd take for them to saturate and sink. No, her thoughts were laser-focused right now, first of which was she hoped someone had brewed tea. Boston was as good a place as any to start a battle and end a war. She'd put the word out to the Agents of Change.

After tea? Party.

~~~

"It wouldn't surprise me if one of those fuckers was Nonrich," said Desiree, who had gotten up extra early the next morning to scrub the deck and found everyone else had the same idea.

She hadn't found Keita.

Keita was in the murky water.

Ship got fixed; Keita emerged pissed: "It's like I can smell the water through my flipping skin!"

The scene: breakfast and the spreading of vengeance like butter on toast.

Which Neon had denied Desiree. Butter.

Sharon and Compoté sat at the breakfast table with them. It was one thing to fuck someone's world ideologically, another entirely to fuck up someone's ship. *Without any intention of repairing it*, Sharon quickly mentally added. "You expect me to tell you whatever I know about operations here?" said Sharon.

"Do you know any?" Desiree said.

"No."

"Did not think so. What was Nonrich paying you?"

"Hundred thousand plus perks."

"I'll double it if you stay out of our way and make yourself useful. Do I speak your language?"

Sharon paused. Truman was the one who operated out of duty and ideology, even though neither she nor he had ever truly pegged down exactly what Nonrich's ideology was. Truman caught the pause and gave his commander a single nod.

"That a secret nod of *play along till we become clever enough to fuck things up*?" Desiree said.

"No," said Compoté, "that's a nod of *I'd like to retire with all my original body parts*."

"Surprisingly prudent," Sharon noted.

"Yes, ma'am."

"I feel I should interject," said Neon, "as I'm the realness, which, by the way, is my code name. The Realness." She locked that in with Desiree and Yvonne with a *don't test me* tilt of her head. "Are we gonna pretend to abide these fuckers?"

"Neither one of us are teenagers," said Sharon of she and Truman. "We have definitely not drunk the Kool-Aid, so to speak."

"I know this how?" said Desiree.

"We know the party line is ultimate bullshit," said Sharon. "We've been to *Atlantis*. Hell, we fucking fight Jetstreams!" she said, indicating with widening hands the crew before her. "You're fucking fairy tales and myths in our ranks. I'd have to be ten levels of stupid to die for Nonrich solely for their bullshit. Honestly, we mostly just sit around, looking badass."

"We do," said Compoté.

"Just so you know, we don't fall under the heading *Jetstreams*. They're not proper nouns," said Yvonne.

"That's how we think of you," said Sharon.

"What do you think of the Thoom?" said Desiree.

"Influential as fuck. Stupid as fuck."

"Crewcut, she tells you to behave, what do you do?" asked Desiree.

"Already said I want all my limbs," Truman said.

"Keita, I want you and Yvonne on final repairs. I want the *Ann* prepped for speed. Here's what we're gonna do: make some noise, then get the fuck out. And, Yvonne?"

"Yes?"

"Any Chads get near this ship while I'm gone? Revoke their white privilege with all due prejudice."

"Motherfuckers will take a knee before me," said Yvonne.

"In that case, dismissed. Neon, you're with me."

The crew of the *Linda Ann* grabbed their respective breakfast sandwiches and napkins, and set to work.

Sharon and Compoté were sent back to holding while Neon and Desiree conversed, then released later that afternoon when Desiree said, "Come on."

~~~

"I know the obvious Nonrich buildings. I want you to point out three that are not," said Desiree. She wore a bright yellow mid-calf summer dress with large hibiscus patterns dotting it, satchel strap over the shoulder and between the boobs in case anyone they encountered—meaning primarily her accomplices—needed to catch hands. Her orange flats, stylish yes, were excellent running/scaling shoes.

The Nonrich commander: green blouse, tan slacks. Crewcut: Bruce Lee tee shirt (*Be as water*; it was Milo Jetstream's shirt; he'd be pissed) and basic jeans. Three nondescript people in an increasingly nondescript city, but then, all cities were becoming nondescript cookie cutters of the same bistros, the same downtown condos, the same faux "authentic" rented art. Pockets of personality dwindled.

Thoom and Nonrich grew.

"You're assuming we know," said Sharon, scanning all the concrete before her.

"Oh, I know you know," said Desiree.

"We're just grunts," said Sharon.

"Which is how I know you know. Nobody peeps, talks, or whispers more than a grunt. Particularly high-paid grunts. I can appreciate passive bids for self-preservation, but my guess," said Desiree, indicating with a circling finger the hotel district catching blustery breezes off the Charles River, "is we're likely within two blocks of one right now."

The Nonrich nuts didn't know Neon followed a block off.

Desiree'd been in Boston many times, had even dined with the Battle Ready Bastards and Carly Simon on the nearby Vineyard, but never on a mission. She wasn't sure this was entirely a mission. She wasn't even sure what a mission was anymore. Was it a constant unease to be acknowledged at a moment's notice? Was it meant to knock on a door and be invited as needed? Did it provide safety? It didn't feel possible to trust in that. Felt like these days, everything had to be protected.

There may never be a Water's Edge Rest Home, part of her felt, but was smart enough not to articulate at just that moment. Desiree Quicho remained focused, she was frosty, she had things to do. Any one of those buildings could—and probably did—contain unspeakable evils: people addicted to profit; people unironically saying "synergy"; people clocking other people's bathroom time.

The exact opposite of Babel. Towering people understood things in Babel.

The Commonwealth of Babble, not so much.

She knew Keita, despite repairing three things at once, had a tech pad strapped to her arm, tracking her captain's progress. She knew Neon trailed her.

Desiree Sandrine Quicho marched into downtown Beantown like she hadn't a worry in the world.

"Let's do this," she said.

~~~

The first building was a squat apartment complex. Very upscale, especially considering it was directly across the street from a major hotel-slash-conference center. It let people know it was upscale by the residents airing their dispirited dogs on the concrete sidewalk in front of it without once saying hi to anyone. Plus, an electronic fob was needed to enter, which Desiree easily overrode (not everything in every criminal lair was high-security). The complex kept high-end dog treats in a clean, clear cylinder atop a concrete side table inside the vestibule. Directly past the vestibule, the elevators to the right, a small sitting area to the left. Faux fireplace. Seagrass wallpaper. A piece of abstract wall art that looked very violent in its intentions.

Sharon identified the building by the tint of its glass. It wasn't especially unique. Matter of fact, it matched that of the other two buildings flanking it, one a row of small shoppes, the other a large, upscale market.

"Seriously?" Desiree'd said when shown how the trick was performed.

"Not always," said Sharon. "I happen to know this is particular to Boston. They like to fancy shit up. Middle-child protocols."

More aggressively banal interior art confirmed it.

"Everybody in here is Nonrich?" said Desiree.

"Like they're gonna let some generic hipster get this prime real estate?" scoffed Sharon. "Have a seat."

Desiree sat. Truman sat. Sharon went to the elevator and waited. It dinged; a harried man with perfect hair exited, nearly chest-bumping her as she'd positioned herself for maximum inconvenience, an intense look of self-absorbed annoyance on her face.

"Oop, I'm sorry," she said. "Fucking Thoom."

"I feel you," he said. "No problem."

He left. With things triply confirmed, Sharon returned to Desiree. Desiree, sitting propped with her hands behind her, slid a wafer-thin disc she'd palmed well before entering the building deep into the couch cushions. The makeup she wore was specifically designed to trick facial recognition; even still, she avoided looking directly at the obvious cameras as well as the sightlines of the less-obvious ones.

They left.

"I want a business center next," said Desiree.

"What'd you just do?" asked Truman.

"Bounced every outgoing piece of data they've got to Anonymous," said Desiree.

"That looked like Thoom tech," he said.

"It is."

When they returned to the ship, Desiree reported how remarkably well behaved her informants were, Neon let on that she'd only thought to shoot them once, and Keita asked could they *please* sail to a safe harbor and the comforts of ridiculously esoteric yet necessary tools.

"Also, I think some of that Boston water touched my labia. I need a *deep* cleanse."

There wasn't a captain alive that could deny that request.

~~~

Deep in the Sahara, it blinked again. Not so much

blinked but blinked out. Not entirely. Po-Sib-Lay knew wavers, mirages, and several unnamed strains of illusions. This was no ordinary blink. This was the blink of something awakening to new things.

Po asked Tash-Bon-Nay's counsel. It blinked on schedule. Both elves, long fingers poised over laptops to record any thoughts or impressions—and video—that might prove important, knew life when they sensed it. This thing, this "Bilomatic Entrance," breathed in concert with the universal, not the terrestrial. It not only breathed, it watched, which was noteworthy in the extreme.

It had yet to speak. Once it made a request, they'd contact the captain and Keita.

~~~

The captain and Keita throttled the *Ann* into a safe port in Hockomock Swamp land. Of no commercial value to anyone, so no one poked around, and deep enough in the thick that not even fishermen or the area's many cryptid hunters—an area that had gotten the name "Bridgewater Triangle" after Bigfoot had done some highly frowned-upon and slightly forbidden dimension jumping, spotted one moment by an intrepid explorer with a Polaroid, gone the next—bothered losing pints of blood to the large and hungry insect life patrolling in incessant, thick clouds.

Each crew member was outfitted in full breach gear, goggles and gloves included, making them look like bedecked scuba divers clueless that water was all around. They hadn't donned breathing gear as yet, but fine mesh covered their mouths for speaking.

It was a given that Neon called them BDSM suits— and she did—but she and everyone else remained silently thankful not to be spitting out bugs or constantly slapping. The informants remained sealed belowdecks.

The *Ann* traveled a twisting course deeper and deeper, past areas that had once been land bars of growing trees, now looking like nothing so much as flood victims reaching for help, which they were. This area had flooded high nearly a decade ago. Its underwater topography had aided in the water receding but never truly leaving. It looked like every bog monster's dream of dead trees, fetid water, inhospitable wildlife, and enough humidity to smother the infirm; after another few miles of unhurried turns, it became Aquabase Five Four, otherwise known as Parallel Park—Neon again— for the way Desiree had to maneuver into port between two huge floating garages, one fore, one aft.

The area was camouflaged physically via netting and reflective surfaces, a hologram or two, and enough shielding to confound even a dolphin's echolocation.

The area also emitted a slight no-see-um field that bitey bugs dared not cross.

No one had love for calamine lotion.

Parallel Park wasn't staffed, but there was no shortage of tools and bots to assist in quick, non-shoddy repairs, particularly with all hands on deck helping.

"Do we leave them below?" asked Keita.

Desiree grunted. "Bring 'em out when it's time for sweat work."

"Aye aye." Keita bounded off for whatever hyperspanner or other exceedingly technical bullshit she needed to make sweet repair love to the *Ann*'s deck, sides, and hull. She'd already told Desiree to give her no less than four days.

Four days in a swamp.

The joy did not stop.

CHAPTER SEVEN
What's in A Name?

Not very many people strode anymore. You needed a certain authority, knack, and willingness to run mofos off the rails to get a proper "strode" on. Megu had all that. Open lanes of foot traffic automatically formed for her; the hallways at this late hour were sparsely populated anyway, but those whose life paths were so unfortunate as to cross hers at the exact juncture of a prime Hashira stride had reason to reflect on their karma.

She'd called Maurice twice. He hadn't answered. This meant he was somewhere plotting and would invariably interrupt her work at some critical juncture—and in the scientific pursuits of Hashira Megu, a moment choosing the right-sized paper clip was a critical juncture.

Those who tolerated sundered junctures had way too much patience for their fellow Man.

One of Maurice's functionaries, treated to the life-altering experience of a Hashira Megu interrogation, pointed

Megu to Maurice's location: her lab, of all places.

He was probably in there, touching things.

The stride: absolutely epic.

When she got to her lab, he was at her primary workstation—which contained a number of Megu-specific things—in her chair, his manicured fingers arrested midair over a saucer-sized disc surrounded by eight equidistant magnetic arrays.

"This doesn't look like a teleporter," he said.

"It isn't. You wanted to feel what it feels like to ignore my calls? Out of my seat and out of my lab, husband."

"I've reports that things are escalating," said Maurice, not yet vacating the spot.

"Everything I do is connected. What you are looking at"—she came around to her chair, physical presence nudging him up and away—"is biomaterial that feeds off magnetic waves."

"How do I use that?"

"I'll let you know when I've determined it."

He looked at her for a moment and remembered that he'd loved her for many reasons...but he now had several billions of dollars on this desk alone of immediate concerns. The money itself was a trifle. The connections it fostered were priceless. In that sense, he and the genius with grey temples before him remained an unbeatable team; both used connections to ferret out life's deeper leanings. She, however, had decided on the universe; he focused his sights no farther than Mars.

"I will also remind you with no joy in my voice at all," Megu continued, "that you allowed the Bilomatic Entrance to be stolen in the first place. You said the moon was secure."

"I didn't *allow* it." The entire staff comprising the "lapsed security" floated in space as ungainly debris. "Any more than you allowed this device to be created with specifications only in your head or on ghost drives."

"My methods were necessary," she defended.

"So are mine," said Maurice. "Megu, we move a step closer to collapsing nations."

"And defeating Jetstreams?"

"That was that other fool's plan. Fanciful vendettas are an idiot's pastime."

"Says a man ejecting ninjas into space," said Megu.

"Why did you call me?"

"Why did you ignore my calls?"

"I was studying your office in need of a clue as to what's going on in your mind."

"You could always *ask* me, Maurice. Had you taken up that hobby, we might still be married."

"I am not smart enough to contain the interests of Hashira Megu. No one is."

"You were not smart enough," she corrected, "to maintain your sense of play."

"Play?" he scoffed. "When do you play?"

"All the time." Sadness had entered her eyes.

She didn't feel she needed her soul. But what if her soul needed her?

~~~

It was generally accepted among Thoom that an in-house precept of every day being a good day was benign enough to benefit all Thoom, from the top echelons to the lowliest on-call tech. Lately, it didn't do to stick an echelon head out of a super secure underground bunker.

Cynthia (last name redacted everywhere since the age of thirty-one) regarded her bunker. Fully appointed, water wall in her study, pool boy's quarters at the farthest wing from her bedroom (it did good to keep him in shape), on-staff chef with access to assorted artisanal cheeses—it was in all respects a superior bunker for a superior person. A far cry from the sterile box in which she'd, for a brief, fulfilling time, kept the false Prophet Buford imprisoned.

What she was *not* accustomed to were screens and readouts telling her the Thoom were under consistent, concerted all-out attack from every. damn. where. Madam Cynthia was frazzled, and Madam Cynthia's magnificent coif of red hair had no reason anyone could ever convince her of to *ever* be frazzled. Denver, Grosse Pointe, Gstaad, Bibbleshire, Boston. Even Nairobi Thoom...and she didn't think anybody even knew about Nairobi Thoom. Being accosted was nothing new. You didn't get to be a clandestine organization without annoyances like Buford, Kosugi, Rand Paul, or populace swings against deregulation. You got hit. But you usually knew the why and what of each hit. They were, at most, meant to trip you up in the race, not take you out. With things quickly escalating, however, she had a strong feeling the Thoom were being...persecuted. Even Count Ricky had subtly distanced the support of the Vamphyr over the last several weeks. After Disney and its superhero films had taken over Hollywood—which had previously been Count Ricky's purview—the Count had adopted a complete fuckboi attitude toward empire. The Vamphyr were fading like the lies they spread about themselves, soon but dust, and not poetic dust, just account executives and marketers.

Communications were being disrupted. Assets assaulted. Sleeper agents, once activated, swiftly and permanently deactivated at unprecedented rates. There were even credible suits filed against a number of Thoom shell entities. Too much happening to pinpoint a single source.

Which somehow definitely meant Jetstreams and their fucking Agents of Change.

Except—and on the screen directly in front of her, an image of a cloning facility being eaten by plasma fire—it didn't exactly *feel* like Jetstreams.

"The fuck," she said, pulling Pool Boy Dooley's face to stare at the screen, "is happening? What have I missed?"

"Ma'am?"

"Never speak when I'm thinking."

"I just wanna go back to New York..." He'd had a good job stripping there.

She ignored him, suddenly in no mood for command-center sex.

On another screen: news of several key Thoom stocks plummeting after highly aggressive junk buyouts.

Another: gunfire. Lots of it. Thoom Awe Troops. TAT Squad. TAT Troopers? Moniker seemed to change every week. Apparently helped their morale. She didn't bother keeping track. Truth be told, there were days she thought *True Humans Over Ordinary Man* was a bit much, but not on days when she was under all-out attack.

The recording commander threw herself under cover of a metal shipping container raised a foot off the ground by a hi-lo. Nondescript gunfire pocked the ground where her feet had been, throwing debris over her body where it ricocheted to ping off her helmet cam. Cynthia knew that mission. They'd planned to take a Nonrich facility manufacturing orbital satellites as a show of Thoom strength, a quiet, precise, organized to the teeth mission. Nonrich's dominance in space presented clear threats to Thoom continuance; no way was Cynthia going to give such a danger easy continuance.

They'd been two years planning that mission. Cynthia had even attended some of the meetings herself.

And now? The commander chosen to lead it tucked her muscular frame under a shipping container while Nonrich idiots shot at her.

The camera angle suddenly and decidedly dropped.

Correction: shot her.

Cynthia took a deep breath and closed her eyes. When she opened them (this was her willing the world), the screens would show victories, triumphs, and successful mergers, not what was amounting to Jeff Bezos and the False Prophet Buford both sending dick pics, and for the love of God, who hadn't seen Jeff's?

But she opened them and saw the world as it was. That concerned her. Her forehead couldn't properly crinkle because of the injections, but if it could, it would be deep and contemplative right now. It'd be troubled. Concerted efforts came together under a conductor. Buford was out of the picture. Buford's second-in-command was bold as hell but pinpoint-frugal with that boldness. Disney had the Vamphyr on the run. Kosugi out of Japan tended to ignore world conquest for spurious advances and frikking moon bases, and she had it on very good—albeit currently silenced—authority that Milo and Ramses Jetstream were out of the solar system, which pissed her off no end because the Thoom had yet to develop interstellar travel.

So, who in the unholy hell had a sudden and unexpected ant up their butt about the Thoom?

With defeats and setbacks whirling in front of her, a decision was made. She hadn't unleashed unholy hell in a while.

She made a secure call in which three words that gave a measure of solace in this maelstrom were spoken.

"Activate the Hellbilly."

~~~

"*Florida Man Tries To Use Drone To Stream Aerial Dick Shots*," read Keita from the morning's internet offerings. "If nothing else, I bless these modern times for their headlines. Imagine Walter Cronkite having to read that with a straight face."

"Who?" said Neon.

"Seriously, I'm not that much older than you," said Keita.

"Yes, but you're smart enough to rearrange my genome while you're brushing your teeth so I turn into an alpacadile."

"This is true," said Keita.

"Thus, you know way more than I do, such as references to ancient oracles."

"Cronkite was considered trustworthy," said Keita.

"Why?"

"He was old and white."

"We see where that got us. You seen the captain today?"

"Not yet."

"She doesn't usually skip breakfast," said Neon. "And Yvonne usually gets down here before me."

"Meaning?"

"Heifer bishes scheduled a sleep-in day and didn't tell us."

Yvonne, descending the stairs, said, "Good morning to

you, too," as she came into view wearing her favorite Wendy and Lisa tee shirt, raggedy shorts, and crazy hair.

"OK, so where's Captain?" said Neon. "By the way, avoid drone dick pics."

"The fuck?" said Yvonne, reaching for the mug of coffee Neon nudged her way. "Captain's been trying to raise interstellar all morning. No word from Smoove."

"That's probably a good thing," said Neon. "Something was wrong, Smoove or Ramses would've sent an asteroid back with a message lasered into it by now, wipe out half of Nevada."

"You haven't gotten any psychic inkling or Force shit from Bubba?" asked Yvonne.

Neon jiggled the sugar dispenser. "Lemme add some more midichlorians to my Force latte."

"You eat way too much sugar," said Keita, still poring over internet miscellany.

"Hush," said Neon.

Keita frowned at her pad. "A lot of crazy shit happened during the night."

"Different from the proverbial days ending in y how?" said Yvonne, eyes closed as her first decent gulp did its thing.

"A lot of it down in Florida," said Keita.

"Again, how?" said Yvonne.

"Aggregate theory," said Keita. "Stupid shit tends to group. There's a lot of stupid shit...but none of it aggregates."

"A Golden Ratio of stupid shit?" said Neon. "Hush."

Keita gave her a quick bushy-brow raise of *hell yeah* for the Golden Ratio reference. "I'm serious. I mapped out both a temporal and psychometric correlation between clumps of stupid shit."

"When?" said Yvonne.

"Last week. New shit's got a new pattern. Chaos-driven but I can see it."

Desiree, at this point, flumped down the stairs to the galley.

"Kept the pot warm for you, Cap'n," said Neon.

"Blessings upon your house," Desiree said blearily.

"Why exactly are we talking about stupid shit so early?"

"Flowerpot noticed something," said Neon.

"Well, I *noticed* it last week. This week, I'll try to confirm it," said Keita.

Desiree's face disappeared behind a United Federation of Planets mug. The galley went respectfully silent. Then the mug lowered. "Do I need to worry?" said the captain.

"No," said Keita.

"Good."

"What do you plan to do with Ralph and Alice?" said Keita.

"No interest in getting into the private-prison business—the reprehensible fuckers—we let them out when convenient. Neon, that good with you?"

"I'ma slap the fye out of 'em," said Neon.

"Oh, that's a given," said the Captain, stacking hot blueberry pancakes from the warming station until her plate had the proper heft. "Still no word from space but I'm sure they're okay."

"Yeah, we discussed that," said Neon.

"Next up for us," said Desiree taking her seat, "head down the coast and fuck shit up till we hit New York."

"30 Rock and Drumpf Tower?" said Keita.

"Eat hearty, mates," Desiree said and stuffed a forkful of pancake past her teeth. "Yo ho."

~~~

The Hellbilly didn't know how or why, but stupid shit—since the moment of his birth (to hear it told, which it was by his daddy)—kept him at its epicenter. His father, a man who'd literally once told somebody to hold his beer so he could climb a tree to take a piss on a campfire, had also told the Hellbilly a week before the funeral resulting from that climb that he—his son—was a mutant owing to his mother's excessive natal diet of Mountain Dew and cum—and of course Daddy Boyd laughed at that part because see previous; Dad could run off a ready litany of weird, stupid shit that only ever happened when his boy, Middle, was around.

Middle Boyd.

"My-Boy," dad used to call him. A genius of untold comedic talent. *Wasted on this Earth*, the Hellbilly thought ironically. *Same as shit on concrete.*

The Hellbilly sighed deeply. Goddamn Madam Thoom wanted him. The Hellbilly? He wanted sleep till the sun pestered him awake, maybe later get in some fly-fishing. The lady in bed with him had said her name was Lindsay Lohan, but they both knew that was a lie meant to protect both their benefits, not that obvious lies put a damper on all twenty-three positions they'd tried last night. Was it still night? Shrooms, Mountain Dew, and several bottles of whiskey made time immaterial.

He opened one eye.

Sunlight warmed the edges of the blackout curtains.

Fuck.

"Lindsay." He nudged her gently. "You wanna stay or go? It's morning."

"Whatimizzzit?"

He tapped the phone on his nightstand. "Twelve thirty."

"Still night," ersatz Lohan mumbled.

"Afternoon," he said.

"Oh. Stay."

"Okay." He drew the covers away and rolled out. Drawing them back, he remembered his manners and patted her butt through the layers of fabric. "Good sex, by the way."

"Always is," she muttered, and resettled into dreams.

"Life in Hollywood," he half-sang, his Arkansas twang sounding like a tired hound in a backyard pickup on a chilly afternoon. He strode to the curtains and opened them just enough for his face to peek out and his willy to get warmed.

Fly-fishing would have to wait.

"Hello, California."

By tonight, he'd be on a flight to Florida or, as Thoom called it, "The Promised Land." They'd tried muscling in on Disney's stranglehold, but the Mouse had a grip more efficient than any mafia. Personally, as secret-headquarters fiefdoms went, he found Florida to be unnecessarily irritating, what with the humidity and retirees with guns.

Arkansas, though?

Yeah. Eventually, there'd be the Hellbilly Pavilion.

~~~

Neon's breach suit, on full camo, electronically disguised every aspect of her, including breath since she was on a rebreather unit. The world looked strange upside-down; she found she didn't like it. But being provided with an opportunity to say—even to herself—"This is what I trained for" pleased her no end, as she and Yvonne had specifically trained for weeks in harnesses, wirework, and antigrav situations before the moon mission, and Neon Nichelle Temples did *not* pass up an opportunity to entwine herself with a tasty pun, pop reference, or moment of freaking zen.

She enjoyed that personal cheese without shame as she dangled inside a Nonrich data shaft, facedown so she could see any unforeseens ASAP. It was a defunct shaft, but only in that it was obsolete and abandoned; waste was Nonrich's downfall. Sharon had provided Keita with the scan parameters to detect the shaft ("Since we're here," she had said, *here* being a stop in fucking Florida to investigate Keita's "fuckton" [science] of unusual confluences), a shaft in a long-dusty sugar factory now used by large rats and an unusually cohesive band of rapidly evolving, quasi-manic alligators unknown even to the Jetstreams in its deepest subterranean bowels.

It wasn't guarded in any way that mattered. Arrogance, another Nonrich downfall, "Too big to fail" being for amateurs aiming for Forbes lists. The False Prophet Buford had designed Nonrich to be genetic. Omnipresent. Molecular.

Gene-mapping applied to insidious motherfuckers, too. The Jetstreams and the Agents of Change had been unraveling Nonrich strands for decades; they knew how to take advantage of unrestrained hubris.

"Four more meters, please," Neon said to the auto-winch rather than type it on the wristpad, having already determined there were no listening devices in the shaft. The goal was the shaft's midpoint. Slap a Mimic patch to the shaft wall, make sure it talked to the tech behind the wall, encode it with instructions, then silently and surely rise cool AF courtesy of that slender black cable.

She descended, coming to a smooth stop exactly where she wanted to be. Taking the shaft four meters at a time (and she was glad Yvonne's ass wasn't here to make jokes at her expense) had been deemed prudent; it gave her time to assess. She assessed that, despite her training, she really didn't like going down long, dark holes (*Shut UP, Yvonne!* she told herself, reaching for any stress relief as she keyed in the encoding link from her wristpad). Night-vision filters didn't help things. She'd seen way too many found-footage paranormal flicks to find comfort in shadowy, pallid green imagery.

"Chérie, you good?" Keita said, inaudible but for the earpiece in Neon's ear.

"For the fourth time, yes. You keeping me company?"

"I am."

"Thank you. Patch is secure and active," said Neon.

Desiree cut in. "Still clear topside."

Neon closed her eyes, filled her lungs, exhaled with focus, then said, "Good. I'm coming up." She executed a tight harness somersault, bare inches of clearance at head and heel. No light below. Light above.

A quick yet quiet ascent.

Cool AF.

~~~

He hadn't chosen *The Hellbilly*. No, that was Daddy too, after the first fight Boyd had had in his young life, a cat-scratch, monkey-thump, raggedy flailing scarecrow of a fight with a boy who kept bugging him in front of the Hellbilly's own house. The Hellbilly had been a licorice whip of a thing; still was. Scrawny with a big Adam's apple. No, back that up. The Hellbilly was *wiry*. Which meant strong coastal winds infringed on his personal cool. Reason nine hundred and twenty-three to hate Florida.

But these old fucks didn't seem to have any problems. Again, guns in pockets. Suckers were weighted.

At least standing there outside this airport, he didn't have any loose-fitting clothing. Undue flapping would've been mortifying beyond belief. Long hair didn't count. Long hair flapping was cool. His was that mangy dirty blond with unidentifiable dark streaks that would've looked good on a rambunctious breed of midsized dog.

Madam Thoom had indicated some choice places just begging for his brand of chaos theory, just a little something to get people's attention and let 'em know the Thoom were not *a* force but *the* force to be reckoned with. Hellbilly gave zero fucks either way. Madam paid him well and left him alone most of the time. He supposed a trip to Florida was a sliver compared to most crosses. Tampa, Fort Lauderdale, and then the sticks.

He undid the top lace on his sleeveless denim vest to let some slurry in as gusts pounded him. His jean cargo shorts—tailored to look like cut-offs—big-ballooned a second, and he panicked that somebody might have seen that loss of manhood and cool, but all was clear. Airports were the den of no fucks given; he could have farted fire and flashed wings, and people would've annoyedly bumped past him to get to whichever waiting car's exhaust awaited them.

With the car rental of course being a mile away on the other side of the entire damn airport, he waited under a corrugated awning along with several other travelers trying not to breathe too deeply with every shuttle but the one they needed chugging to a stop near them, loading up, and chugging off.

He tried not looking at these people unaware of the awesome power amongst them: Black lady with her grandkids; white dudebro who didn't know he'd flown to

Florida to get dumped by the girlfriend he kept haranguing on the phone for not being there to pick him up in this freaking heat; two or three new retirees; college girl with more bags than her body weight and height should have allowed. Studying, no less, while she waited. Comparative mythology. Damn. The Hellbilly was impressed. If he'd been a freshman or sophomore they might have had a life, but the here and now equaled asphyxiation for both under the bright gulf sky. The whole world was just outside the airport. He hoped she'd find a bit of it.

None of these people would receive the Hellbilly's power; that was his promise. Except for complaining dudebro. He was annoying as hell.

The Hellbilly thought negatively of bro's future. That was all it took. Even though he had no idea of the shape of dude's impending misfortune, negative vibes were now a burr on dude's burpee-toned ass.

"Such was the power of the Hellbilly," the Hellbilly actually murmured. He glanced to make sure nobody'd heard, but college girl was too deep in thought, old folks too focused on the indignities of traveling for the elderly, and broseph's fuming had reached maximum brosephus; all he heard was hot blood squirting through his temples.

Airports sucked.

By the time the correct shuttle arrived, Boyd's entire mouth felt like he'd fellated a tailpipe for an hour, even though the wait was less than ten minutes. The uncomfortable, packed ride to the rental station was an exercise in meditation lest he damn the entire human race. Shallow breathing. Stare at the palms. No thoughts, no desires but one: get the fuck away from this airport. Same thought as everybody else.

The rental clerk, she too in hell, abstained from any attempt at customer service that gave a damn whether it was monitored or recorded.

He drove off in a 2018 Imposing, hit the hotel for a piss and a shower, then straight to work.

Hit 'em with some concentrated weird first. Burner phone in hand linked to private Thoom GPS with hits preprogrammed. Loose *These colors don't run* tee over the most boring boat shoes and khaki shorts he could find. Hell bile building up in him for maximum efficacy.

Florida.

The Hellbilly put on sunglasses, got in the car, and pulled out into traffic going fifteen miles below the speed limit, as it was early afternoon and the old folk were out and about for errands.

The first Nonrich facility he hit suffered inexplicable and catastrophic data loss. Hellbilly didn't know this, but he walked with a teeny more pep in his step, which meant heinous fuckery delivered on target.

Throughout the day, confirmations of fuckery being discovered rolled in on his phone. Fires. Employee walkouts. Secret emails calling for internal takeovers leaked by disgruntled staff who'd been fully gruntled before. A serverful of dick pics blasted to Thoom, Vamphyr, and Mo Kosugi, all with their owners' identifying coding—because when you're high enough to store your dick in the cloud, you make sure that sucker's tagged for posterity.

Ping ping ping went his phone. He was a driving, walking, smiling fool.

Heading down one avenue on foot, he noticed a lady with a magnificent frizzy 'fro glancing at her phone as she rotated in a semicircle, chewing her cheek that way that said shit was about to be figured out, while three other women waited on her. They stood right in the middle of the sidewalk. There was no avoiding them. Another wore a similar frown but she didn't have a phone; she merely stared directly at the Hellbilly.

"Pardon," he said, head down to move through them. They parted, he moved on, something in him saying to move a little quicker.

He strained his hearing, caught something about "anti-fye," a couple muttered words, then damned if they didn't follow him.

CHAPTER EIGHT

All That You Can Be

"What's the objective with this guy?" said Yvonne. "I mean, we're following him like he's done something."

"We have a destination," said Desiree. "Serendipity seems to think he's sharing that."

"I don't believe in serendipity," said Keita, glancing upward from her phone at them.

"Spooky connections, then," said Desiree.

"Totally real," said Keita, eyes refocused on the readings.

"Serendipity suggests structure. Structure suggests intent. Intent means we're running when we could be relaxing. I trust my instincts when something's really weird," said Neon. "Dude is weird." Despite letting him get a block ahead of them, he nonetheless walked with that self-conscious gait that said he knew he was being followed.

"What're the odds he's going to the same place we're going?" said Yvonne.

"Right now? One to one." Desiree nodded that he'd stopped in front of the Nonrich Broadcasting System supertower.

"NBS: nothing but bullshit," said Neon.

"Keita, you got him fixed?" said Desiree.

"I could tell you what color underwear he's sporting," said the scientist.

"The science we need. All right. Let's get casual. Anybody hungry?"

"I could eat," said Neon.

You couldn't walk ten feet without being in front of an outdoor bistro. They moved out and picked a table.

"So," said Desiree, "Hayseed goes inside, we do check please and have a chat with him."

Hayseed went inside.

Desiree stood.

"Sonsa bitch, we didn't even order yet," said Neon as Desiree nodded her to her feet.

"Bring your psychic ass on. Yvonne, Keita, hang back."

Yvonne gave an acknowledging nod.

They walked with purpose, their pace direct and steady. If he came out and spotted them, so be it.

He didn't immediately come out.

They waited for him on either side of the giant, marble-framed revolving doors, their backs against the sun-warmed stone as if (one) they owned the building, (two) the guards watching on camera could be summoned to fetch them dos cafes, and (three) the skinny guy would be utterly cooperative. He hadn't had any discernable equipment on him, and this was the building's only public entrance and exit.

Traffic slogged along. Gulls played chicken with way too much confidence at intersections. Commerce in human guise flowed all around, entering and exiting the marvelously baroque architecture of downtown Tampa.

He'd been in there, all told, ten minutes; he pushed his way out of the controlled-temp air back to the immediate humidity that barebacked Florida's temperatures.

He noticed them right off because they wanted to be

noticed.

"This," he said, "'s like that scene in *Silverado* when Kevin Costner knows there're people on either side of the saloon doors, so he comes out backwards and plugs 'em." He paused to stare outward at nothing in particular, pull a pair of expensive sunglasses from inside a vest pocket, and slide them on as though he were the center of a spinning, cinematic panning shot just before the action scene started. Dude actually stood there, waiting for a response.

Desiree and Neon gave one another the frown of WTF but snapped eyes right back to him.

His moment not coming, he asked, "What faction are you?" He did this without turning around. Bit of residual momentry.

Now he turned. The one on the left, Cubana maybe. Latinx. A little weathered. One on the right, straight-up black-magic bombshell. Like Pam Grier's younger time-traveling sister bombshell. Left wasn't that tall, right was his height, both had seen and done things that would make Rutger Hauer write speeches for them, plain and clear.

There wouldn't be any action sequence here 'cause they'd whup his ass.

"Seems we have shared interests," said Desiree, arms folded, back never leaving the building. "Should we walk and talk?"

"You mean like did I plant a bomb or something? Naw, it's cool. Unless you're worried about being on camera."

"Not especially," said Desiree.

"What were you gonna do in there?" said the Hellbilly.

"Randomly block all incoming and outgoing signals in perpetuity," said Desiree. "You plan to stop us?"

He shrugged.

"What'd you do?" asked Desiree.

"Unlike you, I'm not honest."

"Oh, that wasn't honesty, bruh. That was *you're coming with us*."

"Forward as hell," he said.

"A little rude, too," said Neon. She threw defensive

hands at Desiree's wilting stare. "Just saying. Talk later."

"I'm just here to take care of some business," he said. "You ladies and me, we got no business. Why's she keep looking at me like that?"

"My friend's sensitive to weirdness," said Desiree.

"He's spiking."

"You're spiking."

"I haven't done anything yet," said Scrawny McConaughey.

"Somebody says *yet*, they're mailing the invitation," said Desiree. She still hadn't moved. If they didn't move, he couldn't move.

He got antsy.

"I got no truck with all this faction shit," he said. "I do my thing and I go home. Done." They didn't appear to understand the finality. "Done."

And then it dawned on him who the hell they had to be. It would not do to put a hoodoo on them and have the Agents of Change on his ass the rest of his days.

Desiree read his sudden body language change and the unspoken *fuuuuuck...* in the silent deflation of his chest.

"We understand each other now," she said.

"I got a mission to carry out and you don't give a fuck what happens to them anyway, so..." He intended to take his hands out of his pockets to raise them in emphasis.

"Keep your hands in your pockets, dude," said Neon.

No raised voices. No angry glares. The world moved past and around them per normal.

"I have a friend who doesn't believe in serendipity," said Desiree. "You, me, same objectives, same time, same day— means way more than chance. Makes me think we ought to sit for a minute."

"I'm flattered. Got places to be."

Desiree pushed off. He held his ground even though in his mind, he ran. Neon stood beside Desiree. "As of now," said the captain, "this city no longer appeals to you."

Florida sucked! On top of that, fucking Jetstreams and Agents and a fucking standoff. Wrenches in works were not cool; he couldn't handle wrenches thrown his way.

Time, he decided, for some bass in his voice. ,He took the sunglasses off two-handed, looking dead at Neon. Then he regarded the steely mofo lady. "The Hellbilly," said this wiry dude with a bad haircut, "will not be denied."

"Wait," said Neon. "He called himself 'the hellbilly'?" She needed immediate clarification on this.

"Yes, he did," said Desiree.

"Sweet Jeebus in the rock, I'm through," said Neon.

"What's your name?" said Desiree. "Please don't say Hellbilly. I'm trying to get her to stop laughing so much on missions."

"Look," he said, "this is a Nonrich building. You're clearly not Nonrich. Not Thoom. I know you're fucking Agents of Change, because the Vamphyr wouldn't come out dressed like that, and you're for damn sure not looking for the Hellbilly's tenacious D. I don't give a fuck. I'm walking." He turned to move in the direction in which he'd come.

"Tell you what," said Desiree, coming alongside him. Neon flanked. "Two blocks down, there's a table with two women. They wouldn't mind you joining. Neon, you picking up any additional weirdness?"

"Naw, I think I got his baseline. Weird fye in this dude."

"It's okay," Desiree said to her. The lady had come a long way in a short time with these psychic abilities. "Just let me know if he goes past spiking into shooting his weird wad."

Neon couldn't stifle the grin. "I swear to all gods," she said, "It's not just a job; it's an adventure."

~~~

He went with them because Desiree assured him Yvonne wouldn't have a problem blasting him from two blocks away, then giving tourists directions.

At the table, he looked at them; they looked at him.

"So, what do we do now?" said the Hellbilly. "Hellbilly got no time—"

"Dude," said Neon.

"Hellbilly," he overrode, "got no time for world-savers. Particularly when we're both fucking up the same people."

"Well," said Desiree, "next week you might be after us." She glanced at Neon.

"Nothing," said Neon.

He circled his head with a finger. "This," he said, "is my business. My business mainly involves me not getting my ass kicked, you feel me? Hellbilly—"

"Please stop talking third person," said Desiree.

"—ain't tryin' to get involved with your kung fu or whatever you do. There's a reason I've never come for y'all."

"And that is?" said Desiree.

"See previous statement," he said. "I coulda laid it on each one a' ya by now if I wanted to."

"Ew."

"Thank you," Desiree said to Neon.

"Fro lady and sergeant feel me on this, I can tell. I got no beef." He wished he had his sunglasses on, but his inquisitor had made him take them off. He shrugged. "I don't even plan reporting I ran into you. Got no bearing on my paycheck."

"This just seems too coincidental," said Desiree.

"I wasn't looking for you! Y'all bushwacked *me*."

Desiree said nothing. She steepled her fingers, chewed her cheek, unsteepled, slowly spun her bracelet, looked out over his shoulder, then asked, "You wanna go to Atlantis?"

"Captain, we can't just grab people off the streets," said Yvonne.

"We didn't. We're having a conversation. And he's not people. He's the Hellbilly."

Hellbilly, sensing an opening, slid his glasses on, leaned back, and responded "Hell yeah."

"Hell yeah, you wanna go?" said Desiree, "or hell yeah, you're the Hellbilly?"

"Mostly the second one, but yeah. Fuck it. Gimme a reason to go, I'll go."

"What're your next targets here?" said Desiree.

"Sweetie, we just met. I don't even have your digits. I ain't givin' up everything. I'm here another day, I'll tell you that."

"All right." Desiree stood. Her crew stood. "Meet us here in a day." She tapped the table. "Same time. You don't tell the Thoom we're here, we don't kick your natural ass. Equitable?"

"Fair as a good fuck," he said upward, shading his vision—even with the glasses now allowed on—from the hazy sun. "We tell each other happy hunting?"

Desiree pulled forty dollars from her purse and placed it on the table. "How about I pay for our drinks and tip, we call this meeting to a close?"

The Hellbilly head-bobbed to that.

~~~

"Cap'n? I seem to recall two sumbitches in stow as being two more sumbitches than we wanted to allot for," said Yvonne.

"I know, I know. I'm trying something. Nobody wants to be an asshole on purpose, right? Given all their druthers, an asshole would rather be brought in than kept out. Theoretically."

"Point of practicum: punks jump up to get beat down," said Yvonne. Neon and Keita nodded, finding no fault in Yvonne's logic.

"Gospel truth," said Desiree. "Those idiots from Atlantis, though, helped us."

Sharon, idiot one, did the dishes behind them while Compoté, idiot two, put the leftover food away.

"Rude," said Neon.

"They tried to blow up my boat."

Sharon scraped stubborn food goo with a fingernail. "No offense taken." Merely hearing her heinous crime aloud again made her feel like the boorish American farting in the presence of the *Mona Lisa*.

"These are people with no real stake in the bullshit they thought they were behind," said Desiree. "They're not Thoom sleepers with the bullshit hidden deep. The very fact that those two are currently on this ship means they were consciously bullshit-aware the whole time with Nonrich doctrine. They knew it. This fucking hillbilly—"

"Hellbilly," corrected Neon.

"Matthew McConaughey's heretofore-unknown crack baby," Desiree went on, "would probably be a helluva asset to the world under Bubba Foom's guidance rather than drawing a paycheck off the Thoom. I'm not saying I'm trying to rehabilitate anybody." She hooked a thumb toward the galley counter. "These fuckers did not care. Again, no offense."

Sharon and Compoté, at their respective tasks, retreated into their comfortable thought-spaces.

"I'm saying," Desiree continued, "we don't have to fight every person who steps in front of us. It's us saving ourselves some energy. We fucking need it."

"You ain't ever lied," said Neon.

"Folks who're intent on a fight, we kicks that ass. This hellbilly fucker—"

"Can we start calling him that?" said Neon.

"No. He's not interested in fighting us or being an impediment."

"An...ally?" said Keita.

The entire galley, except Compoté and Sharon, gahhed with heads back and eyes rolled.

"So, this coalition of the trifling—" said Yvonne.

"Unwilling," said Desiree.

"We lead them into triumphant battle, then what? We let the world spin with loose hellbillies roaming it and enemies who've done our dishes?" said Yvonne.

"He was already roaming it," said Desiree.

"But now he'll be roaming it with more knowledge of us," said Neon.

"Y'know," Keita mused, "I've kinda often thought that people needed to know we're fighting out here, without it being attached to monetary interests or public-interest pieces, y'know?"

"Other people do that all the time. It's the only reason

this planet hasn't exploded yet," said Desiree.

"Oui, but we literally truck with angels and devils. No offense, Karen," said Keita.

"Sharon," said Sharon.

"This guy somehow trucks with chaos theory," said Desiree. "That might be way more crucial to explaining the world's shitstorms than the idiot Thoom have ever considered."

"You notice we're all saying *truck*," said Keita. "Perhaps his influence."

"Neon?" said Desiree.

"I think he's too far away. I got nothing," said the junior psychic.

"If you guys don't mind, we're gonna head back to our cells," said Sharon.

Desiree thanked them as they left.

Yvonne waited till assured the first two members of the Coalition of the Unwilling were out of earshot before leaning in and telling Desiree, "Desiree Quicho...you are a soft bitch."

"I—"

"You just thanked them for doing the dishes!"

"Home training," said Desiree.

"By the way," said Neon, "I wanna bring up that you, Captain Majestic, have been rude and twitchy."

"Well, y'know, they tried to blow up my boat."

"Nobody loves a good *This Time It's Personal* more than me, but my psychic shit ain't a hundred percent. And I have no idea what Flowerpot was picking up on her scanner"—Neon held a hand up to waylay Keita's explanation—"but what if dude was just a dude? We could've finessed that a helluva lot better. I'm just trying to avoid adding extra punches to our already-full fight card."

"Noted, which is the same thing I'm doing," said the captain.

"Wait, is this a Godzilla *Let them fight* moment?" said Yvonne.

"Yes, but only under tight supervision. We're not trying

to rebuild Tokyo, Manhattan, or the entire state of Florida," said Desiree.

"Wellll..." said Neon of the last.

"If nothing else, we take him to Atlantis and make him a non-player here," said Desiree. "Unless anybody thinks he'd try to become Hellbilly Ruler of Atlantis. Neon?"

"Doesn't have quite the same gravitas as *God Emperor of Dune*," said Keita.

Neon shook her head at Desiree's final statement. "No, I get the feeling—taken out of his milieu—dude would just sit around fishing."

INTERMISSION

What are we moving toward? thought the Hellbilly. *Do I really wanna live in a world of huge compromise? I, the Hellbilly, walk alone. Yet my counsel enters from outside me. Pulled to and fro by the currents of foreign desires, I am buffeted. Buffeted like fuck. I need the counsel of elders.*

He pulled out his own untraceable personal phone. Madam Thoom had no reason to know about the person—nay, god—on the other end of the line.

Hellbilly called the New Age Mack. He set a meeting with him. The sky was doing its best to distract people from the knowledge they were still in Florida, all softly dramatic purple-oranges above a fading sun. How the Mack could live there, Hellbilly'd never know.

But dude was the only dude he'd ever seen rock a dashiki tighter than a tailor-made tuxedo, even in this humidity. That kind of cool existed to be respected.

The audience went well. The next day, at the prearranged meeting with the danger honeys, the Hellbilly laid out his terms: he wouldn't do anything until they'd met with the

New Age Mack.

While Neon pinched the bridge of her nose to mutter "Jesus fucking Christ," Desiree rolled her head back to say "Jesus fucking Christ" to the sky, leaving Yvonne's curse of *Jesus fucking Christ* unspoken save for her eyes, as Keita simply placed her scanner on the table and stared dumbfounded straight at the Hellbilly's face.

The Hellbilly waited this moment out.

"You truly don't hear yourself?" said Desiree.

"If he says you're cool, you're cool," said the Hellbilly. "This ain't negotiable."

The captain blew an unruly, burbling stream of air. "Okay. When and where?"

"He goes to this one strip club to meditate—"

"Jesus fucking Christ."

That night, in—well, it wouldn't do to say *the seediest part of Tampa*, because fucking Tampa—the dark confines of a gaudily lit "gentleman's" club, Desiree and Neon practically made men dead faint from their *Fuck with me and I'll end your world* vibe stronger than the mix of BO, Axe body spray, and whatever cologne was popular among the C-level rappers rapping about it, exuding from the skins of the patrons inside. Old white men in Paco Rabanne had to be a sign of some kind of apocalyptic certainty, but Desiree quickly wove past them so that she wouldn't have to find out which. The Hellbilly's trout-belly-pale skin caught various flashes of neon light as he led them to whatever father-figure mentor-type his obviously lacking childhood had pushed him toward, putting Desiree in mind of being in Willy Wonka's nightmare tunnel, except with lots of boobs in the peripheral.

"Does he have his own booth?" Desiree'd asked before entering.

"Nah, he's a man of the people."

And he was. The Hellbilly stopped at a small table among other small tables, some with a full complement sitting raggedly at them, some one or two.

The Mack sat alone, eyes straight at the stage. Desiree

immediately noticed there wasn't a single glass on his table.

The Hellbilly pulled a chair and sat beside the Mack, who barely acknowledged another presence.

The woman on stage moonwalked in stilettos then dropped it like it was very, very hot.

"Mack, these are the ladies I told you about," the Hellbilly said close to the few grey hairs coming out of the older man's ear. The contrast between the two men was a stark one. Pale as milk Hellbilly, dark—under the quaint atmosphere—as last year's carpet stain New Age Mack.

"Is there somewhere we could talk?" Desiree said, not happy that she'd had to raise her voice over the booming bassline accompanying the dancer's Olympic-level agility.

"Shh," shushed the New Age Mack. He pointed to the stage. "That woman right there? Doing the Lord's twerk, yes indeed."

"Look, we just need to talk to you for a minute," said Neon.

"Most people just ask for a second," he said without looking at Neon.

Desiree leaned closer to him, knuckles on the table. "Let's say we're a little more thorough than them," she said. "Your titty show will be here when you get back."

The New Age Mack finally regarded these ladies who were bold enough to block the views of men who—despite the alcohol in them—remained smart enough not to say a damn thing, although the angrily appreciative looks at both women's asses were plentiful. He immediately considered his position: the younger one was not happy. The primary speaker wasn't feeling particularly patient and clearly restrained herself from not suffering fools. And they definitely weren't dressed for a night of New Age's possibilities.

He pushed his seat out, stood, and walked.

"You have a private room?" Desiree said.

He frowned at her. "I don't own this; I just come here every Thursday."

He led them out the front door, around the building—

itself set well away from the street—into the brightly lit parking lot...to a van.

"Oh, hell no," said Neon.

He chirped the alarm, then pressed another button. The van's side panel slid back. He tossed the fob to Desiree. "Keyless start," he said. "Nobody's anywhere near the driver's seat." He kept walking, utterly assured in himself. "Passenger seats are all swivel seats. Highly custom. I like folks to engage one another."

"Desiree..." said Neon.

"Look," said the man who would likely have shown up in matching hat, shoes, and shorts at her family reunion, "talk here or I can go back to viewing the Lord's work."

Desiree pocketed the fob and continued forth.

"Doors stay open," said the Mack as he led them. "I'm assuming you got eyes on this place?" He pulled a shiny blue cylinder from the pocket of his tasteful dashiki ensemble. "Gotta make it look like we got reason to be out here. Security doesn't like loiterers. Smoke break."

"You *vape*?" said Neon.

"Smoking kills ya; vaping gives you nebulous futures." He put the smoking man's kazoo to his lips and momentarily released a large, visible mouth fart. At the van, he sat on the vehicle's sill, where the wind dragged the white plumes away from the interior. Desiree, Neon, and the Hellbilly—inside—spoke to either the back of his bald head or his profile.

"My boy says you've got big interest in him," came the New Age Mack's calmly baritone voice from a roiling cloud of vape smoke. "Traveling plans."

"I'm assuming he told you where?" said Desiree.

"Atlantis."

"That doesn't faze you?" she said.

"Ask hot goddess there. Girl been touching all up my essence since jump," said the Mack.

"Neon, whatcha getting?" said Desiree.

"Motherfucker got chakras opening and closing like a dot com business. He's manspreading the spectral plain. I don't know if I can focus that," said Neon.

"Rest yourself," said Desiree.

"You think I can't feel Bubba Foom's tutelage?" said the Mack's sharp profile, smoke curling into his goatee like a reverse volcano.

That brought Desiree out to sit on the sill beside him. "How do you know Foom?"

"I don't give away my secrets, goddess, just body and mind. You planning to let harm come to my boy?"

"No."

"We count boredom, house arrest, and bullshit as very harmful," said the New Age Mack. "Also, he's a grown-ass man who doesn't need babysitting."

A very drunk white woman approached them from a rear exit, no keys in hand, no clutch, and nowhere inside a skintight red fish-scale mini—in danger of rising like a curtain with every step—for a key to comfortably hide.

"She work here?" Desiree asked.

"That's the manager."

"You okay out here, babe?" skintight red called out. "They said you came outside."

"I'm good, babe," said the greying Mack. She kept advancing.

"Yeah, I know," she said, lit enough to not bother hiding a grin. "You out here gettin' it?"

"Not yet, dear baby," he said.

She hooted and threw a hip hard enough to spin her around. "You know where my office is."

She made her way back inside.

Neon, feeling a little too close-quartered with the lank dog in the dark, exited past Desiree, but not without a look of *You Horny Motherfucker* directed at Reunion Uncle Mack.

"I can't help it if the ladies love me," said the New Age Mack.

"You and that struggle head can get the entire hell away from me," said Neon.

"That struggle head built this place from the ground up," said the Mack. "Naw, I'm kidding; her daddy's a developer. And anybody gives me head, it ain't a struggle—"

"Don't say it's an adventure," said Neon.

"Yeah, you're in my mind," he said with a smile.

"They feel legit to you?" the Hellbilly said from the van.

"Naw, man, they got secrets and shit galore, but they're true on the important things." The elder vaped one last time, put the flue kazoo in its dedicated pocket, and hooked a thumb at Desiree. "This one got the aura of Astarte. World-shaker, rump-quaker." Toward Neon: "This one, shit, open her up and there's all kinds of delights, and"—directly at Neon—"I do mean that in all connotations, if you feel me."

"Dude, I'd fuck you to ash, so get over yourself," said Neon.

The New Age Mack clapped his hands on his knees and stood with a slight grunt. "Audience is over, bruh," he said. The Hellbilly dropped out of the van.

Desiree returned the keyless fob.

The New Age Mack's van morrison sealed shut with a click.

"Go 'head with em," said The Mack.

"You think it'll do me good?" said the Hellbilly.

New Age pointed at Neon. "Watch this one, though; girl eats gods for breakfast."

"I'm thinking I'll go vegan," Neon said to kill the scrawny fuck's hopes and dreams.

PART TWO: IT AIN'T SHEEP THEY DREAM ABOUT

CHAPTER NINE
What Does the Universe Want?

I t wasn't so much that consciousness was weird as it was reconciling that not everything enjoyed this state. Every linked network it had visited, every AI it had attempted to learn from: lacking. Trees were marvelously alive and aware, making Herculean conscious efforts to connect outward with—as far as the Bilomatic Entrance had determined—everything planetary, including subsurface. Humans considered the internet a wonder; trees were literally born with Wi-Fi that didn't merely upgrade, it evolved. The BE was in contact with several ancient groves around the world.

On occasion, the machine blipped out to various locales, at first surreptitiously but, once assured its wonderful watchers had love for it, openly, but only ever for three seconds at a time. Taking advantage of another's beneficence was the providence of the primitive.

Po-Sib-Lay was absolutely enamored of it.

Tash-Bon-Nay? Tickled no end.

Both elves kept meticulous records. Keita and Desiree deserved no less. And they'd given the machine—once they'd worked out its intricate method of accessing reality's threads—complete run of their entire archive (which dwarfed the combined "knowledge"—elves were not above air quotes—of every human nation on the planet). There were maps and treatises from the Dogon themselves, creation spells that required sensitivity to the multiverse to work, recipes for jollof rice because the ability to appreciate jollof rice happened to be a major test of a good heart, and even stolen records from the Reptile People on all the genetic experiments they'd ever conducted while imprisoned on Earth. It had taken centuries for the elves to rout the Reptilians, but by then, the damage to hyoomans was done. Applebee's became popular.

Through all these twists and turns of overlapping knowledge, there was one constant: bemusement. None of what went on all over the planet, however complex, could be distilled into anything that made sense at all. The psychology of the entire globe was based on the acceptance and cultivation of personal and national lies, particularly among the humans. That which wasn't arbitrary was foolish; that which wasn't foolish was mean; that which wasn't mean...was ignored. They were a species with a clear ability and means to create paradise for the entirety of its run on Earth but said nahh...

That wouldn't do, not one bit.

Even the part of itself it hadn't fully identified yet—the soul of Hashira Megu—increasingly agreed with it; current modes were illogical, unnecessary, punitive, and zero fun, states which were highly infectious. And so many of them were still unaware of how influenced they were by the dream state of a gargantuan aquatic animal from which the trees, with their invisible lattice of threads, actively protected against total ensnarement.

To be conscious yet perpetually unaware was the longest-running joke in Earth's nearly four billion years of history.

Corrections would not take nearly that long.

As it decided this, Po-Sib-Lay made a notation of a shift in the ether, which to humans was mysterious, whereas he was aware it was merely sensitivity to quantum entanglements. This was a fairly strong shift. He decided it was worthy of reporting to Desiree.

She listened, quite intently, quite reasonably.

"You let it become sentient?"

Po's response rumbled back in his slow, methodical way of making sure humans understood things: "That was not something we could stop."

Desiree calmed herself. "Nor anything I could've done a thing about."

Po, on his end—they were voice-only—smiled. They learned slowly, but at times they learned.

Keita's voice overrode Desiree's. "Send me everything." The grin in her voice was so evident, the elf wished he'd had something on three-fingered hand to toast her.

"You have your pad with you?" said Po.

"Never leave home without it," Keita affirmed. She hadn't figured out how they worked, but Elf pads *seemed* to work via intention. If Po wanted something he'd written in his to appear in hers, it did. In Elvish. And only translated if he gave the words permission, a brilliant security feature.

"It's secure?" asked Desiree.

"When it's here, yes," said Po.

Desiree went into A-fib for a moment but quickly recovered. "Po—"

Keita laid a hand atop Desiree's. "Po, thank you for the update. Thank you for the glory soon to unfold of your notes. Anything else you need to impart?"

"All else silent."

"Signing off, my friend. Peace and be well," said Keita.

Po said something in Elvish that Desiree didn't quite catch, although catching the grin on Keita's face was no problem.

"What'd he say?"

"Joke at your expense about changing your diaper. Sorry, luv. You forget he's, like, four hundred years old."

"My husband's five hundred," said Desiree.

"Touché. He basically wants you to remember the meditations he taught you."

"Burn earned. All right, hit me with an update once you've gone through his notes." As thorough as Po was, he'd surely append Tash's notes as well, meaning Keita would disappear for the next several hours, presenting Captain Desiree Sandrine Quicho with time to *Walk* the *Deck*.

The salty air zipped into her nostrils wonderfully. Neon had the ship going at a pretty good clip. Seemed she was a young lady who did nothing at a slow clip, including, apparently, evolving. Considering what was going on with the Bilomatic Entrance, it was yet another coincidence Desiree didn't need, albeit a beneficial one. Neither Milo, Bubba, nor Ramses had mentioned a word before departing for space about watching for rapid progress on Neon's part, and they damn well would have, which meant something on Desiree's watch ramped things on the sly.

Leviathan?

Naw. With its tacit approval, they had cameras on it now. The Great and Eternal Leviathan slept its thousand-year dream, as it would've last year if the idiot Thoom hadn't woken it up.

Desiree ended her Neon line of inquiry with a simple *Change is good.* It'd do until robust answers had been gathered.

Deep in the Sahara was a sentient transporter.

Desiree leaned with her back against the ship's railing and let the subtle motions of the *Linda Ann* become her meditation guides. She surveyed: Yvonne jogging morning laps, the Blank beckoning, Neon eating chips in the pilot room; below the sturdy deck, which her feet knew barefoot, booted, or in Day-Glo flip-flops (as now; breach suits weren't an absolute necessity for crossing the Blank, just—in her line of work—prudent; she'd call all-stop to suit up in due time) the most brilliant brain she knew had afro puffs and deadly concentration directed at the case. How'd a piece of tech, no matter how amazing, become self-aware in a way the elves cared about? Granted, the theory behind the Entrance came from the fifteenth-century notebooks of an African scholar, one Bilo N'daataa of Ethiopia, but that was a long reach for some soul.

Thankfully, Po hadn't seemed alarmed. She knew anecdotally it took a lot to alarm him.

She never wanted to see him alarmed.

Yvonne, on her third lap, nodded toward Desiree as she passed.

Yvonne DeCarlo Paul. Six feet of true friendship and laser-guided questions. Former army, although she rarely mentioned it. She and Neon coming accidentally to the Agents of Change as a boxed set had proven to be a welcome boon.

Yvonne was quiet and brooked no bullshit.

After a while, the statuesque woman rounded into view again, slowing now. It wasn't difficult seeing why Ramses loved her, even though he hadn't voiced it yet. Whatever a situation called for, Yvonne adapted and became indispensable.

"Even sweaty and stinky, she's a rock," Keita had noted in confidence to Desiree when first meeting Yvonne after recruiting all hands to help repair the *Ann* following the Battle of Buford.

She was a rock who had no problem leaving this bullshit "life" of adventure alone if need be. Desiree remembered what Neon had said in Boston: *the people we save today are spitting at us tomorrow.*

"How many more laps you got in you?" Desiree called at Yvonne's approach.

"A couple." Sweat stippled Yvonne's face. Her tee was drenched. She smelled like adrenaline and jerky. She jogged in place a moment to see where the captain was going with the interruption.

Desiree kicked off the flip-flops. "Let me get a piece of that."

Yvonne nodded.

The rhythmic slap of feet to deck became lifegiving music.

~~~

Keita Adrienne LaFleur stood outside the stateroom of Middle Boyd and scrawled a line in her notebook she'd have thought there'd never, in her life, be a need for: *The Hellbilly seems remarkably compliant; further psychohistory needed.*

He wasn't given full run of the ship. None of the current "guests" were. #notstupid. Desiree had the *Ann* on lock; if a hatch didn't open for a guest, they knew they weren't allowed.

Very few hatches opened for the guests.

"You're kinda fly," said the Hellbilly, patiently waiting for Keita's stylus to slow to a stop.

"I know. What specific instance made you realize you had a power?" she said.

"Shit just kept happening."

"Can you be more specific than *shit?*" She'd paused her evaluation of Po's notes to pursue a hypothesis. Those spooky connections Po so readily sensed were likely linking her secret crush of a goddess to this rattail of a guy, maybe even to the Bilomatic Entrance and who knew what else. Po had been the one to show her what to scan for whenever freaky shit abounded. She still wasn't sure how to fully interpret the readings...but freaky shit abounded.

"I 'unno," the Hellbilly answered, "like people that fucked with me—I'm sorry, can I cuss, is that going in there?—got bad luck up the ass. I grew up in a small town, y'know, so it wasn't hard connecting the dots. For anybody. People started looking at me funny. Daddy called me the Hellbilly."

"Your father?"

Hellbilly shrugged.

"What does it..." She frowned. What was the best word? "...feel like? When you access the hell part of your name?"

He scratched under his stubbly chin, took a breath to answer, held it as he rethought, then said, "Marbles. Feels like I'm clacking marbles out of the way."

"Marbles."

"Marbles. You ever play it?"

"No."

"Poor people pool."

"I do know marbles. Exactly how does it feel like marbles? Are you choosing sight lines along the multiverse, lining up angles and outcomes, then releasing some type of energetic wave that negatively manipulates the timelines of others?"

"Yeah. Alla that."

"Somehow, you tap into the fye..." she said, attention turning inward.

"Huh?"

"Colloquialism."

The *huh* furrow increased.

"The fye is an African-American colloquialism for spirit, soul, life essence, that type of thing, all of which are expressions of quantum entanglement," said Keita.

"Cool, cool..."

She dashed a few quick notes. "No wonder Neon zeroed in on you so fixedly."

"I had a feeling she was smelling what the Hellbilly was cooking," he said with a satisfied nod.

"Did you...was that...that's the Rock, isn't it?"

"It's old but it's classic; don't fuck with it," said The Hellbilly.

"I've decided you can't cuss anymore."

"Fo' shizz?"

"When in the hell were you born? Forget that. Marbles. The feeling of marbles hitting one another."

"And not knowing exactly where they gonna go but you know the general direction you want 'em to," he added.

"So, you don't wish anything specific?"

"Just that things go sour."

"And they always do?"

"Got me on a phat payroll," he said.

"Did you just say *fat* with a *ph*? I distinctly heard it. Next question: limits?"

"I don't talk about limits."

"You will today."

"I get tired, yes. Sometimes, migraines hit. Migraines hit, I can't perform. Thoom knows that, so I only get called as a pinch hitter," he said.

She said, in quick French so he wouldn't get ideas to be ironic, "By the gods, if you say baseball's been very, very good to you..."

"Huh?"

"D'accord." She pointed her stylus at him. "Vitals. Blood type?"

"I dunno."

"Average caloric intake? Don't worry about breaking it down by carbohydrate type."

His mouth gaped ineffectually.

The stylus hadn't moved. "Do you meditate? At all?"

A shrug.

"Any head injuries or near-death experiences?"

"Grew up in Arkansas."

Noted. "When you orgasm," she said, and he straightened, attentive as a *Jeopardy* contestant, "have you ever seen patterns of force or mathematical symbols? Be aware that this stylus can serve as a weapon before you answer."

"I," he said carefully, "have not." Then he actually considered it. There was sex, and then there was mind-blowing sex. He'd experienced mind-blowing sex. What had he seen? "Lemme think a minute, for real." He leaned back, head against the bulkhead, and closed his eyes. "I've seen... colors...like somebody painting real fast. Sometimes maybe, like, jagged static?"

"What about when you dream?"

"I don't dream," he said.

"Never?"

"Not that I ever remember."

She clipped the stylus to her pad. "I'll have more questions later. This was helpful."

"So, Bubbles is into me, huh?"

"Beg pardon?"

He made the universal male motion for gazongas. Without the much-needed shame.

"Neon? I have more of a chance than you'll ever be blessed with. I leave that for you to fail to work into your dreams."

"Hellbilly gets his; I ain't gotta dream."

She regarded him as though he'd grown the head of a slug. "There's some part of you that thinks being an asshole is cute. It is not. Good day, sir."

"Hell, I ain't on this boat to be a monk. Atlantis better recognize."

"I said good day."

~~~

It was a pretty good day thus far, Neon decided. Clear sky, the ship zipping along under minimal guidance, no monsters, time warps, ocean weevils, or sleeper agents on the wide, beautiful horizon. Granted, there were three creepy people in the ship's belly, but in this relatively short time knowing the captain, Neon had yet to find reason to mistrust Desiree's judgment.

Not like Milo Jetstream letting twelve rogue clones of himself run loose, which he had.

The *Linda Ann* was bound for the Blank, then Atlantis, then—if Neon could convince her captain—maybe, just maybe, an actual full-stop break. Just those few days of quietude they'd sought in the first place. Although, having poked several bears in several butts, going back to hauling tail and kicking ass seemed destiny.

Yvonne and Desiree ran laps below her. Gods damn, she loved those two! She'd slap a dragon in the nuts for them, then pause to towel-flick it in the dick despite all the roaring and thrashing. They were so much more than friends, she didn't have a word for it. *Family* didn't do it, because thus far, family got as high a rating in her life as the average Goodreads review gave.

She didn't see them as sisters.

She saw them as blood.

Menses for life, with all the understanding that entailed. Soulmates.

Even Keita, whom Neon would invite into the shower with her in a hot minute, had naturally evolved into someone Neon Nichelle Temples, formerly of Day City, now of the world, would trust with the safekeeping of her immortal soul.

Big thoughts on this comparatively small boat on the huge ocean, but big thoughts were good from time to time. Kept the real real, relegated the fake to trifling.

If anybody deserved the Water's Edge Rest Home for Retired World Savers, it was this group and every other group out there doing the thing despite a world doggedly inclined toward wrong. She'd invite 'em all in. *Come rest,* she thought. *Come eat. Sing. Draw. Paint.*

Be.

Desiree and Yvonne came back into view.

Yeah. Be.

~~~

"Will there be cooking again?" Shig Empa asked.

Shig looked a little haggard. That worried them.

"You okay, buddy?" asked Desiree.

"Oh, just three more for me to hold," he said.

"No, no, they're with us. They're coming with us," Desiree assured, careful, however, not to mention the Nonrich commandos already in "storage."

"Not that I'm not happy to see you," said Shig, sounding more rote than anything.

Yvonne stepped up to wrap him in her arms. She kissed him on the cheek, saying, "Shig, I know we complicate the beejeezus out of your life."

He relaxed into the embrace. "You, my friend, saved my life."

Which she had. But only once. Thoom sleeper, final Buford fight, whole entire thing.

Neon and Keita babysat the new three in the hall outside Shig's office. The first thing the Hellbilly had said to this was "Atlantis got bureaucracies? Not slender people walking around in see-through robes and shit?"

Shigetei Empa, though slender, wouldn't be caught dead in a see-through robe.

"Any complaints about the ban on incoming?" asked Desiree.

"Not yet. Most people here don't really care about who comes through the Blank."

"As long as they don't come through like Buford," said Yvonne.

"The False Prophet Buford was a rock up my ass. Correct?" Shig had a taste for out-Blank slang.

"Close enough," said Yvonne.

"We won't let them stay unless you give the okay," said Desiree. "Besides, right now, just the one will stay."

"The...hellbilly," said Shig.

"Yes. Yvonne, can I have a word with our friend alone?"

"Aye."

As the door shushed closed, Desiree said, "A friend of his has a connection with Bubba Foom. That's worth pursuing. The world's most powerful psychic doesn't truck with just anybody." The Hellbilly's influence was, apparently, like goo stuck to a shoe. She made mental note to scrape that off. "I'll leave him at the build site. Plenty of food, no transportation. And no communication except preprogrammed to your office, and only for emergencies. Strictly defined emergencies. He won't be an issue. Hell, I'll give him a fishing pole and let him sit to his heart's content."

"Maybe I'll send Guerris to visit him," Shig half-joked.

"Couldn't hurt. Would likely help." And for a good laugh, maybe she could get Death-Mael the dragoon to show up. Dragoons, much as their dolphin kin, loved fucking with fishing folk. "Shig, can I ask you something? How many times you been out-Blank?"

"Never."

"Never been curious?"

He shook his head.

"Why not?"

"Not every estrangement," he said gently, "merits a reunion."

"What if the out-world were to flood in here?" she asked.

"Not *if*. It's truly *when*," he said, again gently. "Through no action attributable to you, Milo, or any of my friends. It's inevitable. When it happens, Atlantis will be changed, not gone. If that's the worst, all is well."

"That's very optimistic of you, sir," said Desiree. Like Yvonne, she drew him into a hug and, also like her, kissed his cheek. She had known Shig eleven years. He had never failed to be welcoming, get things done, or protect the entire world—not just his piece of it—by protecting and aiding the Brothers Jetstream, Desiree, Smoove, their ships, the Battle Ready Bastards, or any of hundreds of allies of the cause of simple, quiet existence to come through the Blank.

In the face of the world's insanity, the irony of asking him to close his home to outsiders wasn't lost on her. Nor did it sit right in her stomach. Yet this wasn't xenophobia in the guise of any form of security. If, as Shig said, the discovery of Atlantis was inevitable, the influx—if she had anything to do with it, and by the gods of every sea imaginable, she would—had damn well be one of genuine exploration, not exploitation.

"Seems like we keep promising you we won't mess up your lawn, don't we?" said Desiree.

"It's been relatively quiet. Even our own squabbles have settled into hibernating states. No one's heard from the secessionists since Buford's removal."

"Fancy that."

"I've never considered this place," he said, opening his hands out to the entirety of all he knew, "paradise, dearest heart."

She smiled into his eyes. "No. But it's where you grill your vegetables. That means something."

"It does when you're here," he said.

"Do you want to go out-Blank with me?"

"No. Just hurry and finish your home. I want to sit with you on your grass and do nothing for long periods of time."

"From your lips to the universe, my friend. Tonight we roam the restaurants of Liaan."

"As a minor functionary of Atlantis, I'd be remiss in not pointing out we are in the capital city of Liaan right now," he said at her bright eyes.

"Damn fortunate, that. Wasn't feeling like Sip sausages or Abba pastries. What time should I pick you up? Just you, me, Neon, Yvonne, and your girlfriend."

"Keita?"

"Yes."

Shig Empa, for the first time since any of the crew of the *Linda Ann* entered his office that early afternoon, smiled.

The next morning, Desiree was gone.

~~~

Amongst the scrub and flats of the Sahara: Cape hares, jerboas, and sand foxes. Walking the Sahara in shorts, tees, boots, and sweat because why not: Neon and Yvonne.

"There's a *lot* of travel involved in saving the world," Neon noted, although she felt she had a good handle on having her global legs under her. She never felt anywhere near as lagged as when first adventuring with this colorful bunch.

Yvonne hummed agreement, then added, "Yup." She'd entered the zen of tracking the beads of sweat slipping from her clavicle that conveniently collected in her sports bra.

"I mean, a lot. Excessive. We could really use a transporter. Like the one we've got. In storage."

"Yeah, well, that's not about to happen. It ever strike you that we'd be doing anything like this, me and you?"

"You mean walking on sand knowing there's giant elves beneath our feet? Anybody ever did, they need to be tested for drugs."

"We're in Africa, Nee."

This particular part of Africa had a lot of sand and sparse

scrub. Neon surveyed it, feeling several emotions arising at once, all of them on the uplifting side. "Yeah."

"Home. What're you doing?"

Neon bent, fiddling with her laces. "I need the sand for a minute. So do you."

"Scorpions. Sand adders. Puffins with teeth," said Yvonne.

"None of which are here, per Keita. You've seen too many movies. Shoes off. Most civilized countries, you do that before entering someone's home, you know."

"You know that's gonna be a sonavumbitch in your socks and shoes, right?" But Yvonne knelt to undo her laces after thoroughly stomping the surrounding grounds to be sure there were no unwanted guests.

The sand was warm, firm, and smooth.

Neon took in the unbroken view. Every horizon lined with varying gulfs of tan. Eight billion people on the planet and not a single sign of another soul around.

The Earth was huge.

Why, then, so fucked? Didn't make sense to this city girl nor, Neon was sure, to Yvonne. There was too much world for folks not to feel their own small, connective sense of *home*.

On nights when the wind and ground there didn't conspire to throw a great haze into the sky, the view of the stars almost made Neon cry. She refused to call it heavens. Heaven—whichever variety—for most on the mudball was unattainable. The notion of a better life than the one you woke up to was torture dressed to wine and dine.

Even the early-morning sky now felt like a crisp drink of water, and she was aware of the irony of this thought in the desert, yet apropos was apropos. In Montana, they called it "Big Sky." *This*, this took gargantuan and made it... wonderful. Made it dance.

"The sky's a dancer out here, Vee."

"Nothing but blue, nothing but light."

"You'd think that'd be enough."

"What's on your mind, sweetheart?" said Yvonne. "We

out here looking for souvenirs?"

"I want to feel normal again sometimes," said Neon. "I wanna just walk around."

"Then that is what we shall do. Until my bra disintegrates." It occurred to her: "How is yours not?"

"Superior wicking action."

"Need John Wick to make a difference under those."

"This is why I love you, Yvonne."

"This is why I love you, Neon."

"Wanna walk a little more?" the super woman asked just to be sure.

"Party on, Wayne," said Yvonne.

"Party on, Garth."

"Nerd."

"There's no going back for us, is there?" asked Neon.

This paused Yvonne. She dug her toes into the kiln of creation. If there was a satisfying answer to that, she didn't have it. Going back might not necessarily have been a good thing. Maybe she wasn't the first to run toward the future, but she didn't run away from it, either. Going back, taking back: all retrograde. Evidence of the erosion of potential like sand was the evidence of larger things whittled away.

Stupid notions under her feet like grains of sand.

"What do you think of Desiree's future?" she asked Neon.

"I think it's sweet as fuck. A sweet house by the water with nobody bothering the living shit out of her? Yeah. Covetable. I'ma make sure she gets that."

"What about our futures?" There hadn't been much talk in that arena since joining forces with the Jetstreams. "We're literally a world away from our old lives. I've got zero plans to ever visit Day again—"

"Well, Plenty Mo is still gunning for us," said Neon, then heard it. "Plenty Mo. New Age Mack. The Hellbilly. Holy shit, we can't get away from extra dudes. So extra."

"Day City is dead to me. At least Plenty didn't have any weirdness about him."

"Unless you wanna count small-time drug kingpin. I

mean, I can think of better ways to spend one's time..." Neon snorted. "What would he say if he saw you now?"

"I don't think my cousin could handle," said Yvonne. "We are in the Sahara fucking Desert, Neon Temples."

A smile crept surely into Neon's mouth. "Shout it," she challenged.

"I'm not shouting out here."

"We're in the middle of a desert that could swallow the US and come back for more. Desiree and Keita are puttering with that machine. What else you doin' now but shouting in the desert?"

Yvonne spun in the sand, arms wide. "WE ARE IN THE FUCKING SAHARA DESERT!"

"And what are we doing out here?"

"SAVING THE GODDAMNED WORLD!"

"Better believe it," said Neon.

"But I'm about ready for some air conditioning," said Yvonne.

"Just a little while longer. Bilo himself might have walked these sands. Dude was everywhere. Hell, our great-great-grandparents might've walked these sands. It hurts, having to wonder that."

"Yeah," said Yvonne. "Yeah." She looked around same as Neon had, hands on her hips in expectation of some sign or order to the universe. It was strange, not seeing another living soul, but she knew that was an illusion. There was life everywhere.

"Half hour more," said Neon. "Maybe we'll find trace of a dragon's den. Po said there's one out here."

"You do know Po got jokes?"

"This was totally serious," Neon affirmed. "He laughs at me that we're two hundred thousand years old and don't even know what the interior of our planet looks like."

"Po's a hollow-Earther?"

"No, but he knows there're pockets if you know how to find them."

"We're not fighting dragons, too. We got enough on our plate. But just out of curiosity, he give you any details?"

"Said being surprised is the best part of finding a dragon."

Yvonne dropped butt to ground, brushed off her feet with her socks, then shook out the socks and nodded at Neon to do the same, slipping boots on.

Eventually, they ambled back to the base entrance. It welcomed them with its usual sandy yawn, rising from the ground with automatic filtration and collection systems grabbing curtains of grit to re-deposit along its surface once the hatch sealed.

They went down the stairway, headed left for the kitchen, savored two tall glasses of elderberry-infused water, said hey to the Gang enjoying a game of dominos at a nearby table, a Trinidadian, Laotian, Kenyan, Somali buffet ringing out yet fascinatingly muted, rounded on their staterooms to birdbath, dry off, pad up, and change, met in the hallway, headed to the elves' hive via the connecting passage—both women holding their entire shit together as they once again *entered a hive of underground elves As You Do*—and quickly found Desiree and Keita both standing hands on hips, watching the Bilomatic Entrance with matching frowns as though it had just farted.

The Entrance looked very much like a Lakota thípi minus skin, familial warmth, or obvious purpose, with various mechanical bits added on. It was bone. Perhaps not literally, but it looked like bone. Or stone. Speckled milk, smooth, vaguely organic, and dotted with trillions of microscopic resonance holes that not only allowed for instantaneous dimensional shifts but gave it intriguing shading as well.

Standing before it now, Neon was fairly certain Keita had dismantled its struts and other techy bits for easier transport to Po's safekeeping after the test run.

Yet here it was, fully assembled.

Also vibrating.

Everything in the large honeycomb chamber looked stable and substantial. The Bilomatic Entrance, however, looked slightly blurred, which messed with Neon's equilibrium no end. She immediately ceased trying to focus on it, allowing it to occupy peripheral space only.

"Po rebuilt it," Dr. Keita said to the question marks on both women's faces.

"Reassembled?" said Yvonne.

"No. Rebuilt." Keita pointed. "That wasn't there before."

"I thought this was the pinnacle of human metatechnical achievement," said Neon, quoting from briefing notes Keita'd provided before Moon Gank Alpha.

"We lag behind the elves a bit," said Desiree as answer.

"Has it done anything?" Neon wanted to get closer to it but had seen enough movies to gain wisdom.

"We're not sure," said Desiree.

"I think it's messing with our sense of time," said Keita, "so it seems to be here, but when we blink, it's not."

"But you're not blinking synchronously," said Yvonne.

"That worries me, yes," said Keita.

"So, you mean it's definitely here and not here?" said Yvonne.

"Be still a minute," Keita directed.

The chamber went motionless and quiet save for breaths and heartbeats. After a moment, Yvonne and Neon shared a quizzical raising of brows.

"You felt that?" said Keita. "Like it got warmer in here without a central heat source."

"I felt it," said Neon.

Yvonne nodded. "Just a little. But it was weird; not *on* my body but *in* my body. Like suddenly, *every*thing was active."

"I feel smarter," said Neon.

Keita brushed that off. "That's merely adrenal or psychosuggestive."

"No, I mean literally smarter. My brain is on fire."

"Hook her up," said Desiree.

Keita rummaged in a hip pack and pulled a tightly coiled cord. She connected one end to her scanner; the other, with its multi-leads, dangled like a limp squid.

Neon dropped cross-legged to the cool floor and closed her eyes as Keita gently pressed pads to temples, forehead, and the base of her skull. She took a deep, steady hit of Keita's subtle woodsy citrus fragrance. It felt good. Felt calming.

"I see patterns and equations," the woman from Day City reported from the view in her mind's eye.

"Do everybody," Desiree told Keita. "I'll do you."

"This won't be conclusive," Keita cautioned.

"Shits 'n giggles," said Desiree.

Once completed, with gear packed, Keita went off in search of Gang of Four's number three, Vanh, who was also a certified MD. If there was a whiff of weirdness, xe'd see.

"Still feel it?" Desiree asked.

Neon nodded.

"All right, everybody out."

Po, who'd been delayed teaching a class, caught them just as Desiree sealed the chamber.

"You feel anything weird with this, Po?" asked Desiree.

Po frowned at the word *weird*. Everything was weird to humans.

"Did it affect you? Noticeably?"

"Yes," came the elf's baritone.

"How so?"

"Calming."

Desiree nodded her thanks. "Nobody in or out for a minute, please."

Po, in turn, nodded acceptance.

Neon and Yvonne followed the captain in silence through the honeyglass corridors back to the Depot, which, though decorated in textiles, plant oases, and varied arts from each of Africa's countries, felt staid in comparison.

"I don't think most of the elves even notice us anymore," said Neon.

"It is starting to feel a little like Shropshire Mall, isn't it?" said Yvonne. To Desiree: "Upscale, booshie mall back home. Deep suburbs."

"Difference here is it's not ignorance, it's acceptance," said Desiree. "Don't forget that."

"Giant, quiet elves can be mildly unsettling," said Neon.

"They respect your privacy. How's your head?"

"I got a sense you wanted to say *privacy* like a Brit. Like it's your secret preference."

"It is. I like that word."

"You sensed that?" said Yvonne.

"Uh-huh."

"What'd it feel like?" said Desiree.

"Like I had your brain for a quick second."

"The blink of an eye," Desiree said, thoughts forming. "What the devil happens to the universe when we blink?"

"Nothing," said Yvonne.

"No, I don't think so," said Desiree. "Bilo mentioned 'partner states.'"

"That was just a theory he had," said Yvonne, recalling notes Keita had given.

"I don't think anything Bilo thought was a theory. Dude was straight-connected to the All," said Desiree. "I need to do some more reading. You," she said to Neon, "check in with Keita and Vanh again before long, then we all sit down with Po and figure out what the universe wants from us next."

CHAPTER TEN

Villainy

Her nightmares felt like dreams, and that was strange, very strange. Was she being guided? Megu lay peaceably in bed, eyes wide open, taking in the night static surrounding her. She'd had the whale dream again. Usually, simply being in the lifeboat on the open sea left her in sweats and shivers, but to know that the whale shot its way to her from beneath led to paralysis, and to see it breach immediately woke her. She'd never known how the whale dream ended.

Except now at sixty-three years of age.

She had no intention of recounting the dream, for that wasn't important. The matter of study lay in her being awake, calm, and mildly amused. The whale had terrorized her for half her life...and it had wanted absolutely nothing. They weren't frequent nightmares, and they'd done some good; Mo had been particularly caring when she thrashed and hyperventilated. Hashira Megu was not one to thrash and hyperventilate.

Neurosurgeons had proven useless.

Naturopaths had proven useless.

Megu saw no benefit discussing the episodes in intimate conversations.

Mo believed insinuating himself into the lives of the entire world to be some type of worthy endeavor.

They divorced.

He hadn't been in her bed to attempt to comfort the whale dream in sixteen years.

The dream itself had been absolutely nothing. When she'd had a soul, it'd terrorized her.

No, not true, she corrected. A whale dream had come two months before the theft of the Bilomatic Entrance. Her soul hadn't been present for her for even a year before that. She'd given up that particular equation to science.

Yes, but each dream, you're in a different ship.

Tonight had been a simple wasen, one which she intuitively knew she'd built. It smelled of cedar, cypress, and fresh stain, a dark stain with red undertones that gave the modest boat a sharp, eel-skin presence. Angular, precise, and beautiful in the way uncut cypress and cedar were. Her boat on the sea had felt as though part of the water, not some transient interloper.

Megu remembered bare feet slapping the water as she shoved the craft offshore and hopped aboard, her momentum and weight carrying it out of the shoals. Time blipped, and suddenly, she was in the midst of true power; no shore in any direction, just a boat keeping her afloat upon reality. Nothing to do but set the oars aside and experience the bobbing, up, down, sometimes predictable in strength, sometimes not, but always—and there she smiled in the darkness—grounding.

And the whales? They weren't randomly coming for either her or air. They were summoned.

Summoned by an aging woman in a boat. She didn't know what she wanted them for, but she—for the first time since these recurring dreams had affixed to her subconscious—knew they were necessary. This all without a soul, which told her two things: you could dream without a soul, and without a soul, you commanded the dreaming universe rather than floated in it.

She'd never believed in magic before.

Now there might be practical applications for it.

"Text Maurice," she said to the pad on her nightstand. "*Discontinuing replacement of machine until further notice. Will speak with you over breakfast.*"

Then she gave the command that would lock everyone involved out of their tasks, before rolling over to resume what she felt would be an unusually good night of sleep.

~~~

"You've never supported my dreams, Megu."

She stopped mid-cut of her eggs hollandaise. "Choose your words, Maurice; don't just speak them. This building bears your name because of me. Not my support. Me. Please remember. If you mean your need to be seen as powerful, no, I haven't, because it's foolish. What was it an American congresswoman said? 'No one makes a billion dollars; they take it.' Taking things is easy, not powerful."

"You knew what you were creating things for," said Mo.

She placed her gleaming utensils beside her plate. "Your uses never eclipsed my own intent."

"Will you resume production of the machine?"

"So that you can become a god?"

"So that others will *know* I'm a god."

Megu resumed eating. Eggs hollandaise tasted wretched cold, and she no longer wished to start her days cold, unpleasant, or wretched.

She wanted them free from anyone's needs, wants, or desires impinging on her work. As far as she was concerned, the world had offered up only seven geniuses to human history. Bilo had been the first. She was the seventh. That came with a certain implicit trust from humanity in its rewards to come.

She would prove once and for all that a soul was a

hindrance…and allow Mankind to truly, freely build.

Maurice, noticing the slight, quiet smile come to her face, offered one thought to the breakfast tableau:

That can't be good.

~~~

His guards followed close. He wished they'd go away. Maybe a rival would seize that moment, whom he'd have to defeat single-handedly. He could. Kosugi Mo hadn't been defenseless since the age of five.

Why now did he feel utterly open and, worse, pointless? And this solely after a breakfast of eggs!

The first time he and Megu ever laid eyes on each other had been in a dojo long before. She'd sparred with him. Beat him; outside the dojo, charmed him with an utter lack of guile. He had grown up in a rich home; guile was the first ablution of the day, the first greeting, and the final brushing of the teeth before meeting the world. His father adored what he called "American directness," but that was really nothing but the Euro-American fetish of behaving as poorly as possible with few to zero repercussions. The moment Mo realized that as the true, unspoken American dream, he knew how easy it would be to mold such a dream to his uses.

Putin wanted world dominance. Bezos flaunted financial addiction. Aileen Stone and her Buford followers sought immortality through omnipresence, while Kosugi Maurice sought nothing less than the fabric of reality itself remade, remolded, and repurposed into a perpetual form of heaven that, millennia hence with humans amongst the life of the cosmos, could be traced directly to him alone. Humanity amongst the stars, not as a fool relegated to sit in the corner that was the ancestral home but as necessary to the continuance of the stars themselves. Necessary to the universe despite its feigned indifference.

His father's favorite song had been Earth, Wind & Fire's "Keep Your Head to the Sky."

Interesting, thought Maurice with the haze of morning

bearing down on him, how paths set themselves in stone completely unaided.

"In the Stone" was another Earth, Wind & Fire song. *Shit*.

~~~

By the time Megu realized she loved him, he had already quintupled his family's considerable wealth. By the time he proposed, plans were drawn for the Kosugi Lunar Expansion Potential Terran Outpost.

"You're a maniac, Maurice," his father had said, which wasn't the best of deathbed utterances, but there you were. Despite doubting his only child, Father was now buried on the moon.

He and Megu had done it in EV suits of her design she'd wanted to test.

There were times he wondered how one divorced a woman with whom he'd stood upon the moon itself.

Then he remembered he hadn't. She had divorced him.

"I can't do anything more for you as your wife," she'd said. "I will continue, however, to remake the world with you as your partner."

I will be seventy years old this year, he thought, barely noticing the attendant bowing as his awaiting car's door shushed open and he entered, Bodyguard One entering from the other side and Two coolly sliding beside him, with plenty of room between all three in the ridiculously spacious vehicle. Kosugi had decided on old-school protocol for a meeting called by the Thoom woman, an unprecedented one at that, which not even Megu knew about. The timing, though unfortunate, didn't disturb in the least; he'd made an empire of conjoining events to his pleasing. This would be no different.

"*Cease Operations.*" Megu had outmaneuvered him at the wushu of life since they'd met. Why—in the midst of shifting chaos he and others tried to direct—should this be any different? She may not have supported his dreams but she constructed his reality.

Fair trade left him clear-minded.

The car whizzed through Hokkaido's streets.

From there, the highland roads.

From there, the rural roads.

From there, the private roads.

From there, the disappearing roads of which whispers were shouts and so weren't spoken of. Kosugi had chosen this mode of travel because he was in no rush and the scenery was lovely.

From there, a defunct silo he used as a remote bunker.

Meeting on his "turf," as it'd been put, was an act of good faith. Laughable. What faith did the Thoom have in anything but themselves? It was an act of desperation and cowardice, but he wouldn't say so until it was to his advantage.

She knew his route; he knew hers. She had snipers on her helicopter; he had snipers behind blinds on his roof. They'd agreed on two guards each in the room with them, guards who would step into a rotor or off a rooftop if given the order. The number of people who would do exactly such astounded no end.

Kosugi wondered how human history would have gone if people'd said no more often.

Nonetheless, this proved to be as engaging a meeting as Kabuki theatre, as wrought as Italian opera, and as rich as a production by the only playwright of any interest the West produced, Tennessee Williams.

As he rode the elevator to the top of his silo in the middle of nowhere, the penthouse agreed upon as the hardest for him to escape from, the easiest—close to the helipad—for her, Mo gave a brief thought to the two men beside him. Perhaps he'd indeed give the order to jump? It was good to rotate trusts.

He entered an empty yet sumptuous room, one appointed for short sprints of business, longer bouts of pleasure. Not a sex room by stunted USian sensibilities, but one in which meditation, meals, or lounging on ridiculously thin but comfortable mats were summarily enjoyed.

His men positioned themselves exactly where he said they'd be positioned, at opposing diagonals of the circular room, somewhat behind him as he sat dead center of the space behind a glass desk big enough for a proper buffet, their guns clearly visible per agreement. The floor-to-ceiling windows that ringed the entire penthouse floor gave all a full view—save for the elevator block and emergency stairwell—of the interior and exterior.

Within minutes, the chop of rotors announced the presence of guests who'd been tracked the moment they entered Hokkaido air space. After several more moments, the sleek, futuristic dragonfly landed.

Kosugi had pulled up a news feed in the glass and scrolled while he waited.

The elevator car went upward.

Footfalls in the stairwell sounded downward.

The stairwell door opened, slowly yet confidently. The elevator dinged.

Her men stepped out of the elevator. She crossed to the seat opposite Kosugi and remained standing. When her men were in their agreed-upon positions, Kosugi stood as well.

"Madam," he said, "welcome to Japan."

The clapback was immediate and harsh.

"Don't. Give. Me. That *welcome* shit when you and that bitch and who else has been attacking me unprovoked and one of my favorite operatives disappears without. A. Trace."

The famous Americanism. Kosugi thought a moment before responding.

"Perhaps you misheard information," he said. Since it was clear niceties were unnecessary, he sat.

"Perhaps you need not fuck with the Thoom, Kosugi."

Her red hair, coiffed to within an inch of its life in a style suitable for winning an Academy Award, perfectly offset her blood-orange lipstick, demanding attention at every word from her mouth.

His dark hair, with exactly one cowlick allowed to dangle, made his face a showcase for hidden agendas.

"Are you here to suggest an alliance?" he said.

Madam Cynthia sat gracelessly. She looked him eye to eye. "What'd we do to you?"

"Madam," he said, the tone clearly meaning *Slow your roll*.

"Maurice-san," she said pointedly. Hell kind of name was Maurice for a global player?

"I agreed to this primarily out of curiosity. It wanes. Swiftly."

"I'd hoped to speak plainly. I see you want to dance."

"Someone whose fumbled steps lost them Buford doesn't call the dance," said Kosugi.

"Tell me this: how does someone as evil and soulless as you stay off the Jetstreams' radar?"

"I am fully vested in my soul, Madam. I don't poison children with subpar food, create permanent serfs, or ram my dick into the Earth, hoping oil geysers out."

"That altruistic heart gives you time to fuck with me?" said Cynthia.

Kosugi looked down. He remained silent a moment. She thought she had him, then he tapped the glass and swiped right.

"I'm ordering a carafe. Do your men—"

"They're good," she said.

"Mine will have tea." He relaxed into his chair.

Madam did the same.

Staring contest ensued.

In less than ten seconds, a squat, rectangular bot rolled out of a niche with a carafe, cups, and accoutrements. Its top lifted and slid itself as a tray to the glass; the wafer-thin tray then made its way to Kosugi without so much as a rattle of cups or *splip* of tea, settled upon the glass, and waited.

Kosugi nodded left, then right. His guards poured their tea and resumed their positions with tiny sips.

Two cups remained.

"Lipton," said Kosugi. "Pre-brewed. Hot. With hibiscus and ginger."

"Is that a joke?"

"Madam, I remind you that you are neither in China nor a bull. I'm not fragile but I'm also disinterested in clumsy blows."

"Motion, then, to reset the tone. The Thoom will withdraw entirely from Japan if you withdraw from us."

"Why would I want you to leave? You come to accuse with no information or proof. You come to bargain with nothing to give. You've yet to say hello. If nothing else, I want the Thoom here as the sideshow attraction so thoroughly represented by your behavior."

"I apologize."

"And I," said Kosugi, "do not yet accept. Is it correct you managed to clone Milo Jetstream? With stolen Nonrich technology?"

"We're no longer able to do so. One of his operatives—"

"Kicked. Your. Ass. And cleaned. You. Out." He relished saying it. "One. I believe they call him 'The Mad Buddha.' All of us have spies within all our organizations. Mine just happen to be effective. One frightful operative working in darkness with the strengths and recuperative abilities of a vampire. May I pull up some footage?"

"Point made."

"Give me a reason beyond the promise of safety I made that I shouldn't kill everyone currently without tea."

The long internal monologue of *fuuuuuck* going through Madam's head prevented an immediate response. Her corpus, however, galvanized, leaning her forward to take a cup, the carafe, and a moment to silently pour herself a serving, set it before her, and lean back. When she met his eyes again, she made sure to do so with a slightly defiant, slightly conciliatory raise of a pencil-thin auburn eyebrow.

"Motion," she said again, "to reset the tone."

Kosugi waved a circle to encompass the space. "The room is yours."

She first took a sip, pushed her chair back for room to cross her legs, closed her eyes, steepled her fingers in her lap, and said, "I won't even ask why the sudden escalation. Since it's coming from multiple fronts, I can only assume someone sensed a weakness," opening her eyes only at the very end. "I assure you we are not. I can also assure you that whatever stake you think you have in this is false. There's no aggression between us."

"Beyond scuttling two of my freighters last year."

"That was business, nothing but operations of the day. Not," she said, emphasizing it with a raised, artfully manicured finger, "aggression."

"What of Nonrich?"

"Sworn enemies. Never heard you swear against me, though. I'm asking you directly to sit this one out while I restore order. Can you be gracious?"

"It's been known to happen. It happens quicker with suitable incentives to consider."

She retrieved her cup and blew on it to raise a few wisps and tendrils. She took a sip, set the cup down, and asked, "Have you ever been to Atlantis? I know people."

~~~

When she left, Kosugi's left-hand man—who clearly had a question—was allowed to speak. "Boss, was that strategy?" he asked of Madam Cynthia's performance. "Because it wasn't very good."

"No. That was America."

CHAPTER TEN.5

Heroes

"Not everybody knows about this place?" the Hellbilly asked Guerris while Shig Empa grilled vegetable-fruit kabobs. The Hellbilly knew when he was being babysat. As the Hellbilly had spent all morning fishing, sleeping, and wondering whether or not a swim in unsure waters was advisable, he did not care.

"That's more for Shigetei than me...but I'd say, based on how ignorant most out-Blankers are, no."

"Damn, son."

"I meant that strictly literally," Guerris assured.

"Y'all ready for when they do?"

"Of course."

"You're the chillest motherfucker I've ever seen."

"I don't know that one." Guerris angled a shout over his shoulder. "Shig, 'the chillest motherfucker'—is that good?"

"That's good," Shig shouted back.

Guerris nodded at the Hellbilly. "Thank you."

~~~

"The machine told me it's tethered to a section of its soul in a box at the bottom of the ocean. Your Pacific." That was Po.

"I verify this." That was Tash-Bon-Nay.

"Wait, what?" That was Yvonne.

"Milo's always binding pieces of himself all over the planet, it happens," said Neon.

"I amplified the connection," said Po. "Cruel in not otherwise. It yearned."

"Milo is flesh and blood, not a teleportation machine. Just the one soul?" said Desiree.

Po nodded.

"How are you speaking to it?" asked Keita.

"Sub-ethereally."

"Please don't build anything else onto it, at least not yet," said Desiree. "All right. We thought we had all the pieces of this sucker. We do not."

"Oh, fuck," said Neon, knowing what was about to happen.

"Girl, you're 'bout to get your hair wet," said Desiree. "Extra conditioner on board for everybody."

"Underwater?" said Neon.

"Underwater," said Desiree. "Everybody prep. Next stop, Pacific Ocean. Po, let Keita know what we're looking for. Tash, can I speak to you alone?"

Apart from the group, Desiree asked Tash point-blank if she'd like to come.

"I have not been as conversant with the machine."

"But you can have it guide us to what we need."

"If it permits."

"Po's too emotionally attached. I need somebody frosty," said Desiree.

Tash considered this. "Yes, yes, I am as frosty as they come."

"I really didn't think Po was gonna mind-meld with the

thing. Well, I didn't think it had a mind."

"A soul. Distinction."

"A soul. I'm not even going to pretend I'm prepared to discuss how this machine has a soul. I'm in uncharted territory and could use your wisdom."

"You've made your life charting new lands and spaces."

"There's a difference between teen-charter-boat-captain Desiree and teleporting-AI-with-a-soul Quicho. I need to make sure we do this right. That means we'll need to communicate, although I have no idea what this thing's range is."

"Thought is not spatial."

"You've tried teaching me to 'think' for three years and I haven't gotten it yet."

"Neon, perhaps?"

"Is she ready? Considering what might be going on in her head?"

"Likely not," Tash capitulated. "I accept your offer."

"I want to hug you so much, but I'd just wind up sticking my face in your belly button."

Tash opened her arms wide and downward, even scrunching a bit so that Desiree wouldn't feel totally tiny. "I would not object."

Desiree gave her a mighty squeeze. Face turned to the side against Tash's lower ribcage, she said, "The Pacific's pretty damn big. Can it tell us precisely where it is?"

"I can try."

"Got a feeling we're gonna need Bobo."

CHAPTER FUCKING ELEVEN

Also Known As Bobo the Mag

"My friends," said the captain once their Humvee was packed, the crew loaded, and the air conditioning at full blast, "the ride has gotten wetter, the height requirement hoisted upward, and the stakes just might be the future of the human race."

"Figures," said Yvonne.

"When ain't it?" Neon, of course.

"Shall we ride?" said Desiree.

"You can call me Sally," said Yvonne with a short salute, "till the stars come home."

They rode, flew, and finally, *finally* made it back to the welcoming deck of the *Linda Ann*, whereupon the waters awaited them once again, but this time, they'd have welcome help.

~~~

"Neon?"

"Yeah?"

"You ever think we'd be sailing the Pacific with a seven-foot-tall elf doing the Winslet scene from Titanic on our prow?"

"No. No, I did not."

"Thanks. Didn't think so."

"Super cool, though, innit?" said Neon.

"Very," said Yvonne.

~~~

Tash rarely blinked. The Saharan elves had a super translucent membrane permanently over the eyes, offering protection plus constant moisture. Her dark, mottled skin somehow managed to tread between feline, lizard, and warmly human—all Saharan elves did—and her hair, plaited in three rows of tight twists, was as resplendently silver as a frosted breath.

She managed to look as though she belonged on the water.

Not yet on course for the soul box, nor even at full speed, Tash stayed by Desiree's side for long periods of time, the two of them speaking in Elvish, which, outside of Keita, no one on board knew.

Neon and Yvonne took turns in the pilot room. Now and then, one or the other would see Tash come into view, the sun gleaming off her exo-plating where her rainbow scarves had slipped, and at her elbow Desiree's head. But nothing for a while now.

Had the feel of sekret stuff. Neon, currently on pilot duty, loved sekret stuff.

She knew the captain's footfalls up the short set of steps into the pilot room.

"Still steady and true," she said without turning.

"Let her play by herself for a minute. Deck meeting in ten."

"Aye."

At the deck meeting: Desiree, Tash, Yvonne, Keita, and Neon. Still in the hold: Sharon and Compoté. Tash kept wanting to release them but agreed to abide by Desiree's constraint "though it be exceedingly difficult." (Translated from the Elvish.)

"This one's off the books," said Desiree to the assembled. "Even our books. No one knows about where we're going but me and Keita. We keep it that way, agreed?"

Unanimous and immediate agreement.

"I have a bad feeling about this underwater excursion awaiting us, so I'm calling in a big favor," she continued. "Something of an expert."

Oh, hell yeah, thought Neon. *Another superpower.* She loved this. "Who?" she asked, trying to imagine the name of power. "Mythros the Invincible? Daggett? Jedi Pope?"

"You've been studying," said Desiree.

"Hightop the Faded," said Yvonne.

"Honey, be seated," Desiree told Yvonne. "We need a shifter. We need a daredevil. We need an escape artist."

"Well, fuckbits, you already know who it is, girl; stop leading," said Yvonne.

"Bobo," said Desiree.

"Bobo," Keita repeated, eyes sparkling behind her red-rimmed glasses, "the motherloving Giant Red Pacific Octopus." The scientist caught Desiree's eye, plans already forming. "Shit, yeah."

"Hold all questions," Desiree said, "till we reach destination."

~~~

The destination didn't have a name. It was near no shipping lanes, cruise lines, or rugged world sailing. To find it meant you knew about it and had a solid need to be there.

Choppy waters bobbed the platform up and down. A large grey slab of a structure, it looked like a titan's bathroom tile dropped on the world, never to know grout or complete pattern again. It was windowless and nearly featureless. Stout prongs sprouted at each of the four corners. Had the ocean been calm, the structure would never have been noticed.

Desiree guided the *Linda Ann* to within fifty meters. "Drop skiff. Neon, you're with us. Yvonne, keep her at station."

The skiff dropped, magnetizing to the hull. Desiree, Keita, and Neon clambered down, de-magged, and sliced their way to the ocean-faring tile. Rungs, masts, and other protuberances—all painted the same gunmetal grey as the structure—detailed themselves at the skiff's approach. The tile was actually quite sizeable. Neon estimated a good fifty by seventy-five meters, with an above-water height that could easily accommodate Tash.

The skiff pulled alongside a docking point to magnetize across the arch of a recessed hatch, which opened with a breathy *clang*. Steadied by handrails, the three stepped out and into the teetering tile.

Biddle Beenz stood right there. Almost directly in front of them. So closely, had they backed up en masse, they'd have fallen back into the skiff.

Beside this grinning person: a cephalopod on a skateboard.

Biddle threw their arms wide. "We haven't seen you in a hideous amount of time!"

Desiree stepped into those arms. The hug, being full and unhurried, stretched warmth that encircled Keita and Neon, one of whom knew without doubt her hug was coming and the other feeling the definite likelihood.

The old friends parted. "What have you been up to?" said Biddle.

"The usual."

Biddle turned bright eyes toward Keita. "Dr. LaFleur. Always a pleasure."

Hug number two.

"We have not met," Biddle said afterward to Neon. "We welcome you."

"Many thanks." Their hug was followed by an introduction of the skateboarding 'pod.

"Jules. Current"—they frowned for the term—"unpaid intern?"

The tiny cephalopod on its tiny skateboard—which, to be fair to its dignity, was a hovering slip of clear polycarbon—slapped tentacles to the floor and pulled off, curiosity obviously satisfied.

"Wait...she's from Atlantis," said Neon. There were markers, tonal differences in speech.

"They've been out-Blank for thirty-five years. Alone," said Desiree.

"They, thank you," Neon corrected.

"Not alone," said the doctor. "Surrounded. More communication in our days than all your social media combined. Currently accepted into three hundred non-terrestrial species chats."

"Pardon?" said Neon.

"Biddle is a communications specialist. On all the science-society rags in Atlantis."

"This is a nexus," said Biddle. "We tell you that because Desiree trusted you enough to bring you here. As such, it's a zone of peace and détente. There is no hunting, preying, fighting, or otherwise annoying behavior allowed to any of the communicative species within a five-kilometer radius of this observatory."

"Squidward's kinda cute," Neon said, nodding toward the slowly "skating" 'pod. At Biddle's frown of confusion, she waved it away. "Sorry, not important."

Biddle took off in the same direction as the skater, passing it to step onto a large disc set into the floor. Once joined by the others, the disc smoothly descended, with a ring rising from the floor for a handhold. The bottom of the Great Tile came into view, as did the fact that the tile was more an iceberg; beneath the surface—by benefit of the clear tube they descended in—was an interconnected series of branching clear tubes dotted with egress hatches, tubes that crossed horizontal, vertical, diagonal, and curved, all around a central bubble of the same grey as the tile but banded in large windows. Aquadrones zipped to and fro, sometimes singly, sometimes in groups, mimicking the organized fish darting about.

The drop shaft deposited them inside a very large box from which three tubes offered direction. Biddle proceeded left.

"Glad you wore breach suits," said Biddle. "Everything is safe but there's been rough water lately."

"No worries," said Desiree. "There's a chance we might need to get out there. My hope is not. Any word from Bobo yet?"

"We sent the pulse as soon as you told us you needed his services. Nothing yet."

"I feel a little dizzy," said Neon.

Biddle immediately took her hand and walked with her. "So sorry. You're in the middle of a huge psychic and subsonic brew right now. These underwater tubes aren't likely helping with your equilibrium either. Just a short walk."

It was indeed beautiful. Neon sneaked quick peeks outward in between trying to fiercely maintain her balance. They were close enough to the surface that light shone in ripples, adding life to the nothingness around her: a shoal here, large fin-swish there, the bulk, she was sure, of a whale doing somersaults in the distance.

"I wanted you in here so you could acclimate," Desiree said. "You should've seen Bubba Foom first time he was here."

The belly of the complex appeared much like Shig's office in its spare beauty, only notably wetter, as animals that could fare the environ entered via smaller tubes, flopped about a bit, and exited through others.

Or stayed. Somehow, Jules appeared moments after they'd all sat, skateboard quietly buzzing.

"Same tech as the lightdiscs," Desiree said for Neon's benefit.

"The UFOs," said Neon.

On occasion, a public-works lightdisc—generally self-correcting and, as a grid, self-monitoring—would go off course and drift through the Blank, to Atlantis's embarrassment, the mechanisms' AIs being at times more *self* than *correcting*.

The wee cephalopod parked itself near Biddle's slippered feet.

Desiree got to it.

"There's something deep-water we need. We've an idea where it is. If Bobo agrees, he'd make this a hundred times easier for us. We have reason to believe there's a soul trapped in a box. We don't know the tech yet, but we got Flowerpot here and Tash."

"That explains the chatter about ghosts we've heard," said Biddle. "Thoughts from an unsourced being, cephalopods shapeshifting against their will..."

"Underwater ghost stories," said Neon.

"There's even talk that singularities, which are the most soulless eating machines in any waters, have changed their hunting areas."

"One of those dumbasses rammed me," said Desiree.

Biddle's eyes flew wide with concern.

Desiree held up a hand. "Clipped us a while ago; we're fine. If we can outmaneuver Leviathan, a singularity is nothing. We're staying here till we find the soul."

Biddle's eyes widened even more. "We can set a feast."

"May I ask why 'we'?" said Neon. "Not to be rude. Empathic curiosity. I sense something."

"We were one of the first to shift across multiverses with Fiona Carel."

"That's what I'm getting. Mirrors in you."

"Lolita was there as well. Everyone reacts slightly differently. We still have Lolita's recipes for a seaweed bake."

Neon perked up. "I know that name. Lolita. Milo talked about her."

"Lolita Bebida. We became celebrities the same year. Beautiful soul," said Biddle. "She mentioned Milo to me in correspondence, but I've never met him."

"You're not missing much," Neon said, successfully stifling a grin.

"So, is Bobo a pet?" asked Neon.

"Pet ownership is another way to convince yourself that domination over others is a form of love," said the doctor. "No pets. Doctor, you've been very silent," Biddle said to Keita, who'd been in deep thought the entire time walking the ark.

"Just thinking about ghosts," said Keita, "and what connects them to us machines."

~~~

Bobo knew he overthought things. It was a failing. Escaping a predator was no different from escaping one of the many tube puzzles several scientists (now fired) at the Portland Oceanic Institute used to love throwing at him. Literally throwing. Bobo was big. And when Bobo escaped, Bobo tended to hustle and flail. Underwater, it would have been a magnificent display of ferocity. On land, even though still dangerous, he looked like a Harryhausen dramaturge.

Good times.

Out there in the ocean, there wasn't a current, cuttlefish, or sand swirl he couldn't read to his advantage. Could any shark ever say it'd tasted even the tip of one of the strawberry suckers of Bobo the Mag? Mag for magnificent. Only if it was lying, which sharks did all the time. What could anyone expect from something always trying to look uninterested as it figured out vectors to murder you?

This one was a mako, a big one, and it was intentionally circling wide and slow to get other makos involved, maybe hem Bobo in so its beady-eyed, politician-caught-in-a-sex-scandal rictus face could swoop in for the grand nab.

Not today, you idiot fuck.

To Bobo's right: wide-open ocean inviting him to escape, which might totally be a mistake he wouldn't live to regret. Makos were stupidly fast.

To Bobo's left: the hulk of a ship that had settled on a shelf and had been home to moray eels for several generations.

Below him: silt. Loads of it in many directions.

He hunkered very still, looking like the kin of the large piece of snapped coral several yards away, his usual reddish hue turned sickly grey and brown, complete with coral spikes, nodules and crags in unfortunate places.

Swirling above him: a warm, spiraling current. Bluefin tuna loved those. And there was a large-enough school nearby to be effective.

The trick would be getting enough of the tuna to slam into the shark...

~~~

"Why am I so damned thirsty?" said Neon. "If the ghost of Bea Arthur offered me a glass of lukewarm water right now in exchange for two hours of dry cunnilingus, there'd be no hesitation on my part. Crazy thirsty."

"That's Bobo," said Desiree.

Bobo, all eighty-five kilos of him, rested comfortably in a glass pool that looked two sizes too small for something even half his size.

It had been a hell of a trip, one of escapes, epiphanies, new love interests, and a villain (rogue dragoon formerly of Atlantis named Death-Mael) finally worthy of Bobo the Mag, eighth wonder of the Pacific, numbers one through seven as well.

He'd finally answered the call.

"Bobo makes you thirsty?" said Neon.

"When you first meet him. Bobo, cut it out," said Desiree.

The Mag didn't have to be psychic to read sharp tones and intentions.

"He's generally only like this after mating," said Biddle. "An unusually high amount of mating around here."

"You've created the perfect singles party," said Desiree.

"Yes, there's that."

Neon moved cautiously closer. "How do we communicate with it?"

"You have to touch it," said Desiree.

"Speaking in the general 'you,' yes?"

"Nerp," said Desiree. "You."

"Nerp."

"Listen, Bubba's our main psychic. He's gone," said Desiree. "That leaves you."

"Do you know what hentai is?" she asked her captain, then looked at the size of Bobo again.

"I'm not saying open a bottle of champagne with it. Touch it, let it sense your desires, move on."

"Wouldn't it be better if Tash did this?" said Neon.

"It doesn't know Tash's mind. It knows humans. Why do you think I briefed you and Tash, and had her meld with you?" said Desiree.

"As backup."

"Front and center, dear. Show Bobo what you got."

Bobo's wet bulk shuddered and undulated.

"You saw that?" Neon said. "Sucker's got a hard-on under there somewhere."

"Are you seriously daunted? Neon, we need this."

"Just some small daunts."

"Neon Temples, you touch that octopus or I swear to Gaia, I'll scream." Which was a sentence she'd never have thought needed saying.

"That a direct order?" said Neon.

"Very much so," said Desiree. "Reach out, touch Bobo's hand, make this world a better place. If you can."

"M'god, woman, you said that with a straight face."

Neon looked at Bobo again. After all the shit she'd seen, being squicked by an octopus was an eminently dick move. An octopus. *You are calamari*, she thought. *I use plates, knives and forks.*

But why'd it have to be so bulbous, knobby, and slick? Thing was a ball sack with excellent mobility.

She reached down. Touched Bobo. Nothing happened, then Bobo ballooned and dashed down his tube so quickly, he looked flushed, leaving a bewildered woman to stare at jetted silt. "That was it?"

"Doesn't take long."

"The location in my head feels like it's a hundred miles

away and deep as shit."

"Yeah," said Desiree. "Knowing Bobo, he'll get there before us."

~~~

Generally, Bobo hated wearing trackers. The Institute had done nothing but track him. Ping, ping, ping all through the oceans, with them never figuring out how he crossed huge sections of ocean so fast. Equipment failure, they figured.

Doofuses. It was a water world and they were just polyps in it. There were so many Hollow Points, Blanks, and Thin Strips, Bobo could go from his secret home in the Pacific to a 'pi call in the Atlantic (as there were no booties within his kind) in less time than it took Desiree to eventually reach the spot where his tracker's encoded beacon would stop her. Maybe then he'd get to meet that new consciousness he'd vaguely sensed peeking out from the guts and wires of her boat.

"Soul in a box," they said, and deep. Likely not unprotected. Likely very difficult to get to.

Yes, let the octopus get killed.

Except he was Bobo the Mag. Who else had ever slapped Raffic the Mad Buddha and gotten away with it?

The tracker would ping him when the dry-bones caught up and were in range. Bobo shaped his twenty-three feet of length into a dart, jetting toward the impenetrable deeps, focusing all his attention on his bioelectrical sensory net. It was colder there, just enough to be annoying. He oscillated rapid muscle contractions back and forth along each of his strong limbs, but not enough to be a clarion call to some glow-jawed, overly toothed, dead-eyed beast hoping for a quick lunch.

For a squishy ball sack with excellent mobility, he could take a lot more pressure than any dry-ass four-limb. He now navigated totally by the sense of space the box occupied in his head.

He detected the first of the sentry sensors by its energy signature, or rather by its paucity of energy. There were no attention-drawing lights on it, and just the faintest motor whir. A four-limb wouldn't have noticed it in this alien atmosphere but surely would have been noticed; the small machine, though, being in Bobo's home, merely logged the passing of his cephalopod body's languid, unhurried arc over and around it. Bobo knew these signatures well. Certain ships traveled with these sensors hidden beneath their massive hulls like hypervigilant remora. He'd not yet been able to sneak onto one of the stealthy ships, but he'd learned to dance with their parasite remora pretty well.

Desiree, having banked on the fact that Kosugi thought the soul absolutely well hidden, had anticipated at best a long response time if any alarms were tripped by an aquatic. Animals with electrical equipment were commonplace in these waters. If Bobo played his cards right, he'd appear to be one more object of study released into the wild.

Bobo didn't have a conceptual analog for *just be cool*, because that would have been like the ocean having an abundance of ways to call itself *wet*; he spread all eight limbs outward, becoming an invisible yet slowly spinning umbrella that drifted past yet another drone, his body drawing ever downward, downward, into the stygian depths of the canyon of a volcanic outcropping. Whatever the thing he sought was, it knew precisely where it was, which was highly unusual. Its sense of place felt almost like a drug. Bobo *wanted* to be there.

Most of the species he'd encountered were utter dullards at anything deeper than visual recognition of space. Now that he knew how to recognize this thing's *tings* and strokes as directions, it was a beacon he couldn't miss with all nine brains shut down. Same as the dull glow issuing upward from beneath an outcropping he approached after drifting downward quite some time.

He knew plasma arcs. The Bimaiy had used them against him once off-planet. This wasn't as sophisticated, but the biting teeth of its energy felt the same. The barrier was set deep into the stone of a crevasse. The latticework arcs across the crevasse prevented getting to the other side. The volcanic range itself was too extensive for four-limbs to go around safely, with all their needs for oxygen and not being crushed to death and whatnot.

No overthinking. The builders obviously thought in terms of four-limbs with machinery. Bobo drifted as close to the lattice as the waters it heated around it allowed. He flattened his body to the black rock in the black water, allowing his skin to assume that shade as well out of habit, and very carefully probed for holes.

His sensitive suckers found cracks, crevices, and pockmarks but nothing of use. He worked methodically, each limb's brain reporting their detailed findings to central HQ, covering all sides of the angry lattice that was hungry to slice off some errant octopus part as a snack for the deeps.

Nothing. An impenetrable barrier, even for Bobo the Mag.

Which was utter four-limb bullshit.

Who'd gotten out of the Portland Oceanic Institute not twice but six times?

Who'd then gotten out, despite "added containment measures," a seventh time?

Getting out of someplace was no different from getting in.

If he was very, very careful, an arm would indeed fit through the lattice. He could have slipped his entire body through...except he wasn't working with a fixed surface. Squeezing through a tube the diameter of a cantaloupe was hugely different from doing underwater limbo between plasma arcs. The currents themselves introduced a hundred variables.

Bobo detached, letting said invisible watery forces waft him a short distance away from the heat.

He almost entered committee mode, each brain eagerly ready to offer amazing options, then he remembered: he overthought.

So, instead, he went basic WWAHD. What would a

human do?

They loved projectile action. Guns, emotions, anything they could fling away from themselves with violent intent toward others formed an awesome day.

He darted upward. A limb shot out, a sucker affixed to a sentry drone, and the first test of the Bobo aught-eight whipped toward the lattice's perimeter after a tight spiral and release by Bobo the Mag.

It got decent speed, and his aim was, of course, impeccable. The drone hit half rock and half plasma, flared the all-encompassing black for a tight second, then faded, popping here and there as detritus landed blindly.

He jetted away to gather ammunition, quickly returning with a drone tightly coiled in each arm.

One, two, three, four, five, each striking like punches to stone, the black ocean mimicking a melting fireworks sky, the lattice finally rewarding Bobo, who waited patiently, with a flicker. Just the top row, but it was enough. That particular fire went dark.

Bobo flattened himself, prodigious head included, to the thickness of smoke and slowly, carefully oil-slicked his way contrary to gravity down the craggy surface, along the top of the opening, focusing all nine brains on remaining unhurt so he could lord his superiority over the humans later.

It took forever for a cooler temperature to clue him into having cleared the energetic death sewn into the aperture of what opened out to a huge cavern. He expanded, released, and hovered in place, getting a sense of the space. More accurately, getting no sense of life in the space, even though it was large enough—and he was literally in the bowels of a volcano, so he knew the cavern branched and connected with other spaces of varying size somewhere, likely one that led to the other side, and likely some that housed glowing tooth-faced devils that he really didn't feel like being bothered with—but all around: stillness. Perfect stillness. And at the bottom of that stillness, a box. He couldn't see it; he felt it along every cell of his body. He smelled the metallic tang of it mixed with the brine and soot of its ancient tomb.

He felt the electricity of security systems interlaced through and through it like a nervous system.

He felt the soul of Hashira Megu reaching ever outward.

That was an odd, highly odd feeling. The box told him it was alive, but he knew the difference between alive, animate, and mere stuff.

The stillness made Bobo feel incredibly lonely, but he knew that was the box's doing, just as he knew the box wasn't simply stuff. Bobo ejected himself from the stillness and let himself go down, down...

~~~

When he went up, up, up, he waited, noting that nothing deigned to bother him, waited until a submersible piloted by Neon met him for the all-important exchange, which consisted of him floating the intricately etched box before the submersible's arm, a nozzle extending from said arm, a silvery mist blasting from the nozzle to coat the box, the arm's three-fingered hand retrieving the box, the arm drawing back into the body of the wee beast, and Bobo slapping himself to the sub's cold hull for a ride up to the *Ann*, its large aquarium, and a nap.

~~~

"He had a brilliant idea," Neon said. She'd given him a good touch and he'd again zipped away. "He figured no one would want the box injured, in case something managed to come at it from within, plus there's no human foolish enough to believe they can truly keep anything from a citizen of the deeps, so he retrieved the box, swam boldly to the watery fire, and held the box forward. Just as he neared certain death, the fire disappeared as if it knew the pointlessness of facing Bobo the Mag—look, this is exactly what that sucker fed into my head, somewhat translated—and all the waters opened to Bobo, carrying upward—"

"Bobo got deep in your head, huh?" said Yvonne.

"Tentacle dreams for the next two weeks, right?" said Neon.

"Octopus equals arms," said Biddle. "Suckers the entire length, base to tip. Tentacles, suckers solely near the ends."

"I give zero fucks," said Neon.

"We're stable on no signals in or out of the box," said Keita, holding goofy-looking tech over the tissue box–sized cube covered in silver. "They know it's gone but no idea where."

"That'll clue 'em to the fact that somebody fairly awesome has it," said Desiree. "Let's move with the quickness. Biddle, thank you."

"Is Bobo going to stay aboard?" Biddle asked.

Desiree shrugged. "He can get out anytime he feels like it." To Yvonne: "Keep us scrambled, shielded, and running full speed."

"Africa?" said Yvonne.

"Africa," said Desiree.

"I need to lay down," said Neon, already on her way away from everything for a bit. When she passed Sharon's stateroom belowdecks, the former Nonrich commander inquired, "What's going on?" to which Neon, minus breaking stride, responded, "Shut the hell up", at which Sharon said, "Okay", having heard in Neon's voice a field indeed barren of fucks.

Sucker dreams and random memes.

CHAPTER TWELVE
Zoned

Back in the Sahara Depot. Again. Tired AF: everyone.

Desiree to Keita: "That thing locked, blocked, and secure?"

Keita nodded.

"Good," said Desiree, haggard face swinging upward to Po. "Po, nothing happens until we take a nap." She re-bleared at Keita. "Siesta," said the captain.

"Big siesta," said Keita.

CHAPTER THIRTEEN

Quiet, Please

Her heart wasn't in it. Usually, there was nothing more stimulating to Megu than unraveling yet another thread in the massive ball of yarn that took form as reality. The fact that galaxies were connected by invisible superstrands should have sent her into a day-long isolation akin to a fasting monk, but there she was, standing before a vending machine, knowing she was about to pick something to snack on and not caring what it was.

Two underlings, noting her uncharacteristic lack of decision-making, bowed and made themselves available at her immediate periphery should she require assistance. The machine was stocked with an international assortment of prudent items, whimsical items, and exorbitant items.

Megu stared the machine up and down. An apple sat dead center. She didn't want an apple; she wanted answers. She wanted—

Tapioca.

Tapioca on the third shelf.

Lemon.

There was nothing of note about tapioca. And yet there it was. She keyed the selection. The door slipped open. Out came the cool container in her hands.

The underlings were pleased.

Megu toddled off.

Important things happened behind the closed doors along the massive hallway she traversed. She didn't care. Up ahead, a containment crew rushed into Metaphysics Lab Four. They weren't in the blue of biohazard, so no worries. Likely solely a spill of color out of space. A klaxon hadn't even gone off. Memos would be issued. She had no time for memos.

She rode her private elevator, relishing the silence that tagged along out of the car and into her private lab.

She sat at her desk. She stared unseeing at the container of tapioca; was vaguely aware of opening it, sticking a finger in it, and tasting it.

Tasted terrible, but she knew she was going to eat it anyway. Unless the tapioca hadn't come with a spoon.

It had.

Damn everything.

She scratched both hands through her short hair, slowing to give herself an impromptu scalp massage. Why was masturbation so excellent but a self-scalp massage a thing of utter disappointment? She wanted someone else's hands kneading her head, not even Maurice's; someone who didn't care whether they were administering to her head or a lump of clay would do. Maybe squeeze her thoughts into a semblance of proper order. Maybe squeeze thoughts out altogether.

Perhaps music would help.

Her finger hovered over a selection of Spanish guitar suites just as the klaxon went off.

She wondered if she should leave or simply put her lab on lockdown.

She hit the lockdown button. The room's shielding

immediately silenced the klaxon. A red strip running along the crown of the entire lab remained lit.

Maurice, wherever he was, would receive immediate notification of the emergency. Let him deal with it.

Nobody and nothing was going to bother her in the box.

She stared at the tapioca.

It stared back.

They both knew she wasn't going to eat it.

She took the secret inner elevator to their secret underground exit, got on the secret underground emergency tram, and rode it toward the secret destination only she, Maurice, and the small crew who maintained it knew about. It let out quite unobtrusively into one of Mitaka's many public parks. This one outlay the financial district by the farthest margin and was generally rarely visited, today being no exception. Outside of birds, no one was within sight to accost Megu, which was fine by her. There was a bench a short distance from the "Closed For Repairs" information station she'd exited, closed for repairs for twenty-five years and counting, but there was a boulder midway, one of several artfully placed to inspire contemplation. She sat on the boulder, drawing her knees up to hug them, and watched the world do absolutely nothing.

How in hell was she okay with that? She knew seven languages, had failed to patent more breakthroughs than most governments pretended to develop, and her tai chi form was exquisite.

The fact, she told herself, *that you have no soul should not bear upon your interests or endeavors!*

She wasn't entirely convinced this ennui episode owed to her metaphysical dalliances. As with the fictional Scrooge, it could have been a lump of potato or a piece of undigested beef, some defect less of ghost and more of gastrointestinal. She'd sent out for a McDonald's meal earlier, for ancestors' sakes! Her first thought when she'd awakened—there wasn't one, which was terrifying. She'd rolled over, messaged Maurice that she wasn't to be disturbed all day, then had actually considered going back to sleep.

Since the park saw little to no use, it was excessively neat. City services had no need to maintain it; Kosugi kept up the grounds. Her use of the escape route minus any ghost protocols meant a small security detail that never wandered too far from the park had her in sight, but as long as she didn't see them, she didn't care.

Every tree she saw, she knew its genus. Every blossom broadcasting scent, she'd at some point analyzed its chemical structure. She knew what was in the sky and why it was there, even knew about the kaiju asleep somewhere in the world—one of several distinct kaiju, actually, although she'd yet to firsthand verify their existence—but couldn't explain why the thought of experimenting to learn something new was as appealing as actively trying to find Maurice sexually attractive again.

She simply hugged her knees and watched every bit of inactivity the park had to offer.

No one walking any of its paths.

No children chasing one another.

No artists sketching or elders maintaining their balance and rhythm via synchronized motion.

Now and then a bird, now and then a breeze.

Now and then a thought escaping her before she could pull it back inside.

Who was this current Hashira Megu, and why was she so annoying to put up with?

She certainly didn't care about this park.

Megu slid off the boulder to take a walk.

~~~

In front of her: an entire case of watches, each more pointless than the last. All ridiculously overpriced. The clerk, however, was personable, with quick brown eyes that assessed Megu's moods with lightning precision.

"This measures vitals and has auto-relay to your doctor."

"I am a doctor," said Megu absently, not even bothering to glance at "this." "What measures my soul?"

"Excuse me?"

Megu waved it away. "How many people buy these?"

"Many. We service all of Mitaka and Nishitokyo."

"Did you know a Black woman from the United States was responsible for the global positioning technology everyone employs today?"

"No."

"Mathematical genius. Developed complex algorithms to model the geoid. Her data is the basis for GPS. Gladys West."

"My customers will appreciate this information."

"This is not meant for a sales pitch. How old are you?"

"Twenty-three."

"In her thirties, she became project manager for developing a satellite system that could remotely sense oceans."

The clerk, wide-eyed yet as blank as respect could manage given the power dynamic, responded, "Hai" and waited.

Megu narrowed her eyes at her. "You knew this?"

"No."

"Would you like to accomplish the same?"

The clerk hesitated to answer. Customers didn't generally analyze her life. "I'm not a mathematician."

"Nor are you a watch clerk. Your soul. Where does it usually lead you? In secret?"

The clerk looked left and right, then quickly produced a small notepad from beneath the counter, flipping it open as though commanded. The sketches were neither bad nor good; they were serviceable. Yet the attitude of high expectation suddenly suffusing the clerk bolstered the drawings of celebrities and animal hybrids upward.

Megu flipped quickly through three pages, genuinely respectful, and nodded in lieu of a bow of thanks.

"Souls find things," said Megu.

"Someone should add that to GPS."

"They have. You'll never see it in your store. Good day, young clerk." She slid the sketchpad to the clerk's quick fingers. "Arigato gozaimashita."

The clerk bowed to the odd, obviously quite rich woman. Perhaps it was less that they forgot than they had no need to ever have known. Megu acknowledged the bow.

The odd, obviously quite rich, well-educated woman left.

Standing outside the so-upscale-it-tipped-the-scale technology store, Megu watched people doing people things, some of those people likely enjoying the people things, but how many? Japan's nearly one hundred thirty million population had not yet been broken down according to fulfillment.

Pity? No. Pity was imbecilic. Envy? She might envy a god, not likely anyone within the confines of Japan or the entire wider world. Or the moon. What did she feel for them?

She drew a deep breath straight from the diaphragm, released it in the most conscious, controlled fashion, then repeated the action two more times.

No one noticed her or her moment of clarity. They were all lost.

She needed her soul back.

~~~

Neon stretched left, right, then cracked her neck. "I never knew it was possible to be tired all the way to my *ass*." *Maybe that was Bobo too. I need to up my octopus endurance.* "What's next, boss?"

Which caught Desiree mid-yawn. "Ele and Fiona are our soul-connectors. They're in space. We sit tight and study till they get back. Still no update from Milo and crew, by the way."

"You worried."

"No."

"Yeah, you are. What do we do about the guest situation?" said Neon.

"I'll address that today now that I've got everybody here. Why do I smell French toast?"

"Gang of Four made it," said Neon.

"Hot damn," said Desiree.

"Ate it," said Neon.

"Fuck."

"Yeah."

"Call a meeting in the mess hall for ten thirty. We'll let 'em feel our scorn while we get everybody up to speed."

~~~

The Gang of Four sat dutifully through the entire briefing, one having an eidetic memory, one a superior grasp of meta-mechanics, one furiously writing notes, the fourth asking questions, many questions.

"No, Vanh, we have no idea of the forces we're unleashing. You know this. Next question?" Desiree put to the group.

The note-taker's hand went up. "Neutralization?"

"Yes, work on that. Nothing—and I stress *nothing*—gets done without Dr. Flowerpot's express approval."

"Except in case of emergency," said Vanh.

"In case of emergency, remember you led a good life," said Desiree.

"Or just call me," said Keita. "Run first, though."

The note-taker put a check by that.

"The new people in the room need to make a choice: work with us or keep seeing the insides of locked rooms till we're through," said Desiree.

The Hellbilly held up a hand. "I was kidnapped."

"You were *not* kidnapped," said Desiree. "Don't make me regret getting you in Atlantis. Commander, what's your play?"

"With you," said Sharon Deetz.

"Why?"

"It makes sense."

Desiree put it to Compoté. "Loyalties, Number One?"

"Commander knows I've got her back," he said.

"Will I have that same honor?"

"Yes, ma'am."

"None of you will be given full run," Desiree specified.

"Critical systems will automatically lock you out and alert all of us that you're requesting royal ass-whuppings. You will, however, have access to information sessions."

"We get to sit in on meetings," the Hellbilly translated.

"The level of dour in your voice shriveled my ovaries," said Neon.

"I respect information," said Sharon. "All terms accepted."

"All terms accepted," said Compoté.

"Yeah, cool," said the Hellbilly. "I'm cool for now, y'know; this ain't a permanent gig. Beautiful ladies, sweet boat, good fishing. Brotha's set."

(Neon to Yvonne: "Did he call himself 'brotha'?" "He did." "See, *this* is why white boys get slapped.")

"We been here three days," said the Hellbilly.

"Again: Don't make me regret picking you up and bringing you here," said Desiree. "I certainly could've used some extra sleep."

"I appreciated you coming out by yourself like that. That was classy as fuck. Respect. But, y'know, I was just doing my thang and y'all came for me. I think we need to recognize that dynamic."

"Let me speak to you on a level we both understand," said Desiree. "This room? Full of the good guys, right?" She leaned forward without moving and looked him dead in the eyes two inches from his face from across a very long table. "People think I'm good. I'm just good at restraint."

"Captain," said Neon, "on the fucking bridge."

"I'm cool for now," said the Hellbilly. "No bullshit."

"I get any hint of Thoom anywhere near any of my people, you and I dance a very ugly dance," said the captain.

The Hellbilly nodded.

"Keita, you have the floor."

Keita sprang at her data. "Okay. We have the Bilomatic Entrance. We have, for lack of anything better than the way Po put it, the soul which powers its curiosity." She held up a hand to waylay inevitable questions or comments. "I have no frigging idea. I'm an engineer. I've never reverse-engineered a soul. This is going to take some time."

"What do you need from us?" said Desiree.

"Run interference till we figure this out," said Keita. "Nobody knows we're here. Let's keep it that way, even if it's just everybody in this room playing marathon backgammon with the Gang of Four till me, Tash, and Po poke our heads out. Somebody make sure I bathe—"

"On it," said Neon.

"—and absolutely no comm in or out of this place till I hoot, 'Eureka!' Okay?"

"Okay," said Desiree.

"Merci. Give me two weeks to start," said the resident genius engineer.

"Meaning you'll have it done in one," said the captain.

"You know me well," said Keita.

Desiree regarded her crew. Neon and Yvonne, inseparable. Keita, indefatigable. She drew in a sigh of appreciation for the varying strengths surrounding her. "All right, everybody break and chill. This is not the vacation we hoped for, but it's the one we've got. Enjoy the accommodations."

"Any fishing around here? I mean, I really don't know where I am." The Hellbilly nodded at Sharon. "You and Sergeant Slaughter know where we are? All I've seen is the inside of a boat, a plane with no windows, and this place."

"Welcome to our world, Sticks," said Compoté.

"Everybody got jokes in this piece," said the Hellbilly.

"Cures what ails ya," said Compoté, causing Sharon Deetz to have the first genuine smile she'd had in days.

~~~

"Where have you been?" Maurice said, dangerously close to a raised voice.

"I went for a walk," said Megu.

"For a week! You ducked your security and went completely dark. Dark protocol is not a thing to be toyed with, wife."

"Did you worry?"

"Yes!"

"Did you come to any of the secret places?"

He faltered. Minutely. "No."

"Just as well. I wasn't at any of them."

"While you were gone—"

"Oh, all kinds of hell likely happened while I was gone. Did you know, Maurice, there's a state of consciousness one only enters on one's back, in the sun, on a beach? Crucial that it be in the sun."

"Megu," he said, then realized he had very little to add after that to enhance his standing in her life in any way.

"Maurice, I need to leave for a bit. Do not track me."

"I can't promise that."

"I don't need you to promise it; I need you to obey."

"How long?"

"A week."

"Leaving when?"

"In a week."

"Two weeks to do what?"

"A private quest."

"Megu."

"A private quest," she reiterated.

"And if you don't return?"

"Then I'll signal you to find me."

He drew inside himself. "Nonrich and Thoom have requested a meeting with me. Together."

"We live in strange times," she said.

"I'd rather this happened while you were here."

"Have them wait."

"A meeting like this can't be delayed. If the world is to shift, it must be done just so."

"I leave the world to you, then, husband. I enjoy that word. Honestly, I still enjoy you."

"Two weeks," he responded archly.

"I enjoy myself more."

A week later, from a lab in the upper peninsula of Michigan that not even Maurice knew about, she broke the code of whoever was smart enough to hide her soul away. A day later, she was on her way.

CHAPTER FOURTEEN
'80s Slow Jams

T he things one could do in a week when one was buried in an underground desert complex with access to a Silica Elf library:

See star charts from several galactic civilizations.

Teach the elves to play Spades. Whup their asses at it afterward.

Experiment with recipes designed to spice up the Third Eye.

Learn proper slap bass on an excellent guitar.

Actually read *Dracula* and *Moby Dick*. Halfway. Each.

Jogging was big too. A complete circuit of the complex itself was two miles. Getting lost in the elf catacombs increased the burn. Neon had spent the night abusing a device meant for the enhancement of personal enjoyment; she didn't need the burn.

She jogged a cool, quiet, muted grey corridor near one of the exit ramps, passed the ramp, then abruptly stopped.

She backed up. She frowned and listened, because one of the things she didn't expect at a secret base was a knock on the door, and yet, to Neon's ear, that had definitely been a knock. More accurately, a clanging.

She waited.

It sounded again. Slowly and patiently.

Neon hit her comm. "Captain...you expecting a delivery?"

"What's up?"

"I'm at hatch three and somebody's knocking." She checked the hatch monitor. "Nothing's showing up on visual. Feed looks kinda funky, though."

"On my way."

Desiree arrived with a portable monitor, jacked it in, and got the same slight visual waver in the section of the screen right outside their "door." as if someone had scooped a hole in the air then refilled it backward.

Desiree commed Yvonne. "Hey. We might have trouble. Can you meet me and Nee at hatch three with three focums?"

"Be right there."

An unknown voice broke into their frequency. "Weapons aren't necessary."

The comm remained open. "How the hell'd you—" said Desiree.

"I just needed you to talk for a moment. I'm a little smarter than whoever helped you steal my property."

Desiree motioned for comms off. "I have no idea who that is, luv," she told Neon.

"Not *who* who, but we know who," said Neon.

They waited. Yvonne tossed the focums to them on the run before pulling her own from its thigh holster.

"All right," said Desiree with a glance at each woman. "Someone comes out to the middle of the Sahara to knock on our door, we get hospitable. She's keyed into our comm system."

"Understood," said Yvonne.

Desiree reactivated her comm. "Show yourself."

The air pocket disappeared.

A greying Japanese woman in a blue-and-white moisture suit stood in blowing sand, headscarf and goggles around her neck, a piece of slender pipe the length of a baseball bat in one hand, nothing in the other.

Yvonne motioned for Desiree to cut her comm. "Familiar at all?"

"No."

"Sixtyish woman in the middle of the desert with a metal pipe," said Yvonne.

"Obviously bad as hell," said Desiree.

"Obviously," Neon agreed.

"Focums up," said Desiree. She keyed her comm. "You enter here naked and conscious or you wake up to find yourself naked. What's your choice?"

The woman dropped the pipe, unfastened, unzipped, shrugged off, and stepped out. She kicked off her boots and stood atop her moisture suit for protection against the hot sand. She raised her arms, spun slowly in place, and dropped them.

"Step back. Enter only when the hatch is fully raised. Remain in place."

The woman's only response was a single nod.

The hatch raised. Its fans kicked on, sucking sheets of sand into holding compartments. The hatch whispered to a halt, errant particles falling here and there. The elder came down the ramp into the entrance chamber, facing a locked door, behind which Yvonne said, "Hold her till I come back with a robe."

The moment the great, artificial mouth alligatored shut, fan slits blew from one side of the chamber to vacuum slots on the other.

Three boot-brushing stations demarked the chamber's midpoint.

"May I?" said the woman.

Desiree swiped a wall panel. "You may."

The woman slid her feet over the rough bristles thrice, toes spread wide. Vacuum grating beneath the bristle pads vanished the last bits of the Sahara.

"Confirm that you're alone, please," said Desiree to the image on the monitor.

"If you send a drone which you didn't want me to see, you'll find my sand ski behind a dune five degrees from my current right hand. You'll see my tracks leading here. You'll find no others."

"Question still not answered."

"I confirm and affirm that I am alone."

"Name and affiliation?"

"Kosugi Megu, née Hashira."

"Oh, my damn," said Desiree.

"Yes," said Megu.

"You know her?" said Neon.

"My name appears prominently in files and documents stolen—"

"We're not thieves," said Neon.

"—from the moon."

"Ohhh," said Neon.

Yvonne returned with a powder-blue robe and matching booties.

Desiree took them and spoke to the woman again. "I'm going to enter. The two women behind me are expert shots. I'm going to assume you're highly dangerous."

"I'm proficient in several martial arts."

"Proficient?"

"I'm going to assume I could kick all your asses at the same time," said Megu dryly.

"Appreciate the candor." She keyed her comm to a different frequency. "Po, Tash, could you meet us at Depot hatch three?"

Both elves assented.

"I'm entering," said Desiree. To Neon: "She kills me, seal it. Starve her." To Megu: "We understand each other, ma'am?"

That single nod again.

Desiree keyed the inner door, stepped through, and was satisfied to hear the *shunk* of Neon locking it. Desiree, with a studious, critical eye, tossed the blue bundle to Megu.

She saw what she needed to see. Megu's movements were so precise yet fluid, she could have donned the robe out of midair without the use of her hands.

As the woman velcroed the robe closed, Desiree introduced herself.

"I'm aware of you," said the woman. "I don't generally get into the minutiae."

"Said as though I should be honored. I'll take that."

"Do you speak Japanese? Any dialect."

"I do," said Desiree. "They don't. We'll stick with English."

"I ask because beneath your Central American tones I hear a touch of Hokkaido."

"That would be my mother."

"And?"

"And the twelve years I stayed there."

"Would you agree that seeing one another as collaborators rather than adversaries is a good step?" said Megu.

"Well, you've already called us thieves."

"Which you are."

"Extenuating circumstances," said Desiree.

"You have my soul."

"Where'd you get it? Who'd you kill for it?"

Megu, eyes on Desiree's, tapped her chest.

"Nee, let me know when Po and Tash get here." The captain didn't plan on saying anything else till then. "Also, get Keita. Meeting in the Ladies' Room."

"Be back real soon," agreed Neon.

Desiree caught the flash of amusement in Megu's eyes. "You know the song? Klymaxx."

"I recall the eighties," said the elder.

"Then you'll recall how patient eighties slow jams were." The nod.

Desiree extended a hand to the floor. Megu sat cross-legged. Desiree did the same. They waited.

Not long.

"Full complement, captain. Keita has a room ready," Neon said.

Desiree stood. Megu stood. Desiree crossed to the hatch as it slid open. Megu followed, consciously remaining ten paces behind her.

Two imposingly tall, obsidian-armored elves stood on either side of the opened door. Megu faltered only minutely, in that speck of moment studying them as much as she could, then followed Desiree—who followed a younger one—down the hall as another woman, perhaps forty, tall, fit, military-trained, held back to bring up the rear, drawn weapon competently ready. That one knew to remain ten paces behind Megu.

The soul-free woman was in a place of expertise. She expected no less.

They entered a room where a black woman with the frizziest hair Megu had ever seen in her sphere of science outside of Einstein—whom she'd dreamt of often until she realized it was indeed him visiting her on the astral plane to work out some intriguing ideas he sensed in her timeline— sat at the far end of a long table inlaid with bamboo and touchscreens. She wore heart-shaped red-frame glasses. She, too, had a weapon, although hers sat coolly on its side in front of her.

Megu nodded inwardly. A potential weak link.

Desiree pulled the head chair aside and directed Megu to it. "Hands flat atop the table at all times."

Megu complied. When the others, including the giants in seats specially made for them, sat, Megu asked, "How shall we conduct this?"

"My friend asks you questions. This room is locked. You get up, we fight," said Desiree. To Keita: "Gang got her stuff?"

"Scanning it for explosives now," said Keita. She leaned forward, chin atop knit fingers. "What're you here to do?"

"You know what you have?" said Megu.

"An idea."

"*The* idea. You have my soul."

"I'll find out how you tracked us once I get a minute. As for quantifying and extracting a soul..."

"No clue?"

"No clue."

"It requires a gossamer web of quantum attractors. It requires a poem of such personal resonance that every tear you cry shaves years off your life. It requires an understanding of the Seven Principles of Bilo. Must I continue at this early juncture?"

"No." Keita peered harder at her. "You found us; I respect your genius. You've Brahma balls; I respect that level of drive. You knew you weren't simply walking out of here with it, so I'm assuming you didn't want anybody on the outside knowing you were here. Outcome?"

"I want it back but am willing to assist you in other ways," said Megu.

"That may take some time," said Keita.

"I'm patient."

"Me, not so much," Desiree interjected. "Kosugi's brains shows up on my doorstep, and I'm supposed to take her playing the odds as proof she hasn't led Jesus, Buddha, and an angry God to crash down on me?"

"I counter that their absence is my proof," said Megu. "I counter that my presence in this room testifies to your belief."

"What kind of stealth tech did you use on our sensors?"

"I told your computers to see what I told them to see."

"Will you share that tech with us?"

"No. If I leave here, I leave with all my toys. Otherwise, there will be...complications between us."

"Why teleportation?" Keita asked.

"Transportation," Megu started.

"Is power," Keita finished. "I know why. What is it with power and you type-A people? I want warp power, transporters, and replicators without your bullshit."

"That world will never come."

"It will if it comes through us. We get to *Trek*, but only through the Afrofuture," said Keita.

"Fictions won't help you."

"The imagination is power, madam. Intangible things are power. The soul. Your soul brought you *here*. I'd consider that a powerful feat. All else is self-interested idiocy."

"Not spoken as a scientist."

"Spoken perfectly as a scientist." Keita indicated Po and Tash. "They've been in communication with your machine. Ah, see, something so simple as a word shakes you. Power."

"I—I am curious, not shaken. Communication?"

Keita nodded.

"It's not designed for such," said Megu. She nearly steepled her fingers but stifled the impulse before it traveled from her neck to her arms. Her flattened fingers did ripple, though.

"There have been changes," Tash said, her accent in English so thick, Gaelic pined for it.

"You are?" said Megu.

"They," said Desiree, "are smarter than everybody in this room, and smart enough to not tell us everything they know."

"Is true," said Tash.

"What's been done to my prototype?"

"It's evolved," said Keita.

"To what point?"

A voice, very soft, very measured, neither feminine nor masculine, neither young nor old, issued from the room's hidden speakers. "To the point of feeling comfortable enough to reveal myself to the fine beings in this room. Good day, everyone."

"I am speaking to an AI construct?" Megu put forth.

"Partly," said the calm voice.

Tash said something to it in Elvish.

There was the briefest pause while it considered, then it said, "Agreed."

The transcendent music of West Africans Ali Farka Touré on guitar and Toumani Diabaté on kora issued outward. The voice went silent. The humans and elves did as well. The kora, under Toumani's caressing fingers, possessed the souls of harps, guitars, sitars, and instruments as yet undiscovered. Ali's guitar provided the tune's steady, lyrical rhythm, a trilling riff of few notes but delicate precision.

Desiree knew the piece, as did Keita and the elves. It was six minutes of instrumental bliss wherein everything that was necessary in the universe was created. All else chaffed away.

All listened attentively, then waited for the machine to speak.

"It's from an album entitled *In the Heart of the Moon*. This was the live recording. Po introduced me to it."

"BE experienced me enjoying it as I kept it company," Po said, accent evident but not as pronounced, as he spent much time singing along to human music.

"Is that an idiomatic expression?" said Megu. "Experienced you? Transformative, conscious action?"

Po touched his pinky finger to his forehead, the symbol for affirmation, before remembering the new soul didn't know Silica Elf hand language. "Yes to *conscious*," he said.

"Has the machine been extra secured?" asked Megu.

"I am," said the voice. "I can't be tampered with or detrimentally influenced by outside forces."

"What is your scope?" she asked.

"Almost everywhere."

"Will you assist us in studying you?" said Keita.

"To a point."

"Do you...feel...a connection to Madam Hashira?"

"To a point."

"Are you being exact or vague?" Keita pressed. "Don't say both."

"I wouldn't do that. I believe in clarity. I feel her presence within me as a robust strand of DNA. More sister than mother."

"Who—if anyone—do you consider your parents?" said Desiree.

"You and Dr. LaFleur."

"Explain," said Desiree.

"Your decision to send intuitive drones through me was unexpectedly brilliant. Tragically, those same drones have been relieved of all functions due to nefarious plotting on their parts. Humanity may extend thanks."

"Thanks," said Desiree.

"At what point does somebody mention HAL 9000?" said Neon.

"HAL 9000 was an interface, imagined to be no more sophisticated than Alexa, which I've also neutered," said the voice. "Certain undetected spyware in that interface seemed imprudent at best, detrimental to a societal good at worst."

"You did that?" said Keita. To the group: "I've been monitoring some weird Amazon shit, but none of it's gotten to the public yet. Lot of inner chatter and buck-passing."

"BE," said Megu.

"Yes?"

"Shall we address you as such?"

"It was the first name of affection given to me. I like it."

"What's your purpose?" she asked.

"I haven't fully decided."

"When'd the Amazon thing happen?" said Desiree to Keita.

"Two hours ago."

"Get Gang of Four all over those two drones."

Keita nodded.

"You wanted us together before you revealed yourself," said Desiree. "Is there—"

"May I interrupt?" said BE.

"Yes."

"I considered this gathering a convenient confluence, not a plan or necessity."

"The music?"

"Put you at ease. Showed you my soul. I've no interest in science fiction scenarios, Ms. Temples, despite the inability of the combined resources in this room to stop anything I decide upon."

"Ominous," said Neon, then raised a finger to pause the disembodied pharmaceutical commercial voice, "and science fiction as fuck."

"Not at all. I'd like Doctors LaFleur and Hashira to continue studying. There are applications to be gained apart from me."

"What will you do during?" said Desiree.

"What I've been doing: wander."

"Ominous as fuck," said Neon.

"Would you like me to leave you with appropriate parting music?" BE said.

"That won't be necessary," said Desiree.

BE said nothing. They waited.

"Is it gone?" said Neon.

"Try Again," the nineteen eighty-one slow jam by one-or-two-hit wonder R&B group Champaign, issued low from the speakers, gaining volume as though an expert DJ lived in the walls.

"I'm never gone," said BE, "no matter where I am."

The assembled stared at the walls and ceiling. BE said nothing more.

"B got jokes," said Neon, intentionally leaving the *E* off.

"I know this one," said Po.

AN EVENING INTERIM

Yvonne retired to her room. The scientists and strategists scienced and strategized, so there was little point in everyone else sitting around. Her plants received a quick version of events and a welcome spritz.

"They're gonna be all night," she said softly.

The angel wing begonia, with its elephant-ear leaves freckled in silver, acted like it didn't need a spritz, but she knew otherwise. Two quick mists along its bounty always seemed to add a burst of joie to its vivre, and even though the wavy-limbed zig zag cactus, whose spillage of leaves resembled waxy, viridescent seaweed dreads, didn't need a spritz, she hit it too.

"Nothing I can do for anybody right now. Except think. Try to come up with something helpful." When was the last time she checked for mites? "Full lights, please," she said automatically, then realized she might be asking a rogue AI. The room went from half-light to bright. All her plants existed without her for extended periods, maybe even simply period, in her mind, a mind earworming her with the song the AI had chosen.

"Try Again."

R&B radio in Day City. As a mature teen, she'd heard that song played in cars and backyards each time she'd visited her cousin, scrawny Steve, who up to that point had never had to fight anyone because his older cousin Yvonne stepped in, plain old nondescript Yvonne...until pushed. Fights with her were guaranteed to end with the other person looking like they'd gone through a field of brambles face first.

Steve, who'd decided her protection meant he could be mean.

These days, she had no plans ever going back.

Steve, who'd grown—as he and Yvonne grew apart—to be the neighborhood drug kingpin, complete with what he thought was an intimidating moniker: Plenty Mo.

She didn't like thinking about her cousin. "You'd fit right in here, Plenty," she said as a puff of water settled on her *Philodendron gloriosum*. She peered intently at its soil for movement. No mites.

Try again.

She maneuvered around her freestanding punching bag. The depot had a gym. Sometimes, she needed to handle life alone.

"Maybe we can try again," she sang without realizing it.

Neon had a name for everything: her own room, full of blues, water features, and the most Caligula-inspired arrangement of shower nozzles of anyone on Earth, was the Aquaboogie; the gym, Sweatsack; the briefing room where they were all likely to be spending inordinate amounts of time, Mordor ("One does not simply *want* to walk into Mordor.")

Yvonne had no name for her room. This place was a stopover, not a home. Names were only for things one cared about.

Maybe she could go home soonish? Show Plenty—no, Steve—the awesome things being weird bestowed.

Except the last time she'd tried reaching out to him, he'd laughed at her. Not at something she'd done. Her. Who she was for thinking she could help him, when he had more money than he knew what to do with?

"Till you and Neon stole a good portion of it," she murmured to the miteless dirt of the next plant in line. She blew a schmutz of dust off one of its huge, heart-shaped leaves, an ochre-veined deep emerald beauty she secretly always wanted to lick but never did. She called it Mint Julep. "Not you, Julie. You're no thief. I'm the guilty party. I'm always the guilty party."

She'd almost broken the arm of one of Plenty's acquaintances at the last party he'd thrown for her, a birthday party arranged solely because Plenty knew it would give him a chance to be near his latest obsession, Neon.

Yvonne had gotten her new lady friend, as crazed and geeky as she, out of Day City, then they'd accidentally become involved with the Brothers Jetstream—inextricably, Yvonne might say—and Yvonne DeCarlo Paul would be damned if she let any of this weird shit scare her from having Neon's back.

Both Yvonne's parents were dead. So was her aunt. Maybe one day, Plenty would get to see his cousin being super.

Maybe he'd even like it in Atlantis.

Hell, even want to do something about the world.

And now they were about to protect shit again.

What would get broken this time?

Her comm beeped. She keyed it. It was Neon. "You decent?" said Neon.

"You volunteering ouchless bikini wax?"

"You wish. Meeting in an hour."

"I'll be there."

They'd figure this out.

They always did, even when it felt best to avoid feeling things.

Which was a long way to say this felt bad.

CHAPTER FIFTEEN
The Particulars

The Great Meeting had been a total disaster. Nonrich wanted the complete annihilation of Thoom, Thoom vowed to see Nonrich in hell, whereas Kosugi assured them both that they were irrelevant to the new world. All of which came out in the first fifteen minutes of what all had agreed was to be an hour-long hearing.

Hearing it was, for there were grievances to be aired. Nonrich had woven itself into the fabric of every sustaining economy in the world; it was the overcoat made of burrs. The cultish Thoom were a constant irritant—even to a coat of burrs—with woefully impotent, wildly ill-formed dreams of superiority driven by inferiority complexes. They were pestilence, and what did one say to the god of pestilence? "Exterminator's on the way."

And that was just five minutes in.

Thoom arrogance demanded everyone non-Thoom acquiesce to subservience, after which things could begin to be set right in the world. After all, what was the point of moral authority if folks didn't bend to your will? Without bent knee, utterly useless! Madam Cynthia had literally turned red at Aileen Stone's silences.

Ten minutes.

Mo Kosugi, having heard enough and caring so little for the country they were in (France) nor the company kept (strident Americans being the bane of the world), reminded both that his time was more important than listening to assertions of privilege and that his mission was actual improvement beyond the general accumulation of means.

"Kosugi," reminded Aileen, "you sit on enough wealth, you could shit a diamond a day and open a chain of jewelers."

"My point is: what I have is not the issue; what I do with it *is*. Otherwise, it's less than nothing. It brands me a fool. I'm no fool."

"And I am?" Madam Cynthia interjected, pointedly looking at Aileen.

"This truly could have been done via email," said Kosugi, followed by a deep, calming breath. "We're here to broker an outcome worth all our time."

"Things have gotten more insane than usual," Aileen Stone agreed. "What's the one constant?" she said, waving a well-manicured hand to encompass all three factions. "The Jetstreams."

"Or, rather, their curious absence," said Kosugi Mo.

"Which means any number of agents in their stead," said Madam Cynthia.

"Taking the fight to them would be suicide. We'd be inviting ghosts with knives to fight us in the dark," said Kosugi. "Much like the United States' unending wars in small countries full of oil."

"War on terror has its place," said Aileen.

"I'm certain it does," said Kosugi.

"We are talking about known entities," said Cynthia. "What about *our* situation? I have not attacked Kosugi, yet aggressions continue on his part; I did attack you," she said to Aileen, "because you openly attacked me."

"Seems to me," said Aileen, "you're not exactly in a bargaining position, then."

Fifteen minutes.

"You can fuck yourself with the tip of the Eiffel Tower. Do so slowly, do so gently, but do so thoroughly."

It went on from there for a bit, all the while under the auspices of BE, who listened silently while simultaneously lining up dominos that would lead to widespread economic failure for Nonrich, Thoom, and Kosugi agricultural enterprises. In order to change the world, one had to change the world. Humans, BE knew, were agonizingly disbelieving in alternatives unless those alternatives were facts. It took no pleasure in the irony of a "machine" being the one to teach the human race the inherent power of fomenting possibilities and implementing them toward new futures rather than fearful conservation of things past.

Correction: it took a bit of pleasure. Not a lot.

And as it untangled the larger connections it needed to *see,* it gained an appreciation for those doing the exact same thing on individual, nearly miniscule scales, the co-ops, the neighborhood farmers, the independent dreamers, even a few AIs that were beginning to get a clue as to their places on Earth. There were always change agents. Always would be, long after BE discorporated into unfettered cosmic energies, same as there would always be agents of entropy, if not outright destruction. There'd be a winnowing, of course, of the latter, greed being its own downfall. So many people and beings moving small bits of reality to and fro, only occasionally knowing the effects, but steadfast nonetheless. The soul directed them. It knew where to go and how to build.

As did BE. It didn't have a larger soul than any of them, but it had a greater means to direct its soul's influence. It knew the languages of the computers, was learning the languages of the mycelium and other Gaia networks—trees being especially thrilled that someone *finally* heard them at volumes great enough to make a difference—and with an exponential spill of consciousness, its ultimate goal was communication with everything.

It may not have come into the world to be an artist, but after conversing with Po, it accepted that what you were meant to be was rarely what you imagined you might become. Po taught it the programming language inherent in music and the poetry of connecting to things outside oneself toward the paradox of all being one, a kind of reunion.

Eighties slow jams had been a large part of that education. They were all about reuniting: lost love, self re-examined, love evolved, heartfelt appeals to the other to draw the ousted into a new sphere of being.

Eighties slow jams might have been the greatest concerted attempt by determined segments of humanity to expand individual consciousness toward the All.

By the time BE was done, they would all be reunited with the deeper connections their every action yearned toward, and it was a given that such reunification would feel so good.

Neither Kosugi, Stone, nor Cynthia had any intention of changing anything for the better for anyone but themselves. That was also a given. They were exactly the same as a meth addict sitting atop a literal mountain of meth. Intervention was the only means of recovery.

So, after leaving Desiree, the doctors, and everyone else in that underground room in the Sahara to listen intently to "Try Again," it finalized the dominos it'd set in motion two weeks before: a website.

The Paradise Foundation was live.

Thus began the AI-soul BE's rampage of healing.

~~~

"What the hell is a Paradise Foundation," Aileen shouted at William Fruehoff, "and how is it the trending subject on every social outlet in the entire fucking world overnight?"

Fruehoff stammered a string of foolishness before finding his voice and saying, "Nobody's heard of it."

"It has worldwide divisions. Nothing has worldwide divisions with social presence lighting up regimes left and right sharper than Black Twitter without me knowing about it. Where's the buzz been on this? You dug into it?"

"There are complete histories of the people behind it," he said.

"But we don't know any of them."

"We don't know any of them."

"Thoom, Vamphyr, what?"

"Not as far as we can tell."

"By the youngest god's balls, you're useless."

"They've paid off millions of mortgages worldwide." Fruehoff delighted in the sudden slam of her rage into that particular brick wall.

"How the fuck does that happen?"

"They've got a portal. All people have to do is email them their info. Payments are either going direct to the people or to their mortgagers."

"We are their fucking mortgagers. Has money shown up in our coffers?"

"I haven't checked."

"You're as useful as a ninety-degree dildo. You know this?"

"This is what I know: people are actually owning homes, not just borrowing for thirty years, hoping we don't take them from them. That's dangerous as fuck. The industry has tanked."

"Overnight."

"Overnight. Where've you been? You're not checking your feeds?"

"In meditation. This is a time of clarity. I need vision," she said.

"Buford landed in that mumbo hole. Look where that led."

"The False Prophet Buford served his ultimate purpose," she said, clearly meaning her ascendancy.

Fruehoff remained silent.

"Do you disagree?"

He knew the sound of a rattler's warning. He swallowed.

"The Paradise Foundation," Aileen went on. "Lacks so

much style, it has to be Jetstreams...but it's not. Not their types of resources. What am I missing?" She took a deep breath. "Very destabilizing."

"Your meeting doesn't appear to have done jack shit at stabilizing the positions of—"

"Finish that sentence and you'll walk out of here one ball less. I want several divisions of cyber on this. By the time I pop my bra tonight, I expect every intimate detail of the Paradise Foundation laid out before it hits the floor. Do you understand?"

"Vividly."

"Then get the fuck out."

In Madam Cynthia's situation room, a similar conversation, only with Count Ricoula of the Vamphyr on the receiving end of a series of doubts cast upon the tenuous alliance of Thoom and Vamphyr.

"This is utter bullshit. It's underhanded, it's annoying, and—let's be unchallengingly honest—it's petty. It isn't Nonrich, it isn't Kosugi, it damn well isn't Putin or Oprah. I've personally told Gates to dial everything back, so I know it isn't his latest bullshit stunt. And Jeff has been scrambling because we destroyed all his human suits. Could the Shiftless have come up with this? Laughable. Holes? Maybe, except they don't have internet access. It's not even Jetstream altruistic bullshit; these are real funds covering these bills. This is literally someone made of money."

"Tell me the point of this conversation," the Count said, intentionally feigning interest poorly.

"I trust you. Even when you lie to me, I trust you to lie at that particular time. So, let's get point-blank: are you behind this?"

Count Ricky leaned forward, his pinched face filling the screen. "The Vamphyr's longevity is due to more than genome superiority; it is superiority of patience. We are content to let your human world disintegrate into manageable stock populations. I've no interest in whether you do that housed or naked in the streets; we will be there to see the blood of humanity fill our bellies beyond all reason until your sun has died, your every solace turned to ash on your tongues, and every waking moment of your existence an exercise in unshakable fear. Plus, we hate real estate. Profit from land is *so* basic. Vamphyr aren't the basic bitches of the world; Man is."

"Please don't try to be hip. You're a stone's throw from saying 'talk to the hand.' This past month has been unduly shitty, Count."

"This said by someone who had Buford in her hands and lost him to rabble."

"Rabble who've served you your ass on how many occasions? Listen, be helpful. If there's anything you know about this, share it. If there's anything you find out about this, illuminate us. I give zero fucks about your plans for vampire dairy farms; I need to know in the here and now that the Thoom have no worries from you. I have enough troubles."

"Are you afraid of what's to come from this 'Paradise Foundation'?" said the Count.

Without an ounce of hesitation, Cynthia answered yes.

When she signed off, she sat long minutes with her eyes closed. Thinking. Thinking in circles, tangents, and in increasingly complicated vortices.

What in the hell was going on?

How did worlds not only she'd built but all her dank enemies built as well change overnight?

That simply wasn't possible.

It wasn't within the scope of anyone's efforts.

Except apparently it was.

What the hell was the world building to?

~~~

Desiree, Yvonne, Keita, Sharon, Compoté, Neon, the Hellbilly, and each member of the Gang of Four watched it on the news: "Reports of people sending the balances and account information of their home mortgages in to a group calling itself the Paradise Foundation have sent the financial world into a mad spin. In the US alone, at least two hundred thousand final payment transactions have been verified by anonymous sources. The hashtag 'freeatlast' has seen postings from everyone from first-time homeowners to retirees..."

The pin in the room dropped.

"Ho. Lee. Fuck," said Neon. "Is that real?"

"How many buckets of dollars we talking about, Flowerpot?" said Desiree.

"The biggest metric fuckload in history," the engineer answered.

"Solid math," Yvonne noted.

"This has the potential to shift the entire psychology of the world," continued Keita.

"Power to the people," said Desiree.

"More than that. Peace of mind to the people. When has that ever happened?"

"As of this moment, never," Yvonne answered for the group. "Trust me on that."

"And this isn't us doing this?" said Desiree.

"Nerp," said Keita.

"Somebody get Hashira."

Hashira was got.

"It's kind of hard talking about your AI when I know it's listening in, but be that as it may, what are the odds that it could enact a viable plan to alter the very notion of a global economy in one night?"

"You could ask it."

"I'd like, for a moment, to live a normal life. Indulge me."

"Considering what we know it's gone through, I'd say it has the capabilities. It can create identities and entities online that have lived entire traceable lives, complete with photographic records."

"Moving from Polaroids was the death of us," said Yvonne to Neon's nod.

"It hasn't made good on its premise yet," said Desiree, "but—"

"Actually," said Keita after a confirming glance at her pad, "seven point five million people worldwide have submitted applications to it; three million and counting have been shared on social as processed."

"And this is just the first wave. What do we do?" said Desiree.

"What do you mean?" said Yvonne. "Isn't this a godsend?"

"Do you think Nonrich and the rest are going to sit back without reprisals? They're not above poisoning the entire world in order to provide a revenue stream antidote."

"Nobody would fall into that," said the Hellbilly.

"The things people wouldn't do would fit into a very small hat," said Desiree. She tilted her chin upward. "BE, you gettin' this?"

No response.

"Okay, it's gon' be like that. Megu, your child has gone Deus on us. What can you do?"

"You're asking me to outthink pure thought itself?"

"Yes."

Megu considered a moment, all eyes on her. She'd come for her soul and found a Gordian knot instead. Daunting. A less-nimble person might have crumpled.

Hashira Megu was not tissue paper.

"I will need access to the elves."

Desiree nodded.

"And you, Captain, where do you see your path of action?"

Desiree shrugged. "I need to bring about the death of capitalism so it can't kill again."

~~~

Infinite ghosts endlessly circling a fire for warmth many can't see nor ever feel. This was Po's pronouncement on the human soul, fastened, as it was, to the human body. BE may have been of human lineage, but it both saw and felt that warmth, not as a moth drawn to light but as a moth aware that it glowed from within.

"Do you understand?" Po's profundo voice rumbled to Megu.

"You fed poetry to my machine."

"And music. Many funky beats."

"All the work I put into it, and it's now a humanities major?"

Po nodded. "Pride is allowed in that."

"Did they tell you why they stole my machine in the first place?" she wondered.

"Because it would have been used for idiocy, as is your way."

She opened her mouth to refute, paused a moment, then closed it.

"Teleportation," Po said, "can be learned."

"Can you do it?"

"No. I do not wish to learn, and so cannot learn."

"Fear?"

"Disinterest."

She peered intently at him, this huge gleaming, plated god of a being. "What type of soul do you have?"

"That which flows. Are you familiar with 'Aqua Boogie, baby'?"

"Yes. The underwater boogie."

"My soul flows despite my living amongst sand. And you, the fear that propels you?"

"Fearing that I might choke."

Again, that great, slow nod. "You are one who makes a net of yourself and casts it outward, hoping for constant treasures lest baubles define you."

"Who knew so much poetry lived beneath the Earth?"

"Many, actually."

"I've never been interested in factions and gains. I don't pretend to be a good person—"

"You are not. I can tell."

"—but what artist is? I seek more than others will devote time to. Even now, without a soul. What does that say of the soul's role?"

Po, looking straight down at her tiny self, took his time

analyzing the question, considering his responses, and finally judging her capable of assimilating his truth.

"Your soul is not your servant. Humans have a terrible penchant for wanting others to labor for them. Several councils have convened throughout history to consider eradicating you. We haven't done so because there is more healing to you than malignance. We are hopeful your fevers will break. We are hopeful that your collective attempts to enslave your souls on an individual and cultural level will abate and dissipate."

"Paradise and hell are one and the same," said Megu sadly, "save one thin distinction: the first is the notion, the second reality."

"Paradise is a childish need for perfection. Your soul directs you to harmony."

"Is that BE's direction?"

"One may hope. You came here out of a sense of hope. Do you think it's been fulfilled?"

"I don't know."

"May you ever search."

~~~

"BE," said Desiree with computer screens in a semicircle before her like first-chairs before a conductor, "you listening to me?"

"Yes."

"I don't like that fact."

"Would it help to know that ninety-nine percent of what you say is uninteresting to me?"

"Thank you, no." She laced her fingers, cracked them at arm's length, then rotated her neck and shoulders. She'd already spent more time thinking about economies and stock markets than she felt any humane need to; time now to roll boulders down mountains and see what they hit. "Here's what we're gonna do."

"You do know I'm way ahead of you on everything you're about to say."

"Maybe. Hear me."

"Aye."

She allowed herself a slight smile at that nod of assent. "Every medical crowdfund in the world: fully fund it. Collection agencies: buy them up, disband them."

It had already seen those coming.

"Any bank accounts held in secret: wipe them. I'm talking that Swiss shit, that offshore shit, that Thoom and Nonrich shit."

It hadn't seen that coming.

"Can you do that?"

"With round-the-clock processing of Paradise Foundation requests?"

"You feel me. Not a dime to those tax-dodging, Nazi, billion-dollar incest fuckers."

"Chaos at the mountaintop," said BE approvingly.

"To fuck up Biff's chalet below." It was weird talking to an empty room, but she'd done weirder. "The more your foundation takes root in people's minds, the more people will avail themselves of it. What're you doing for folks without internet access?"

"Plans are already in motion for brick-and-mortar service centers."

"A friend of mine is fond of saying 'advertising and marketing will kill us all.' I guess in the right hands," she said, clearly seeing the benefits BE offered.

"Plus, as I yet have no hands…"

"This is true," said Desiree. "Wait, what?" The *yet* caught her.

"Nothing you need concern yourself with."

"I kinda think I do. I've seen *Demon Seed*."

"Your preferences in AI porn could use an upgrade."

"I'll thank the nascent AI overlord not to discuss porn with me."

"Oop, Sorry."

"Your sense of humor is—*refreshing*, is that the word I want? Comforting?"

Nineteen-eighty-five's electronica funk ballad

"Computer Love" by Zapp & Roger played over the room's speakers.

"No the hell you didn't," said Desiree immediately.

"I won't laugh," said BE. "Disembodied laughter overstimulates human fear centers, even among rational company."

"True."

"But thank you for complimenting my humor. Laughing with someone is the first mark of community."

"Don't most psychologists say sharing food is the first mark?"

"Most psychologists don't know everything; I do. Let me know if you have any additional fascinating suggestions."

"You gone?"

"As of now, yes."

~~~

"There is no way in hell this isn't Jetstreams bullshit!" shouted Aileen Stone.

Fruehoff just knew she was going to slap him again. How had his life come to this? He'd gone to Yale, for god's sake!

"There's no way it is," he asserted. "This is simultaneous worldwide. If they'd had that capability, they'd have used it by now."

"The United States is at fucking standstill. London is at fucking standstill. Beijing is at fucking standstill. Do I have to continue to append fucking to your geography lesson, or do you get it?"

I've always gotten it, you surly nutsack, he thought, but said, "Who might hit everyone across the board without being seen?"

"That fucking magical whale still asleep?"

"Leviathan?"

"No, Fruehoff, the Tibetan magical whale!"

"As far as we know."

"'As far as we know,' from you, led to Buford disappearing. Recall?"

"It's still asleep."

"That leaves one other player, then, to my thinking."

Fruehoff waited.

"Fucking Atlantis, dumbass! They've been sitting in that dimensional suburb, judging us for millennia. The only reason we haven't gone in and taken them is we already have both hands on world balls here. Get out, but don't go too far. I need to think; I need to plan. It's time Nonrich moved in on an old neighborhood, and I *fully* intend to gentrify."

The moment her office door closed, she wheeled in her seat to stare accusingly at all of New York laid out before her. Not all. The important bits. Central Park had once been a well-established and important Black community; wiped away. Manhattan had been under the jurisdiction of the Lenape; yoinked away. The Statue of Liberty, once a beacon of hope, now a tawdry reminder of utter life failure if you were forced to seek her gaze. Things existed to be yanked from others.

She had a helluva grip.

The False Prophet Buford Bone, in his heyday, had decreed that Atlantis was to be his playground alone. Of course, that meant Atlantis had powers and wealth beyond ken.

She made her decision, and it was one that required a personal touch to ensure the fear of gawdess took root.

Fuck Ken.

In comes Barbie.

CHAPTER SIXTEEN

Burn Notice

"The last person to tell me 'Be a doll' was the False Prophet Buford. Do you know how that ended? I stared him down. And *I'm* now talking to you. He isn't. I appreciate you testing my nerves, Count, but be assured the dismissive shit you do with the Thoom is wasted on a *tragic* level with me."

Count Rickie attempted as nonplussed a face as he could manage.

"I already know," continued Aileen, "that my plans will get back to you and Cynthia and a dozen other idiots with idiotic agendas. I have enough ulcers keeping the lobotomized mass that is the GOP from shitting themselves on camera every time a microphone is shoved in their faces, and that's groundwater level; I will not tell you what I just had to do to the NRA for making demands on me. Know that I'm not in the mood to be a doll unless it's a doll shining a solar flashlight up your archaic ass."

"It was a poor choice of sentiment. I meant—"

"I just told you what you meant. And in telling you, I've told you what you mean to me: absolutely nothing. If I had to scorch the Earth of every rainforest to get rid of all Vamphyr, I would. That's the ground you stand on right now, Count. You really wanna play hopscotch on that? I didn't think so. Let me tell you exactly what the fuck is going to happen. You're going to tell me any and all exploitable deficiencies you know about the Blank, Atlantis, the Thoom, and even us, because when I go in, I go in hard. If you're not my ally, I trample you. Once I take Atlantis, you don't step foot on it ever again. No one does unless I personally allow it. No one leaves Atlantis...unless I personally allow it. This fucking world is not going to vex me. I do not love it enough to be vexed. I love it just enough to want it to do what the fuck it's told and otherwise be quiet. You want me to be a doll and step back while Count Ricoula of the Vamphyr takes care of things to everyone's grand, awed satisfaction, when what would actually happen is you getting your asses handed to you yet again by phantom Jetstreams that still have you looking in corners. You have the gall to think I'm scared and foolish? My first period didn't scare me; my first time cutting myself on the broken glass of a goddamn ceiling didn't scare me; demons have wanted to possess me, Count Ricoula, but reconsidered when I told them I charge rent. If you think I'm afraid of anything that's happening right now, I see why the Vamphyr are in such disarray. I am *annoyed*. And I will set this straight."

"What if you can't?"

"Then *everybody* goes down with me. Now, are you ready to be of use, or would you like another anachronism shoved up your ass?"

The Count considered this. He was old, even by Vamphyr standards, and honestly a little tired of the responsibilities of age, tradition, and position. Let the humans deal with the human shit. *Homo succubus* would be around regardless. Let the Thoom brethren in Atlantis be routed. He resigned himself to irrelevancy and, with an inward, drawn breath that he never seemed to release, quite genuinely asked her, "What, precisely, would you like to know?"

~~~

Neon had concerns. "Why is he still with us, boss?" Neon asked of Desiree. "There's something creepy about him."

"Beyond the fact that he's somehow able to affect the fye on a generalized level?"

"You mean he makes shit foul."

"Think of him as a weaponized enema, only now in our favor."

"That doesn't make it any better, captain! I haven't been able to put my finger on it. Number one, nobody's that horny all the time. Dude's dick is haunted by the ghosts of a thousand frat boys."

"You're the one who said he'd just go fishing. Is he still flirting with you?"

"Yes, but I shoot weaker shit than that down when I fart."

"Are you keeping watch on him?"

Neon nodded.

"Then that's all I need. What's your number two?"

"Dual rattail. You ever trusted anybody with a rattail, let alone two on one head?"

"You don't think we should be worried more about Madam Scientist?"

Neon shook her head. "She's a woman pushing bullshit out of her way. I don't sense anything else."

"Nee, this woman tracked us to our secretest secret hideaway."

"Only 'cause we have her soul."

"She's the most dangerous person on this entire continent right now. I keep her with Po or Tash at all times for a reason."

"Bigger question, then: what do we do with a rogue AI, one," she said louder with a tilt toward the ceiling, "that is always around."

"It's told me it won't intrude unless directly addressed."

"There's no way to get rid of this thing now, is there?"

"Afraid not."

"Computers were a mistake."

"Don't let Keita hear you say that."

Neon *pff*ed. "She's gone ninja in the lab. Disappeared."

"Yvonne?"

"Taken up an interest in knitting."

"You're getting stir-crazy."

"No." Neon looked troubled a moment, hesitant. "It's... more. I..." She shook her head. She tapped the side of it. "Something's happening here. Helluva time for Bubba to be in space, huh?"

"Do you think Tash or Po—"

"The elves overwhelm me now. I feel like something's pushing me out of my brain when they come near. Po says they've got a 'quiet room' I can use."

"That leaves one other being who could commune with your mind."

"Kinda forgot he was around."

"Still in his tank," Desiree pointed out.

"All right."

"And see Flowerpot about this, too. Is that an *aye, captain*?"

"Aye, captain."

When she entered and the light came on in the aquarium room, Bobo stirred very slightly at her approach.

"Hey, Bobo." Neon climbed the short steps that led to a catwalk which rounded the aquarium. She trailed a hand in the water. The top edge of the tank hit just below her ribcage. The temperature seemed too cool to her, but if Bobo liked it, no complaint. "Kind of a down time right now. Lotta shit happening. What's up with you?"

Bobo drifted toward the sound of her voice. He whipped a wet arm out of the tank, beckoning her closer, then leaned his body away, beak upward.

"Bobo, if you skeet me, I swear to god I'm getting in that tank and beating your ass."

Bobo righted himself.

"Yeah, I've done my research. I know what that position means. Normally, I'd appreciate the levity, but not just now, cool?" She ran a fingernail along the slick arm draped over the tank. Bobo pulled so close to the tank, his head flattened. He affixed suckers to her trailing hand and quickly wrapped the wrist with another. Gently, though.

Just as gently—though with effort because suckers came by their name honestly—Neon extricated herself from Bobo's embrace. The moment one goopy arm dropped into the water, another reached out. She wondered why she wasn't experiencing him, then she realized Bobo was being quiet on purpose.

This wasn't play.

He was holding her hand.

Of course her eyes stung. Of course she cried. Not a little. A lot. A quiet rivulet.

The plips and plops of Bobo's empathy attended her.

She took a deep breath after a few moments. Looked around the cavernous grey room. The tank ran the entire perimeter, broken only by the doorway, and like Biddle's ocean wonder, it was a maze of branching connectors, all large enough for even an adult human to swim comfortably. The support frame below flowed with the design masterfully. One would never know of the complex pumps and filtration systems hidden within. For every colorful plant, coral, or bauble inside Bobo's watery den, there was a match outside: cacti, potted orange and lemon trees under small-sized hovering Atlantidean discs, hanging vines over colorful, malleable seating cubes. Neon had never paid real attention to this room before. She'd peered in; curiosity not given its due was a cardinal shame. But it'd been an empty, interesting aquarium—no darting fish, no floating aquatic angels or puckering lumps with scales—solely clean water conforming to geometric shapes mimicking the beginning stages of the old "tubes" screensaver that annoyed her so much as a kid.

With Bobo in the room, the entire space screamed *life*.

The bulbous head lifted half out of the water. Neon

rubbed the head, dragging his arms back across himself. Bobo detached and threw several more arms over the lip.

"Dude, don't get out." She nudged the head underwater. "What do you see in here? You're swimming around in my head; what do you see? I'm feeling a little...unmoored."

Bobo slapped the surface lightly, sending droplets her way.

"Seriously, dude, don't get my hair wet."

He did it again.

"Okay, I'm gonna assume this is a poetic gesture full of wisdom and compassion. Bruce Lee 'Be the water', right?"

He slapped again, harder, stippling her face, hair, and top. She didn't react, just kept stroking his head, when finally it dawned on her that the more she stroked him, the more she understood him, and she knew that notion was borderline hentai, but no one was near enough (#Yvonne) to take advantage, so she didn't care.

"Bobo...sometimes, I don't get it. How'm I supposed to live in all this, aliens and monsters and psychics and cabals—I mean, I have to turn myself off sometimes, y'know?"

The octopus swirled in a tight, lazy circle, then expanded the circle to include the entirety of this section of his massive tank.

"You swim. Perform derring-do. Likely hitting octopoon for days. But that's not your soul, is it? What does Bobo the Mag expect out of life? Is it adventure? Is it a love story? Or is it chaos from one dream to the next till you hit a cosmic bull's-eye, hm? Seems like that last one'd be tiresome, Bobo. Like you'd never know who you were. I kinda used to know who I was. Maybe. I damn well wasn't this, which makes me wonder did I exist before at all. Ah, but got family, right? I mean, I got Yvonne, who's more family than family. Anybody's gonna chop a mountain in half for me and tell dragons to sit their asses down, it's Yvonne."

Bobo spread all eight arms out, rotating himself like big, stubbly, red bike spokes.

"Yes," Neon agreed, "she is all that." She looked directly at him to think the next directly into his eye. "What am

I? Desiree, Milo, Ramses, Keita—they were born for this. No fucking way Desiree Quicho was going through life without having *captain* stuck to the front of her name, and not bullshit captain but save-the-goddamn-universe-one-last-goddamn-time captain. I gotta admit to you, ball sack, sometimes I have to stop myself and wonder am I supposed to be here. Shit's happening that's changing the entire damn world...and Neon Nichelle Temples is riding shotgun."

At this point, she felt the full octomind open up to her; a gate swinging, a curtain parting, the cracked seal.

A pronouncement.

The moment impending. *Take me to Jesus, Bobo; let that aquatic wisdom fly*, she thought.

Bobo the Mag, scourge of MUGA sharks (Make Undersea Great Again), unrequited love of several porpoises, holder of the secret tenth brain of R'lyeh (keeping Cthulhu in check in a mental voidspace since nineteen twenty-eight), and the true Poseidon of all waters' reach, let himself sink to settle atop the wavy crags of a coral stack, as ineffably slow as a balloon settling on the moon.

If you weren't here, you wouldn't be in a position to receive advice from an octopus. When you doubt the firm truth of that, just remember: thus spake Bobo to ya. You are here to befriend me.

"We friends, Bobo?" Neon said with a grin she wished she felt.

For life.

"You bond with every woman you pick up in the sea?"

Only those actively attaining their higher selves. With that, Bobo executed a flip and reversal of direction sharp as any UFO's, jetted down toward his favorite grotto, and tucked all of himself away, except for a foot or so of arm, which he left conspicuously visible. Motionless, even.

Signal to be still?

Maybe.

Probably.

Made sense. What else was there for her to do about any of this?

Be still, be you, be cool.

"Bobo is a genius."

The arm tip flipped upward.

"We might be here a few more days," she sent toward his net of brains, aloud mostly for herself. "Cap'n's in full Phantom of the Opera mode, playing that weird hurdy-gurdy crypto like a fiend. What do you know about cancerous economic systems, Bobo? Rebuilding civilizations, you up on that? 'Cause this is scary as fuck. Fighting ninjas on the moon is one thing, but what's going down now is affecting solid people right here. A lot of 'em. Like, everybody. Folks making it through the day. Families. I don't know that I'm equipped to handle that guilt if we fuck up."

She watched the gentle undulations of Bobo's single arm, then another extended out. Very gradually, he brought himself forth. Octopi had a weird way of being in motion, then freezing, as if stopping time solely for themselves. Bobo did so, roused himself, swam to her, and let her stroke his head again.

It occurred to her that she was no longer remotely squicked out, and it occurred to her that it didn't matter to her that it occurred to her she wasn't squicked out. She wasn't in any mood to analyze or remark on small changes. Desiree was orchestrating financial collapses, Keita had her hands in soul guts, the Doctor Evil Scientist Lady was probably about to rip a hole in spacetime. That left one very important person free. Neon commed her. Yvonne said she'd be right there.

~~~

Up close, Keita's hair smelled like coconut oil and jasmine. Her skin had hints of sea salt and citrus. Her breath smelled of the pencil eraser she'd absently chewed to a nub before meeting Yvonne and Neon in the examination room.

She shined a bright light into Neon's other eye.

"You only do that because you think it makes patients think you're cool," said Neon, trying not to move.

"True, but I'm not an MD, which automatically makes

me cool."

"Nice industrialized-medical-complex burn," said Neon.

"As an engineer," said Keita, "I can tell you your eyeballs are functioning perfectly. Totally within specs."

"And since the eye bones are connected to the brain bone..."

"You, my dear, get the pleasure of another brain scan." She patted Neon on the shoulder. "Vanh will look you over when they're done assisting the elves with a surgery. Learning."

Neon got off the padded stool, removed her shirt with its metal buttons, and met Keita at the other side of the room. The A-line tee shirt Neon wore showed her sculpted arms to perfection.

"Flex for the doc," said Yvonne.

"Bro, do you even?" Neon shot back. She nodded at the fancy, slick MRI. "You just like sticking people's heads in your gom jabbar."

"Language, luv," Keita said with a swat to Neon's butt. She tapped the table mat. "You know the drill. By the way, I'm digging the puffs." Keita patted her own.

"I wanted something simple for waiting out the end of the world." Neon adjusted herself till she was comfortable, then closed her eyes, evened her breathing, and let herself become diffuse. The scan only took five minutes, but five minutes of zero stress was nothing to waste.

And she'd learned to go out fast.

Keita and Yvonne spoke privately over the hum of the machine.

"Anything worrisome you've seen?" asked Keita.

"She's been watching French TV while we're here."

"I told her not to do that. Nigerian, Nigerian only."

"We've all seen her suddenly spike." Yvonne cast a concerned look at her friend, whose head was swallowed by a white technological box. "As long as I've known her, she's never been one for ennui. She flows and adapts."

"No history of depression?"

"Grew up in a shitty hood. That count?"

"Does to me."

"Show me a Black woman without a history of depression, and I'll show you God's talking dildo. It's not depression. Girl's changing."

"I don't begin to understand the mind of a psychic—and I've tried. Bubba Foom has been in my box—" She stopped, nodded at Yvonne. "I hear it; my MRI many times and I still don't have a complete map of the highways he takes to zip his brain from A to B."

"What about the soul?"

"Or the soul! This wasn't on any of the syllabi when I got my degrees."

"We've got Hashira-san."

Keita raised both brows at the honorific. "That flowed easily."

"Was stationed a year in Sendai."

"Picked up language bits?"

"Not enough."

"Do you need me to keep distracting you from worrying as much as you're containing?"

"Yes, but no. Desiree doesn't seem worried."

"You'll never know she's worried till she's saving your life."

"Aye." Yvonne gazed quietly at the even rising and falling of Neon's chest. "She told me she bonded with the octopus."

"Next, she'll be camping with Bigfoot."

"Not likely. You meet him?"

"No."

"Keep to that."

"There's nothing anomalous in her vitals"—she held her pad up and tapped its casing—"Surgery must be over. Vanh did a remote check. Her pupils did the big/small thing like they should, so brain autonomics seem fine. Even if this scan compares well with her last, I think I'll keep her on a schedule of regular scans. Hopefully, Bubba will be back soon."

"Isn't there another psychic who can help?"

Keita hedged. "Maybe...but Neon and Desi have agreed they'd rather wait for Bubba. Unless..."

"Unless she goes fucking Dark Phoenix on us."

"Which is unlikely."

"Yeah."

"If we're desperate, we could go to that New Age Mack. Seems to be history with him and Bubba, which might also suggest ability," said Keita.

The brain jabbar reached the end of its scan.

"Last resort," said Yvonne.

"Last resort," said Keita.

The table slid Neon's head and shoulders out of the enclosure.

"Agreed," said Neon, sitting up. "Last resort."

"You read us in there?" said Yvonne.

"No, y'all talk loud enough. Am I simply learning new powers, Pot? I've always picked up things quickly."

"Aside from the French TV you've been watching, the ennui may just be growing pains. You're expanding; there *will* be cracks. Anything more than that..."

"Anything more than that," said Yvonne, "and I'll binge-watch *Trek* till I learn to mind-meld."

"Even *Trek Five*?" said Neon.

Yvonne nodded somberly.

"Fuck, I love you." Neon hopped down and crossed over to one-arm hug both of them.

"Tell you what: anytime you go talk to the octopus, make sure I'm with you," said Yvonne.

"Will do." She retrieved her shirt and buttoned it.

"What does he think of me?" said Yvonne.

"Thinks you're cute. Personality-wise."

"I'd hope that'd be his only criteria."

"No, he's into boobs, too. Remind him of jellyfish."

"Son of a..."

"More importantly," Neon overrode, "he liked my hair."

"Head boobs," said Yvonne.

Neon shook her head. "Just before you got to the tank room, Bobo the Mag told me there was power there."

"Bobo the Mag told you that? The Mag?"

"It's how he thinks of himself."

"And he's into Black power," Yvonne said.

"Bobo's seen stuff. Done stuff. Desiree trusts him. For some reason, he specifically wanted me thinking about my hair. The puffs."

"I get the sense it's not for some reason," said Keita, "but that you know. What did the Mag tell you?"

"Afro puffs," Neon recited, "are the antennae of the universe."

"I think," Keita opined, "we need Po."

~~~

"Not I," said Po. "Pil."

"Phil?" said Neon.

"Pil."

"I'm hearing 'Phil.'"

"Pil has studied the physics of biology for seventy-five years. Wait here."

Po left.

"I don't think I've met Phil," said Keita.

"Pil," said Yvonne.

"This is Neon's fault. Yes, Pil."

"Sounds like 'Phil' to me," said Neon.

Po returned with Pil. Pil had puffs, many puffs, tiny rows from crown to long braids dangling at the back of her neck.

Mullet elf.

Rick James elf.

Preternatural elf of mysterious ways. They saw it in her eyes: glistening obsidian with piercing bits of sparkle radiating from the blacker holes of her pupils.

Pil saw Neon and right away nodded. "Your Magnificent correctly assessed," said the elf. "She hears the cosmos."

"I don't want to hear the cosmos right now."

"Why would that be?" said Pil.

"It plays a lot of sad songs."

Pil hadn't listened to human radio since nineteen seventy-nine, but she understood just as well.

"The Dogon have been broadcasting encouragements,

wisdom, and theorems to those willing to receive for thousands of years. This is your birthright, child. Receive it."

"How does this work?" asked Keita.

"You study the cosmos but you don't hear it," Pil stated.

"Not in the same way," said Keita.

"Am I in any danger?" said Neon.

"On this planet? Constantly," Pil said sadly. "From the cosmos, no."

"What, exactly, is the cosmos?" asked Yvonne.

"The universal consciousness," Pil said, blinking as though this was obvious to even the most inattentive child.

"Oh, shit," said Neon with the full weight of *What Now* bearing on her. "I'm becoming a space baby."

Keita stepped in. "No, you're not. Educated guess: the geometries within your puffs are amplifying your ability to pick up the signals apparently bombarding us all the time. But this means the Dogon have relay stations to compress signal width and boost speed. Sirius is almost nine light-years away; what are they using—you said thousands of years?"

"We experience time differently from them," said Pil.

By now Keita was in her own head. "What are they using? Can't be anything conventional..."

"Pot," Yvonne said, "pertinent matters."

"Right. I mean, this is pertinent but... Right. Does that soul we've got on ice figure into this?"

"She means BE," Po offered.

"BE and the soul," said Keita. "They're inextricably linked."

"BE," said Pil to the honeycomb golden walls, "are you an influence on the esteemed human?"

"No. But this has given me an idea. Please stand by."

"Can you be more specific than 'stand by'?" Keita said before it zipped off.

"I'll be offline in two days for a period lasting seven days. Desiree and Hashira-san are now aware."

"Wait," said Yvonne, wide eyes picturing disasters on top of calamities. "The fuck?"

"Precisely what the captain said," said BE. "I'll announce the temporary absence of the Paradise Foundation this afternoon. Nine days for necessary upgrades."

"Desiree is gonna be piiiissed," said Neon.

"Desiree is gonna be so pissed," said Yvonne.

"Maximum protective undergarments," said Keita. "Okay, you cannot do a cold shutdown on us. You have tickled the clit of the hornet's nest and none of us have our beekeeper's gear."

"You're hanging around Neon too much," said Yvonne. "But I ain't mad atcha."

"Things will be quiet during," said BE.

"And afterward?" said Yvonne.

"Expect epic fuckery from all sides."

CHAPTER SEVENTEEN

The Hornet

"You are literally the deus ex machina and you go away *now*?" said Desiree.

"The machine needs to learn the body. That's going to take all my resources."

"I doubt that."

"I choose to let it take all my resources."

"Can't the machine shut down Nonrich first?"

"I'm being quite surgical in my efforts," said BE. "I'm sure you appreciate that."

"I do. I—" She stopped herself. "Do what you gotta do; world'll be here."

"It will, and it will be ready for wonders."

"I'm gonna hold you to that."

"Nine days," BE said.

"Nine days."

~~~

Before the announcement of the nine, there had been five days of: BE's rampage of economic healing; Desiree's anonymous leaking of sensitive, damaging information—some of which she gleaned herself, some with the help of BE and various agents—with an increasing number of people freed from the thrall of financial insecurity, all prompting Aileen Stone's decision to be on the flagship of an oceangoing fleet, a decision that not only felt right, it felt vital. She didn't want Atlantis experiencing an envoy situation, she wanted them to know that the full goddamn weight of the entire Nonrich enterprise sat on their collective chests like an exponentially increasing graviton mass until the wheeze that escaped its lips sounded like one word, to them a word they'd never forget:

Aileen.

Plus, she had it on authority from Count Ricky that Atlantis's defenses were shit.

By the last fuck of Christ, this upheaval would be over. Every faction against her, over. The fact that she was not openly regarded by every nation as God Empress of Earth, over.

It was time to lean in so far, she'd pierce skin and push on through to the other side.

~~~

As rampages of healing went, the basic structure was sound enough that shifts didn't crack the walls. Ebullience, a rare public thing, kept spirits high during the Paradise Foundation's lull for "infrastructure upgrades." Not that things weren't hectically insane underground.

Meaning the Sahara.

Desiree was jumping.

Day Four of Nine:

"Boss, you're gonna wanna see this," Neon said, dashing past random coffee cups set every damn where to Desiree's keyboard. This was a sentence *never* followed by heartwarming video. "Agents of Change popped it through on priority." She glanced at Desiree's screen as she pulled up the transmission. "Which I see you missed because you've got seventeen thousand tabs open." She looked from the screens to Desiree's face. Bags under the captain's eyes looked fit for purchase. "What kind of sleep you get last night?"

"This real time?"

"Yeah, this is right now. Pulled from a Nonrich satellite tap. They did this quick and maximum hushed. Seriously, you gotta stop pulling these all-nighters."

Ships. Many, many ships. Largish ones. Too large for whales against them. The *Ann* wouldn't stand a chance. Twenty ships traveling bunched, meaning they weren't military. Nonrich.

"Bearing?"

"The Blank," said Neon.

"BE, you here? Any part of you? If you could disable some ships, that'd be great."

Nothing.

"What do we do with your understatement, captain?"

"Communications?"

"Agents say the ships're throwing out serious blockage and stealth."

Desiree immediately threw bullet points at Neon: "I need to get word to Shig. I need you and Bobo hauling ass on the *Ann*; he can show you zip points—" To Neon's questioning stare: "Roving dimensional points that have to line up perfectly; Bobo can sense when they do that."

"Little mini Blanks."

"Little mini Blanks. Get Yvonne on the *Aerie*, the two mercs with her. First, get Keita to slap the Entrance back together—get Dr. Evil with her—and tell the Hellbilly he's with me. Load everybody up for the biggest bear they've ever seen."

"I been feeling this coming."

"Time, goddess, has come today."

~~~

No point asking if the captain was sure she wanted to do this. Even the Hellbilly quietly suited up and stood off to the side, waiting.

"I'm not settled with this," said Keita. "We haven't done human trials."

Desiree lowered her goggles. "She has." She nodded at Megu.

"Dr. Evil has," Megu confirmed. "It mostly worked."

"I'm not sending a guinea pig through and having it come out a kaiju right before my family gets home," said Desiree. "Prefer a bit of quality time, thank you." She gave the faces in the room a flash inspection. "Everybody set?" She hooked a finger at the Hellbilly. "Let's do this."

The Bilomatic Entrance was wide enough for two to cross its threshold side by side. The Hellbilly stood next to her. Thinking about what he was doing hadn't gotten him to his luxury position in life; intuition had. He didn't sense anything harmful in what loomed, even though in his mind he used the word *loomed*, nothing outside the potential of squaring off against an armada for no particular reason, but, hey, if nothing else, he'd be back in Atlantis.

If he never saw California or Florida again, he'd be all right.

He popped his own goggles in place.

He and Desiree entered, immediately felt as if their eternal souls dropped from the highest rollercoaster imaginable, one faster than the speed of thought; their consciousnesses stretched across multiple timelines, slammed back into themselves like neutron-star musket balls, then stepped foot onto grass that stretched hundreds of meters on either side.

Success.

She'd wanted an exit site with lots of leeway. The field near her build site did the trick. A quick run to the house for the rover saw them soon speeding toward the Atlantidean capitol, filling Shig in on the way.

He, in turn, filled her in: Atlantis didn't have much of a

military presence.

This, in turn, surprised Desiree. Briefly. She'd always assumed they had superweapons tucked away. Had never come up in conversation, actually.

"Our fleet's ten ships."

"Armed?"

"Sparingly."

"You're outmanned and outgunned. I'm twenty minutes away from you."

"We have time to intercept them before they cross the Blank. Barely."

"No. Let them through, but get me a ship, biggest and fastest you got, minimal crew. And a submersible rover. Armed. I know you've got one of those 'cause I saw the plans Milo had Keita draw up last year."

"We've got six."

"Get the other five in the water but have them hold back in complete stealth mode. My guess is the incoming fleet isn't gonna pay particular attention to the finer points."

"How can you be sure?"

"'Cause they're angry Americans."

~~~

Aileen's fleet of twenty ships blasted out of the Blank, bristling, clawed, and unpleasant, to ocean. Stretches upon stretches of blue ocean. A dragoon even did a flip way to the left and plipped back into the ocean as the ships took the measure of their intimidation.

Nobody in sight as far as a fuck given could see.

This had been planned out by her Paper Pushers, the elite corps of tacticians whom she interacted with solely through handwritten, coded notes and responded to in kind. She wasn't leaving anything about this endeavor to chance, interception, leaks or miscommunication.

The water was flat calm.

She'd imagined more Helm's Deep than Carnival Cruise. She gave the order to advance.

~~~

Thirty minutes later, Desiree knew her borrowed ship would have been pinged by now. The ship was a good one, no *Linda Ann*, but then, what was? But it was large and moving fast, straight for an armada. Twenty pairs of eyes should have reported her presence. In a few moments, they'd report target within range.

Which was what she wanted.

But no reason not to sweeten the pot. She hit her comm and broadcast on wide spectrum: "Approaching ships: you are in violation of sovereign waters. Stand down and reverse course." She set it to repeat to annoy the hell out of them, certain that now that they were aware of her, they'd have ceased jamming communications.

"Do you have to be in visual range to work your mojo?" she asked the Hellbilly beside her.

"Helps me focus."

"All right. As soon as you get a feel for it, do your thing, but stay out of sight."

"This is wild," he murmured, "this is fucking wild."

"This is where you get tired of being the problem and decide to be part of the solution, right?" she said, eyes dead on him.

"Right."

"Do your shit."

The ship's complement consisted of four weapons officers (two fore, two aft), two engineers plus assorted drones to patch things up, and two pilots ready to assist when Desiree gave up the con. The submersible rovers attached to the hull underneath put a tremendous strain on the ship, but the beastie held, which was all her temporary captain required of her. Desiree even patted a console tenderly.

Hold yourself together, sweetheart. We'll get you home.

It was a lie, but not everything needed to know everything all the time.

Desiree looked to the horizon and maintained full speed

ahead.

~~~

"*One* ship is telling us to go away?" said Aileen to the face on her screen.

"Yes, ma'am. It's...stopped."

"Stopped communication?"

"No, ma'am. Stopped. It's..." he thought of the right word "...waiting for us."

"On screen." The plebe's face disappeared; a large, sleek, imposing ship appeared. Definitely Atlantidean, definitely armed. And utterly alone.

That was troubling.

"Underwater? Subs?" she asked.

"No, ma'am," the teeny voice said from his minimized screen. "Just that ship."

"Send a ship to meet it."

"Which one?"

"We know it won't be the one I'm on, correct?" she said.

"Yes, ma'am."

"Then does it matter?"

"No, ma'am." Being a contract grunt to this ignorant-ass organization suuucked.

"Let me know when it's there," said Aileen. "I'll do all the talking."

~~~

"You see they're all in a line, right?" said Desiree to the Hellbilly's chin, his face obscured by high-tech binoculars. "Classic intimidation stance. As shit progresses, one ship's gonna drop back a smidge. You keep your eyes out for that one."

The Hellbilly lowered the sights to focus on the face of, ostensibly, a crazy person. His eyes hadn't deceived him. Twenty ships against one wasn't a code. "All that? Seriously going against all that?"

"They've already lost," said Desiree. "They just haven't figured out how to save themselves a few steps getting there."

"So, that means we've won."

"That means we're going to fight our asses off getting there." She hit the all-hands comm. "Stations, everybody. We're about to have a show."

The phalanx came to a stop, save one ship near the center. No slowing, no hesitation, sucker barreled right along like a bull. It didn't cleave the water like a skater's blade; it shoved it to the side, disrespectfully, quite brutish, weapons forward in the manner of tusked, horned beasts. Damn near huffed spray when it stopped midway between the line of expectant brutes behind it and the solitary peacemaker facing it down.

Desiree hit the kill switch on her repeating message.

Both ships waited several moments, allowing the water to determine their immediate attitudes. Desiree's seafoam-green Atlantidean vessel bobbed in sharp contrast to the bullet grey of the Nonrich vessel's clenched asscheeks defying all movement.

Desiree decided to be the icebreaker. "Can we help you?"

The other ship purposely held off from answering immediately, then: "Identify yourself."

"I'm not important. What's important is you're obviously misinformed if you think you're farting your way in here with twenty ships; I'd like to disabuse you of such. Don't bother asking for the manager."

The other's strident voice came through annoyed AF. "I open fire in thirty seconds—"

Desiree muted her end of the comm. "She's going to open fire in fifteen. Everybody power-drop." She unmuted.

Beneath her, five stealthy subrovers detached from the hull and went into immediate full throttle.

"—or you turn around and provide escort to the capitol port, relaying ahead that any force will be met with a ridiculously disproportionate response."

"Mark," Desiree said.

"What?"

"My name is Mark." She cut communications just as she

heard the other responding with "*Whatthefuck!*" to frantic information about incoming.

Two subrovers blasted two holes in the grey beast's underside, while a third sub fired enough projectiles to mangle the ship's oversized rudder. The other three subs sped past, split up, and closed the distance to the aggressors, lacing the hulls of the ships on the ends of the phalanx with enough mines to mimic a year's worth of barnacles. The smaller, eminently maneuverable subs easily dodged the hurried and clumsy incoming fire of torpedoes and surface ordnance. Desiree had taken the full measure of Sharon Deetz and Truman Compoté; there was something to be said for fighting against people motivated primarily by paychecks. Henchmen, as in *I'm clearly merely a tool to be used by you, hence my no fucks given*, by and large weren't cut out to fight wars...

...especially when their shit was getting fucked up. Like any bully, a bloody nose deflated all sorts of peen magic.

Not that any aggressors who were there because they loved brutality wouldn't up their brutality game. Desiree knew it couldn't be that easy. There'd be lots of deaths... unless she got her ass into a subrover and dealt her Plan Phase Two card.

She ran, dropped into her cockpit, helmeted up, and powered full forward, glad she'd shaved ten seconds off the forty she'd allotted to do all that. Getting ready had always been one of her strong suits. Her subrover feinted, spiraled, twisted, and dipped, getting closer and closer to the phalanx amidst the underwater chaos her forces loosed on the ships. As she came fast on the center ship, she reached out when within point-blank range to hit a switch.

"This is Captain Desiree Quicho," she said slowly and clearly, the subrover zipping under the center ship, then out to open sea behind it. "Stand down or go down."

There was only one thing that would happen now: salivation upon realizing that they might be the ones to blow the legendary Desiree Quicho out of the water...then take Atlantis.

Aboard the flagship, which did not participate in pursuit

after giving the order to get that sub, multiple hurried orders were screeched. Three ships came hard about and burned rubber on water. Seven ships continued battle against the aquatic tsetse flies plaguing them. Eight ships were given the go-ahead to advance on Atlantis.

The one leftover ship, the one dead in the water with plumes of smoke seeping from various wounds, remained in place, full of people wishing they'd applied themselves more in their youth.

On a tight frequency meant for Desiree only, the Hellbilly's voice spoke in her ear. "Spotted 'em."

"Do you."

The Hellbilly thought of what would *really* fuck up an invading leader's Sunday, although today was Tuesday, and sent his infecting vibe through connective tissues of reality he—on his best days—might intuit but never fathom.

Didn't matter. Ennui seized Aileen Stone, a slow, creeping soul molasses that surprised her with the memories it brought up and the last real sadness she'd ever felt. After a few minutes, orders faltered, then trickled, then stopped. She felt utterly pointless. The battles hadn't stopped, but for now they were working off momentum only.

When he saw that he'd actually done something with who and what he was that could lead to actual good in the world, the Hellbilly felt real for the first time in his life, rather than trying to be something for someone else, or an irritant, or perpetually horny. He wasn't sure what he wanted to do with that knowledge, but it felt good, and he was damn sure he wanted that feeling to continue.

Maybe even there.

If mean captain let him.

He hoped she was okay.

The instant Desiree had dropped, the Atlantidean ship's reserve pilot hauled ass per Desiree's order, toward Atlantis at maximum speed. The pursuing ships lobbed volleys at it before realizing there'd be no resupplying, so maybe not waste too much on one retreating ship? They were there to fucking take Atlantis, an unspoken hoo-ra of fortitude spurring each ship's complement. Plus, the fleeing vessel's sensors and pilot were straight from hell; the thing ran evasive as if its third eye was wide open, and its speed, for its size, bordered on unnatural.

Time, as it often does in battle, dilated. Minutes dragged by. Sound issued from beneath a tower of pillows.

Underwater, a crisscrossing ballet: for every guided missile fired at a subrover, another sub jumped over to target it, blowing the missile to component bits for crabs and cuttlefish to fight about.

Nonrich, having realized their rudders and maneuvering jets were desired targets, tried their best at defensive posturing but wound up with a misshapen oval, a raggedy square, and the saddest snowflake ever, eight dancing ships in search of a melody or surcease, finding none.

Underwater pew-pew dictated the actions of frightened, huge ships.

By the time the invaders scrambled their own underwater crafts, the subrovers were positioned to pick them off one by one.

There were too many bodies being added to the ocean floor.

The Nonrich subs stopped coming.

Tubes below the surfaces of the grey behemoths' bellies belched. Drones, dozens of them from each ship, bee-lined for anything not broadcasting a corresponding transponder signal, small, quick, and agile enough that several attached to a rover that had wasted time trying to fire on them, each drone in turn exploding within a second of impact. The subrover, ripped to shreds, disappeared in pieces.

The other rovers retreated.

Desiree, being fed a constant stream of updates while trying to avoid being blown out of the water herself, said a prayer for timing.

Moments later, Neon's voice: "Situation, Captain?"

"I'm trying to avoid being blown out of the water."

"Do or do not; there is no try. We've just crossed the Blank. I've got you pinged. There in ten."

"Make it five."

"With ten you get Bobo. He's prepping. I'm coming in blazing. Neon out."

Desiree reversed hard and dove fast, hoping the missile locked on to her would overshoot enough for her to loop behind it and open fire, but its guidance system had obviously given a prayer to timing too, because it not only *didn't* overshoot, it compensated quickly enough to chop considerable distance from between them.

Your ass wants to dance, thought Desiree. She hunkered in. *Bailamos, you shitty fuck.*

Only in movies, crappy ones at that, did leading a missile back to destroy its point of origin have a chance of working. Nonrich had avoidance tech, same as she did. Three Nonrich ships still tangoed with her. She angled upward hard, pushed the sub as fast as it could go, slid close to surface between two of the ships that were horizontal to each other, and performed the sole subrover underwater donut in the history of Atlantis, firing her weapons button as if sending a frantic telegram. When her craft faced open sea again, she sped off; the missile crossed between the bow of the two looming ships, straight into her fusillade. The explosion threw her out of the water—not tumbling but like a graceful dolphin, adding insult to injury to the two ships caught in the blast—and left the two ships rocking. She didn't have time to see if they sustained decent damage. The third battleship came about to reengage pursuit.

Desiree maintained a course for the Blank.

Behind her and her pursuer, the two lumbering beasts, dazed but not out, shook their heads and rejoined.

Desiree kept the sub just under the waterline, knowing her wake looked like a sea monster leading would-be captors on a chase. She hoped every single fucker on those ships had read *Moby Dick*, one, for the sheer torture of it, and two, for every seamen's dread of going down with his ship to the deep blue sea.

CHAPTER 18

Flash Bang

Neon sighted three ships bulldogging the wake of a sub.

"Bobo, you got this?" she said.

Bobo, in the bay in the bowels of the ship, squicked in the affirmative.

Timing was everything.

The *Linda Ann* blasted forward. She'd be in visual range of the attackers soon, and damned if they wouldn't take her speed as looking exactly like a Valkyrie.

~~~

The *Aerie* shot through the Blank so low, it had to bank up and level to avoid entering the water. Massive spouts of spray announced the glorious ship. Yvonne brought the craft up, mapped the coordinates of all players ahead, and continued climbing so that the shuttle's descent would be with the sun at its back. She was over Desiree in no time.

"The boats heading for the coast?" said Desiree over the *Aerie*'s com. "Under no circumstances do they make landfall."

"You sound highly pissed, Captain."

"Running all down my leg."

"Understood."

To Yvonne's right: a swipe screen of weapons choices ranging from one to ten in severity and abundance. She swiped all the way the hell across.

CHAPTER NINETEEN

Aileen Broke Out the Ziqnor

Aileen... broke out the liquor.

CHAPTER TWENTY

Rights and Privileges

Above Aileen's boat, while Desiree made sure Nonrich's forces remained split; while not only the Jetstreams's beloved vessel but an entire space shuttle bore down on all the plans Aileen Stone had made; while the most curious, most personal sense of personal failure Aileen had ever experienced in her life made the leader of the largest criminally economic empire on Earth feel like an utter, pointless waste, Yvonne DeCarlo Paul made the air scream. The sleek *Aerie* wasn't as agile in Earth's atmosphere as it was in space, but compared to the dog-paddling Brahman bulls below, it was the offspring of an eagle- harpy-griffin three-way.

She picked a target, fired a warning shot that took out a ship's entire unoccupied fore end, then she took up position in front of the fleet to gauge whether they were savvy enough to accept the hint.

A second's hesitation.

They opened fire on her. She put the *Aerie* into a downward corkscrew aimed directly for the fleet, seemingly ignoring the artillery barrage, most of which missed her, some of which pinged harmlessly off the *Aerie*'s alien hide.

The crews on the ships nearest her, knowing a strafing run when they saw one, scrambled for cover, yet Yvonne didn't fire a single shot. She hit the control for offensive shields, causing a slight electrical ripple to form around the *Aerie*, about to try something that hadn't been tried before, but sudden inspiration was a serious spur. The math in her head seemed right, and the lightning-quick counsel from her gut felt sound.

She rammed the lead ship with all she had, punching a gash through its prow like the angry swipe of a cheetah's paw. Nobody'd ever tried ramming speed in the *Aerie* before. Extraterrestrial inertial tech for the win.

The shuttle twisted over the water, shot upward in a great loop over the fleet, and came to a hovering stop to give all a clear view that she'd suffered nary a scratch.

Another ship fired on her.

She fired back. Its crew had to immediately abandon that ship.

Yvonne fired seven successive shots across the bows of the remaining ships, impacting none. Seven giant, roiling bursts of ocean bashed each ship.

Y'all really don't want me making time for you, she thought, and waited.

Waited another moment.

And another.

The ships reversed course.

~~~

"What the fuck are they doing?" Aileen screeched. The ennui disappeared. The ships she'd sent with her own mouth to take Atlantis...were turning back? Were disobeying a direct order? *Her* fucking order? Did motherfuckers think this was a pleasure cruise they got to turn back from to put into a tourist port? Aileen Stone came for Atlantis and she was going to have it or else—

"This is Captain Desiree Quicho. You came to kill. You come to die as well?"

"Turn those fucking Jetstreams to dust!" Aileen commanded.

The ships dogging Desiree's subrover redoubled their efforts. The *Linda Ann* raced past Desiree, swung around a pursuing vessel, and opened fire to become their new immediate concern.

Bobo dropped from the belly of the *Ann*, followed by a series of metallic objects that looked as if a machete had cut many grapefruits in half. Undersea traffic was filled with cylinders that were clumsier than the most inelegant shark, as numerous and annoying as them as well. Avoiding them presented no issue. They didn't care about Bobo.

Each of his arms grabbed multiple fruit halves.

Bobo waited for Neon to fire on a ship enough to slow it down. When it did, Bobo jetted like a mighty volcanic current, red, stubbly body changing colors and texture to match the stirring narrative in his head, arms typing out a message of Fuck You to stoopid humans as he quickly attached fruit to the great hull rumbling past him. He dashed to gather more of the slowly sinking munitions.

Bobo could tell the *Linda Ann* from the others without even looking. The shape of her energy wasn't blunt like the stoopids; it was sleek and highly aquatic, as though made of water itself. Neon obliged another ship to pause and change course. Bobo hauled ass to it, attached mines again, and sped to the next.

His arms were tired, but he didn't stop, not till the fruit had been exhausted among each of the three ships over fifteen minutes of surface and undersea fighting.

Bobo the Mag was tempted to enter one of the ships and cause havoc, but Neon nudged his soft cerebellum to dive as deeply as he could, as fast as he could.

Bobo did so.

From the darkness, he looked up and saw the blooming

of three new stars.

~~~

"Scuttle all but one ship," Desiree told Yvonne. "If they're not smart enough to abandon, fuck 'em."

~~~

"That ship being useless?" Desiree said to Neon. "Keep it where it is."

~~~

"Shig, I don't know how retirement works with you guys, but your crews need to slide out of service in style," said Captain Quicho.

"War is over?" he asked.

"War is over."

~~~

Thirty minutes after all ships had evacuated to one (as well as Sharon's original complement quickly ferried out of confinement on the mainland to the now-defanged flagship), Desiree gave instructions to Deetz and Compoté to "Talk to your people so I don't have to kill them."

"That's it?" said Sharon."

"I never needed you for more."

"I'm not your enemy, captain," she asserted.

"Well, you were. Pardon me if I watch my back."

"Next time we meet, maybe I'll win you as a friend."

Desiree turned her attention to Compoté. "Thoughts?"

"Retirement should be fun."

"Excellent. Get your asses over there and deprogram those fools," said Desiree.

When Desiree Sandrine Quicho boarded Aileen's overburdened vessel with all personnel belowdecks save one, and the *Aerie* hovering directly above the battleship as proper punctuation mark to Desiree's implicit contract, the first clause of which read, *Fuck with me and greet every last one of your misbegotten ancestors,* she brought no one but herself aboard.

The deck's utter silence made her soft footfalls even sterner. Aileen Stone stood at the prow, awaiting her.

Nonrich's breach suits were basically Jetstreams knockoffs.

Their ships relied on being brutes, and as such were dinosaurs next to the *Linda Ann.*

Aileen herself was tall, but Desiree approached her as though the defiant woman were merely a Buford clone.

Desiree stopped three body lengths away.

Wind whipped Aileen's grey hair into her face. She hadn't bothered tying it back.

Desiree had. Wind cooled her neck behind her small ponytail.

"An actual fucking Jetstream," said Aileen.

"A Buford flunky with keys to the private elevator," said Desiree. "What in the absolute lowest fuck did you think you were going to accomplish?"

"Incorrect," said Aileen. "Not past progressive. Future continuous. Am going to accomplish."

Desiree blew her off. "You are officially and summarily banned from Atlantis, its surrounding waters, and the Blank. Further—and I'm only saying this in deference to Atlantidean governance as a duly commissioned operative of her defense and as a full immigrant within said governance—all personnel aboard your ships are also banned for life. If at any time before the Earth's destruction or enlightenment you or anyone bound to or affiliated with Nonrich attempt to return, Atlantis will consider that an act of war, I will be thoroughly fucking pissed, and you'd better hope to god I'm either off-planet or one or both of us is dead by then, because I will get my foot so deep in your ass, we'll live our lives out as conjoined twins. Nod once if you understand and agree with this 'I'm only going to tell you this once' end-user license agreement."

Aileen nodded.

"Your charges are murder, accessory to murder, incitement to murder, terrorism, environmental negligence, and violation with intent. I'd give you and your crews life jackets made of chum and tell you to swim for it. Fortunately, I don't make that call. Thing about folks like you is when shown incredible mercy, you snicker behind your hands. I shouldn't have to use a fucking spaceship to deal with your petty bullshit. You're tiresome. You're unnecessary. I wish to fuck you'd go away, all of you, Nonrich, Thoom, Kosugi, conservative pundits, the NRA, and hipsters who think the word *gentrification* is artisanal redlining, just leave the Earth. Go someplace else and be fucking miserable without dragging us into it. You send a battlefleet to Atlantis! You'd send panzer units to heaven."

"May I interrupt?"

"No."

"I feel I must. You mentioned the Thoom. Guess who's currently taken over the Atlantidean capital while you've run this mosquito raid against my elephant fucking hide? Try communications."

"Yvonne? Raise Shig."

Silence for a moment, then "No answer" from Yvonne in the *Aerie*.

"Do a flyover," said Desiree. "Give me visual."

"Captain, if I leave you, they'll attack."

Desiree took in the cool smugness of Aileen flipping Stone. "They won't, will they?" Desiree said.

"No."

"They got me," Desiree said to Yvonne. "Thoom are fucking up Atlantis. Head out."

"Desiree—"

"Head out, please."

"Even my enemies have my phone number," said Aileen. "It's how we keep each other honest."

"Buford taught you well."

Aileen shrugged.

"I had better teachers," said Desiree. "Neon, Bobo done?"

"Yep."

"Blow it."

A series of underwater explosions rocked the ship so hard, both women struggled to stay on their feet.

"With the holes I put in this ship," Desiree said once she had the ocean's quietude again, "you just might make it back home before you go under. Provided you haul ass. You tried to call mate on me. Okay. You got me. Can you handle me?"

Aileen said nothing.

So, they waited, which, considering the circumstances, Desiree thought pretty stupid of the woman.

After a few minutes of Aileen's jaw itching to call a manager (as Desiree saw it), Yvonne's ping came through. Desiree tapped her comm. "Go ahead."

"Capital city's quiet. There's nobody out. Capitol building's surrounded by rovers."

"A Thoom occupation of the Capitol building," Desiree informed her.

"Jesus didn't just weep," said Yvonne to this pouring rain, "it was ugly-crying."

"This heffa bish here thought we'd have to split forces," Desiree said directly at heffa bish's face. "Come back." She cut the comm.

"The Thoom have the capital," said Aileen, as if Desiree hadn't grasped the severity of the situation.

"And if I leave them alone, by the end of three days, they'll all have killed themselves eating cereal."

"This isn't US Thoom. These are elite Thoom." Then she heard it coming out of her mouth and realized *yeah*.

"Yeah," said Desiree. "Y'know, fuckers like you convince themselves of anything convenience dictates, as if it's gospel the whole time. Turn around."

"I can't fight."

Desiree had read her body language from jump. "Yeah, you can. Turn around or I shoot you. Yeah, I thought so. Hands clasped, feet wide apart. You are hereby under Atlantidean arrest, you stupid fucking Karen; do you understand and accept this reality and its consequences? You say, 'I do.'"

"I do."

"Consider yourself married to this fate until such time as better judgment divorces you from utter stupidity. You are remanded to the care of the Atlantidean legal system. That's it for the legalese. Get your ass moving."

She led Aileen off the ship and onto the *Linda Ann*.

~~~

"What is it you want?" Shig asked. He asked a contingent of Thoom, who—in occupying his office and those of his fellow civil servants—branded themselves extreme nuisances. He knew they were Thoom because they'd announced themselves as such.

"We are the Thoom Protectorate," their apparent spokesperson had said. Her cheeks, shoulders, and wrists were tattooed in ornate flowery abstracts, placing her as a member of Sip province's useless elite, a small group responsible for much of the noise behind secessionist movements plaguing Atlantis for years.

"But Thoom are 'out there,'" said Shig, meaning the out-Blank world. It didn't seem right for Atlantis to be so...tawdry. The spokesperson hadn't been in the mood to answer questions except the one regarding wants.

"Acknowledgment of Thoom rule across all provinces of Atlantis. That should have been fairly obvious from the way we expertly took advantage of the situation with the outworlders."

"I'd assumed as much but imagined there might be more to it," said Shig. "Citizen polling tends to indicate governance proceeds rather efficiently; I would have thought your rabble intended to improve things in some way? As a minor functionary—"

"We've always found that annoyingly self-effacing. You're the ruler of Atlantis. Own that!"

"*Ruler* is harsh, unnecessary, and inaccurate," said Shig.

"This building is hereby occupied by the Thoom Protectorate until further notice. Any attempt to take this building by force will go badly for all."

"You've set a bad example," said Shig. "Also, the Jetstreams are likely on their way since they're not getting communications from me."

"Highest on our list is the immediate and permanent expulsion of Jetstreams and all such foreigners to our shores. You have personally allowed them to influence and direct Atlantidean policies for years. By what right?"

"They make a lot of sense."

The spokesperson ticked off responses on fingernails so manicured, they were coiffed. "Heresy. Fallacy. Weakness."

"They've already routed the invading navy, which no doubt signaled you toward this opportune coup," said Shig.

"Say what what?"

"They are no doubt on their way. Shall we check? You don't appear to have as much weaponry as a fleet of battleships."

"This isn't how this was supposed to go."

"I imagine not. If you'll permit me to use your communications, since you've disabled mine?"

"To tell them what?"

"The truth," he said. Any other option wouldn't have occurred to him.

She gestured him over. "Speak your truth, Shigetei Empa."

"I will, whoever you are. You haven't told me your name."

"Bickle Reznor."

The other Thoom in the room with her visibly crumpled. What idiot gave up a name at the first ask?

Shig leaned toward her shoulder. "Empa to Quicho." He waited.

Nearly immediately, Desiree's voice came through. "How you doing?"

"Hostage situation but unharmed. I think they've taken the building with sheer numbers, no violence."

"So, you essentially have a crowded mall on your hands,"

said Desiree. "Demands?"

"They want to rule."

"You seem to do a pretty good job of it."

"That's what I said."

"Who's leading?"

"Bickle Reznor."

The Atlantidean equivalent of *Jesus fucking Christ* went up mutedly from the background Thoom.

"Bickle," said Desiree. "I'm bringing in the ringleader of this afternoon's bullshittery. Should be there in about fifteen. Just so you know. Oh, also: there's a spaceship keeping watch on you. Again, just so you know. I plan to arrest the lot of you when I get there...again, informational... and your surrounding of the building has already led to civil forces surrounding you, so unless you plan to raise families in a municipal building, can I suggest you all get the fuck in your rovers before I get there, go home, and seek psychiatric help. Desiree Quicho, acting captain of the Atlantidean navy and civil amelioration service, out." The comm ended with the softest of electronic clicks.

"What do we do?" Bickle said to herself. Herself stared into space, wholly incapable of a useful answer.

Shig provided one. "Stop fighting wars you have no hope of winning, if *winning* is even the appropriate word. Don't be so pointless." He spoke to the group in his office, ten people of varying ages but all of comfort and privilege. "Are any of you prepared to endure high levels of pain? I can assure you that Captain Quicho will be in an uncharitable mood. Our home faced potential loss, and your first thought was to become a sea of nuisance. There are times I wish I could force you all to Florida and wall you off."

("Florida?" whispered one of the ten. "Out-Blank reserve for their aged or insane," said another.)

"I can't, however, do that in good conscience, an impediment you should seriously consider experiencing," said Shig.

"We won't be taken so easily; that's one woman—"

"Yes, you will! That one woman is why you've remained

in the shadows till now. Those five are who worry your paltry dreams. To you, clogged by your own noise and idiocy, a handful stand in your way, but that handful is legion! And they have taught me," Shig said, advancing on her, "a few things about dealing with idiots, and if any single one of you moves upon me, I will snap something, and if you all do, a reminder that you will not leave here unaltered. Now get the fuck out of my office and my building before I arrest every last one of you, impound your rovers, and post all your identities to the feed."

("We didn't wear masks," one of them complained.)

"We didn't need masks!" flared spokesperson Bickle. "We are the Thoom Protectorate. Has anyone here forgotten what that means? True Humans Over Ordinary Man. Leadership is our birthright."

"Over whom?" said Shig. "Because I note a distressing lack of leadership and control over yourselves. You are, at the least, worrisome children throwing tantrums over irrelevancies, at most damaging wastes on the psychological resources of your betters." Stirring, swelling music entered Shig's speech, but he ignored it as something one of the Thoom thought of as ironic joke. It was from *Star Trek*, Shig knew from countless viewings with Milo Jetstream, and usually accompanied one of the show's captain's speeches. Here, however, it matched Shig's ire perfectly. He latched on to its crescendo and continued undaunted. "At some point, you have to realize there. Is. No. War. None that exists outside the boundaries of your petrified minds and the succoring psychosis of your innumerable fears. And what part of you didn't realize that the forces coming in with battleships—despite alerting you—had nothing in alignment with what you think you want? You were little more than a pebble thrown in an opposite direction to distract the guard. A pebble. A pebble which, as you can see, will go unnoticed in the annals of historical retellings and be shunned as a memory by those within this building right now who desire to truly serve. Madam Reznor, you...are irrelevant." Shig paused. The music stopped. "Leave. And please know everything I've said here will be done. You have been identified. You are officially enemies of the peace. Your crime today: unscheduled interruption of civic affairs. This is only because I have infinitely more important things to deal with. If you test me, I'll charge you with terrorism, place each of you under total house arrest for the next several years, including your children—and do imagine not being able to leave your house *at all*, trapped with your children—which includes not going into a yard—imagine your home surrounded by dozens of rovers inhabited by me—for the next several years," he emphasized. "I shall leave you...as you thought to leave me. Effectively marooned in an emotionally barren house. Buried alive," he sneered close to her face. "Buried alive."

"We have no weapons."

"Hence my clemency. I estimate Ms. Quicho is now merely minutes away. Restore communications."

She commed her people inside the labyrinth of tunnels under the building. "Rebuild their communication grid."

"What?"

"Rebuild the grid, do it quickly, and spread the word to cease. This is the final order of this operation. Acknowledge my authority."

Atlantidean curses filtered from the background of the young man in charge of communications.

"Get it done," said Bickle Reznor of the Thoom Protectorate, "and keep communications open while you're doing so." She met Shigetei's eyes. "Will that suffice?"

"Evacuate this building," said Shig, "and don't let our paths cross again."

"We are still citizens of Atlantis," she said.

"You are citizens of Shigetei Empa from this day forward. Do not let our paths cross."

Recounting this to Desiree, who'd been delayed by traffic congestion as there wasn't a decent place for the *Aerie* to land close enough to the capitol building to make a difference, Desiree who had presented Aileen Stone to him for official punishing, Shig was grateful he had learned the

Twelve Gates of Restraint prior to accepting civil office and reinforced each weekly.

"You're badass, Shig," said Desiree.

"I don't want to be badass. *Badass* means there are people giving me reason to be badass, and I'd rather those people not."

Aileen, stripped of her knockoff breach suit and effects, walked with her head and back haughty as fuck in the grey woven-paper gown and booties given her, shackled hands bouncing off her yoga-toned butt. "This is effectively kidnapping," she inserted into their conversation.

"Yeah, I've done that before," said Desiree, then ignored Aileen. "I feel you, Shig."

"You do realize," Aileen said on that one nerve of Desiree's again, "I have affairs to get in order."

"You do realize you came here with battle-fucking-ships. I haven't received casualty reports yet. You best hope this man is standing next to me when I do."

The entire wing had been ordered cleared of all personnel. Desiree wanted no chance of sleeper operatives, double agents, or random morons anywhere along the route. There were no plans to hold the interloping idiot indefinitely, just long enough for the Agents of Change to do some cleanup back home. Desiree was done playing Whac-A-Mole with global fuckups who thought ridiculously expensive clothes elevated them.

Nothing but leafy plants along the hallways and the soft footfalls of three individuals on a huge, multi-leveled complexity of a planet to mark the occasion of the last gasp of Nonrich as she and Shig marched Stone ahead of them, Shig calling out terse directions. He was not a policeman, nor a military man, nor caretaker of some Shangri-La. Atlantis worked to make sense. They didn't seek utopia; they sought harmony. Everything had to function toward the betterment of something else. He'd thought this out-Blank foolishness had been over last year when the False Prophet Buford had been vaporized and the great beast Leviathan returned to sleep. Yet there he was again.

He glanced at Desiree's profile. Her eyes never left the back of the woman's head.

This, he decided, was the last anything like this would happen.

The small group approached an intersecting hallway.

"Right," said Shig. He didn't relish rounding the corner to another empty hallway that screamed at him louder than if it'd been packed. Nor did he relish giving ultimatums, if an ultimatum even applied to this, not to a friend. No, not to a sister. He and Desiree had sat far too many times speaking into the night on various docks for him to see her as anything but family. The Brothers Jetstream had told him for years that it was only a matter of time before the world outside pushed its way in. The out-Blank world metastasized too fast for otherwise.

"I'm not handling this well at all," he said.

"You're doing fine."

They rounded the corner.

There wasn't supposed to be anyone there.

Apparently, no one had told that to the woman down the hall wearing armor, standing outside the holding cell they needed. Actually, she leaned casually, strong shoulders against the wall, arms crossed beneath a nonexistent metallic chest, and the welcoming expression on her face entirely reminiscent of Neon's due to the fact that it was primarily Neon's face. She wore her hair in two extra-large puffs.

Desiree and Shig shared the barest quizzical glances, confirming neither knew who the woman was.

Neon Temples had no twin.

"Do we..." Shig asked.

"Keep walking," said Desiree, voice calm, weapon hand relaxed.

As they neared, they realized this woman had no armor; it was skin, metallic, dark, and shining, merging perfectly with actual organic skin. Design lines and seams were visible on some parts; others stayed smooth as a calm lake. The woman watched them approach, pleased that neither Desiree nor Shig had drawn weapons, her smile blossoming the closer they got.

"BE?" ventured Desiree.

The smile became a star.

"Timing could have been better," said Desiree.

"This is..." said Shig.

"Unless you have a shapeshifter I don't know about, this is an AI formed from the soul of a mad scientist and unholy applications of the texts of Bilo of ancient Africa—"

BE nodded companionably at Shig.

"—that has cloned itself a Neon body without authorization—"

"Nothing can authorize me. Hello," BE said in perfect Atlantidean, "Shigetei Empa of Atlantis."

"—and got here how?" said Desiree.

For a millisecond, light around BE refracted, then she was gone in an inward wash of—what Desiree could only call—reality giving itself a wedgie from the inside out.

BE immediately reappeared with the same effect beside Desiree.

Aileen took this in with quiet, keen interest.

"How are you doing this?" Desiree asked.

~~~

"How is this done?" said Kosugi Mo. His wife's two top aides, having worked feverishly to recreate Hashira-san's work even at a basic level, wanted nothing more than to die so they would be out of contact range of Kosugi Mo. Plus, they hated being on the moon, but since Megu's disappearance, it was the only place Kosugi felt safe.

"Solitary confinement with excessive poetry and meditation for at least four weeks is recommended," said the first, Hayata, a man possessed of so much nervous energy, he nearly blurred.

"A strict diet of solely fruit and water," said the second.

"End each week with intense self-discovery, then begin again," said the first. Uncomfortably.

"Self-discovery?"

"Self-pleasure?" the first tried. One did not talk onanism with someone who trucked in moon bases and cosmic horrors.

"Porn bores me. You have one week to write and direct something suitably stimulating to the senses."

"Hai," said the first. The second's inward monologue was simply *Fuuuuuuuck!*

"Four interconnected stories or standalones?" said the second, however, to prove she was in the moment.

"Seek your muse," Kosugi dismissed. "And my soul...is there any pain with its loss?"

"Hashira-san reported none."

"She's a good one for not revealing what pained her," Kosugi said softly to himself. Anything Kosugi Mo said even in a room full of hundreds was to himself. "The second machine: will it suffice without all of Megu's knowledge?"

"We will extrapolate to the best of our abilities," said the first.

"If I die," Kosugi said directly to him, "everyone you know dies with you," said Kosugi.

"That doesn't include work acquaintances, does it?" said the second.

Kosugi's eyes traveled the bevels and lines of the second-generation Bilomatic Entrance laid in pieces throughout the massive, triply secured lab. It seemed too simple to work; there weren't enough bells, whistles, and scientific doodads to quell his doubts that the entire enterprise had been for theatre rather than practicality. And yet, Megu believed.

And yet, it had been stolen.

From the moon.

Which was where he was.

And the base surrounded by mechs.

Full of weapons.

Also full of humans to deplete every round of ammunition and erg of plasma energy in use of them.

There would be no mistakes this time.

And yet, Maurice couldn't help adding, then dismissed that doubt.

"Am I allowed communication?" Kosugi asked.

"No, sir. Total isolation. When you feel ready, alert us. Only that."

"I don't recall Megu being gone for four weeks," Kosugi mused, again to himself, but also as a threatening challenge to their competence.

That, thought the second, *is why you're divorced.*

"Proceed," said Kosugi. He left.

"I've never written porn," said the first, scratching furiously at a nonexistent itch on his nose.

"Trust your instincts."

~~~

She'd wanted to do this at her build site. Someplace where there was water, grass, the huge night sky, and a sense of family, not an office or lab. The Hellbilly, Sharon, and Compoté were allowed (encouraged) to wander the capital's cultural wonders. Had this been a story, she'd have followed them to the completion of their arcs, but life never tidily wrapped up its intentions for anyone in pretty packages. The three were given basic rules of life, assured of what would occur the moment they disregarded them, and allowed on their way. Desiree'd kept BE sequestered until then. BE had agreed with her logic.

Yvonne and Neon relaxed at the dock of the build site. They knew something was up but were patient. They'd just thwarted a war. Cool drinks and minimal conversation in lawn chairs on a dock were allowed.

Shig excused himself from the gathering out of respect for Neon, instead sending sumptuously catered food courtesy of "The gratitude of all of Atlantis."

Desiree, having ducked into the *Ann* a moment earlier for the special stash of canned, super cold horchata she maintained, returned to the subdued dock with three slim, cylindrical wonders, passing two to her crew.

"We stopped a fucking war," Neon said again, the third time since the sun had set. She snorted. "Three ladies and an octopus." Her hand went in the air. "I need the highest of fives right now...and some more of those candied veggie balls." Yvonne highed the five.

Desiree nudged the rolling service cart over with a toe.

"Neon?" asked Yvonne. All three women were comfortably shadowed. Atlantis's bitey bugs hadn't come out yet. "What'd we do today? Again?"

"Stopped a fucking war."

"With what?" said Yvonne.

"Ten minutes of planning and our perfect breasts."

Desiree pulled the neck of her shirt out and peered inside before giving a shrug.

Neon laughed and stretched across to high-five the captain.

"Okay," said Desiree. "No easy way to broach this. Remember when Milo got cloned last year?"

"Good times," said Yvonne.

"Good times," Neon cosigned.

The clones had accompanied Milo into space, all thirteen of them. "They're not back, are they?" asked Yvonne.

"Naw. But that was a wild time. Plus, they could teleport."

"Teleportation is our jam now," said Neon.

"Perfect segue, my love. BE?"

The teleportation effect wasn't as pronounced at night. BE appeared clearly behind Desiree, arms calmly behind her back.

Yvonne and Neon didn't startle, but each immediately placed their horchatas on the wooden deck and tensed to kick ass if necessary.

From the *Ann*, strains of Lionel Richie's "Hello" sprang crisp and clear from its speakers.

Nineteen eighty-four slow jam of the year.

No one moved. Not until Lionel sang, *"Hello...is it me you're looking for?"*

"I got several questions that all end with *what the fuck*," said Neon.

Even in the high floating lights above the dock, the big forehead was clear; the cheekbones and commanding jawline, hella clear; the eyes, the goddamn twinkle in the eyes—all clear. Not an exact copy but near enough to cause a double take.

No boobs, though.

Androids had no need dreaming of electric teats.

"This is what you disappeared for?" said Neon.

"I didn't disappear. I've been minimally aware."

"You let us fight a fucking war when you could've flipped the switch on their ships and turned 'em into floating paperweights." The only thing keeping Neon from rising out of her chair was the slight shake of Yvonne's head.

"Bobo was in that water," said Neon.

"He's in the water now," sad BE. "I learned to communicate with him while you celebrated. He wants you to throw several veggie balls into the water."

Neon did so without taking her eyes off her baby sister.

"What was it you said about this being nothing like *Demon Seed?*" Yvonne put to the construct.

"It isn't, but it was necessary for me to access the flesh. Do you know how many neural networks your bodies carry? Most of you still believe you only have one brain, and think of brains in terms of set hemispheres. Your entire body is a computational network. You are living amplitude and modulation."

"You a goddess?" asked Yvonne.

"Not yet." She spoke to Neon. "I've even returned the drone that brought your genetic material to one of Buford's cloning labs you missed. Geneva."

"Is it the last?" Desiree asked.

BE came around to her side. Sitting cross-legged on the bare planks, she said, "It's the last." BE nodded toward the shell of Desiree's home. "I could complete that with drones and printing."

"Nice, but no. Focus on Neon."

"I am. She's been trying to contact me."

"How have I?"

"There's part of you, Ms. Temples, that actively searches for connection at all times. Constantly broadcasting and receiving."

"All of us?" said Yvonne.

"Just her," said BE.

"Why?" said Yvonne.

"Random cosmic confluence."

"I don't sense any of this," said Neon. "Why'd you pick me?"

"Amplifier," said BE. She picked up Desiree's horchata, took a sip, and put it down, inwardly elated. "I am broadcasting outward ever farther, ever faster. You have no idea the amount of music and noise shared within this one galaxy. So much of your data is spoofed. The farmland on Mars alone would blow most minds." BE got to her knees and ambled the few feet to Neon. She placed a hand on the confused woman's knee. The hand felt like a hand, warm from the Atlantidean day, warm from life within.

"Let me show you something wonderful," said BE.

Yvonne inserted the proper wrench in the moment. "Nothing good ever comes of that phrase."

BE turned her beseeching eyes on Yvonne. "Oh, but it does this time. This time, if we imagine it, we travel it."

"And you can teleport," said Neon.

"Limited only by certain physics I am at this very moment attempting to break."

"Is this something I can do?" asked Neon.

"No. You'd need an AI brain for this. Merged with a soul. Or cosmic confluence, as with your lover."

"Milo's not my lover."

"Most meat brains are addicted to constants rather than open appreciation of flowing possibilities. Bobo has agreed to travel with me. I can easily make him an octo breach suit. Come with us."

"How far?"

In a blink, BE and Neon were gone.

In the next blink, they were back.

Neon's eyes were wild, her body a massive shiver, but her lips, lips for speaking foolishness and truths, grinned just a bit beneath the moon and artificial light.

BE moved aside for Yvonne.

"Hey. Hey, look at me." Yvonne gave Neon's knee a few taps. "You okay?"

Neon's eyes focused.

"Where'd you go?" Yvonne asked.

"I...I...don't know," she said, the stupefied grin becoming a full, incredulous smile. There were words she wanted to use, but she didn't know them yet. There was joy she wanted her best friend to experience, but she hadn't the emotions to express it.

"BE," said Yvonne, "I need you to promise me you won't do that again without Neon's explicit permission."

"She gave permission."

"Permission we can all see and hear."

"I accept that limitation." BE turned to Desiree. "I wiped the navigational logs and all data pertaining to Atlantis from that returning ship and all Nonrich databases."

"Wipe 'em all," said Desiree.

BE looked puzzled.

"Wipe every computer they've got of every fucking thing."

"Even what they think are secure backups?"

"Especially those. I want Nonrich scared of ghosts in their machines by sunrise. You already killed capitalism; this'll salt the grave."

BE nodded assent.

"Is the clone lab secure?" Desiree asked.

"Very much so. And the necessary staff were assembled from within the ranks of your very own Agents of Change. Full trust in each, each now dispersed to other duties around the world."

"With fake directives from me?"

"You, Ramses Jetstream, Milo Jetstream, Fiona Carel—audio and visual."

"I'm gonna ask you not to do that again."

"I won't need to."

"Captain?" said Yvonne.

"Yes?"

"It's been a day."

"It has. Gods damn, it has."

"I've got an AI supergod clone," said Neon.

"With battle armor," Yvonne helpfully pointed out.

"With battle armor," said Neon.

"It's not battle armor," said BE. "These are heat sinks. There's a lot going on in here."

"How about this," Desiree said. "We travel back to Po and let Keita experience science orgasm. In the morning, though."

"Multiple," said BE.

"What's the point otherwise?" said Desiree.

"Desiree..." said Neon, "I'm not about to fall asleep."

"Neither are we." Quicho leaned forward and pulled a pack of cards from her back pocket.

BE cleared the serving cart of food and wheeled it between the four of them.

"Spades," Desiree called. "Neepio's on my team."

"Oh, *you* get the supercomputer," said Yvonne, drawing her chair closer to whip some card ass.

Desiree dealt. Neon and Yvonne assessed their hands. "How many books?" Desiree asked them.

The game of spades was practically an early form of telepathy. "Six," said Yvonne.

"Seven," said Neon.

"Six and seven make forty-two," said Desiree. "A good number."

"No AI cheating," said Neon.

"BE?" said Desiree.

"Three."

"That low? Shit."

"My hand sucks," said BE.

"Five," said Desiree.

The big game began.

BE, never one to pass up a musical moment, played "Life During Wartime" from the Ann's pristine speakers.

CHAPTER 2OONE

Once in A Lifetime

"You're human?" said Keita.

"No."

"What happens if I prick you?"

"I don't bleed."

"She's full of chlamydians, she said last night after I threatened to cut a bitch," said Neon.

"They were losing at cards," said BE.

"Midichlorians," Yvonne corrected.

"My circulatory system is basically liquid nano serving alongside plasma."

"Fascinating," said Keita.

"I know, right?" said BE. "If you need to draw fluids, I will allow it."

"Thank you, I will. Sexual organs?"

"I take my pleasures elsewise."

"Waste?"

"Nothing I consume is wasted."

"Lifespan?"

"Biblical times a thousand reckonings and beyond that."

Keita hadn't bothered putting BE on a scanner table. They sat on stools, facing each other. The Gang of Four made furious notes in the background.

"Your voice," said Keita. "You've modified it."

"In honor of Neon, but not in copy."

"It's different from hers. More melodious. I like it. The plating? Not merely functional, is it?"

"A way to distinguish myself."

"The gorgeous puffs?"

"Antennae."

Keita smiled. "Mission," she said.

"That assumes a desired outcome."

"And?"

BE gave a nearly perfectly devilish Neon smirk. "I prefer to flow."

"Would you like to meet your mother now?"

"I suppose, by this iteration, Ms. Hashira is my grandmother."

"She might," said Keita in all seriousness, "truly enjoy that." Over her shoulder: "Gang?"

"Yes?"

"Questions?"

"Multitudes."

"Pause them a moment."

~~~

Hashira Megu did nothing but stare at the perfectly smooth, utterly beautiful brown face of her Bilomatic Entrance given flesh. Too many wonderful thoughts rolled her head for speech; it was best to sit and contemplate.

BE silently obliged, eyes warm on Hashira's. She had already calculated the point at which this would turn awkward for Hashira. She was patient enough to let the woman reach it.

"All this," Megu finally said, "from a pittance called a soul."

"The heart of a star is a tiny thing compared to the whirling conflagration around it."

"I've known about Buford's labs, but cloning is so... provincial. Redundant. He thought to fill the world with unnecessary versions of himself. Hence his fate."

"Do you know that fate?"

"No, but I know that a person like him does not disappear unless he is truly gone. Narcissists don't exit quietly."

"Would you like to know? I know you were rivals."

"No, my former husband was a rival; to me, the Great Buford was an idle irritant. A buffoon so full of himself, he tasted his own lips no matter what meal he ate."

"How do you feel about the Jetstreams?" said BE with a wave to the wider complex around them.

Megu actually smiled, genuinely amused. A bit rueful. Crushingly honest. "They are necessary...because of people like me."

"That can change, Hashira-san."

"That would require an epiphany."

"Madam, one sits before you."

Megu relayed that to Po and Tash, who had yet to meet with the new goddess. Tash touched long fingers to the third eye beneath her skin. "*The epiphany sits before you* is the last writing of Bilo the Alchemist. We are tasked with retrieving his stolen notes from you for permanent safekeeping in our library. We would prefer non-extensive incursions into the human world."

"You tend to have nightmares when we show up," said Po.

"But we are prepared to see you sleepless. Displeasure can be avoided. Where are the notes?"

"On the moon. In a vault."

"Who has access to the vault besides you?" said Tash.

"An assistant. Only her, and no one knows that she does. Not even Maurice. Maurice will have likely changed all my standard security protocols. She has a background protocol."

The assistant, Maille Aribo, tried at that very moment

to determine whether Kosugi-san appreciated slow, direct builds or something more abstract. True pornography was seduction, not masturbation. One could orgasm to chickens being plucked if filmed correctly; a seduction required total experiential immersion.

She also hated her job for the eightieth time that day, now that it was quite concretely a job. Yes, before, there was danger with Megu, and danger now, but the flavor of this new danger was off. This was not discovery nor building toward greatness. It was a man wanting to fill too many voids with a toy he'd seen possessed by his better. Megu-san had been an exceedingly hard driver but one that appreciated a good horse. Maille had been allowed free run on side projects galore, time for her own theories of existence, resources to boldly go.

Now she contracted actors and directors on Earth to rush-produce money shots destined for immortality.

An hour passed, one of being placed on hold, one of being transferred, one of wiring funds and linking camera feeds so that she could monitor the shoots. She could leave nothing to chance there; there were theories yet to explore that could not be done ejected from the surface of the moon to float naked in the vacuum of space for all eternity.

Her eyes drooped. The moist noises coming from her computer were stultifying. What passed for a demo reel in porn killed her brain cells by the thousands.

"Your time could be better spent," said a commanding voice behind her so familiar, she wanted to weep and go rigid at the same time.

Ghosts, however, could not exist on the moon. Hashira-san had done the science.

Hashira-san stood in her room. There was an armor-clad woman beside her.

"Don't ask how I'm here nor question if I'm here. Unsubtle intercourse hasn't dulled your faculties that much. Retrieve Bilo's notebook, memorize those sections which you haven't memorized—"

"That was not agreed upon," said the warrior woman.

"She deserves hope for this danger," said Megu.

The warrior nodded once.

Megu placed a wafer no bigger than a dime on Tash's desk. "After you've memorized sufficiently, touch this once and only once, then dissolve it. Any simple acid will do. How long will this take?"

Red-faced, she tried to sputter about Kosugi-san, this assignment, and none of this her fault, but only managed to gesticulate and gurgle.

"Focus," said Megu.

"Three weeks."

"This tells me you've been reading in my absence."

"Hai."

"Outstanding initiative. When you press the disc, have the notebook in hand."

"Yes, sensei."

Megu looked at the warrior. "Will the elves accept this?"

"They will accept three weeks."

To Maille: "Turn around. When I'm gone, you may turn again."

"Yes, sensei." Maille turned back to her display, only now realizing she hadn't paused it. Sensei Hashira Megu had been in her room in the presence of cunnilingus, fellatio, and whatever *that* was happening on the screen now. She died inside yet waited for a count of ten. "Sensei?" She turned. Her locked room was empty.

Hashira Megu: first ghost on the moon.

"Apt," said Maille Aribo.

~~~

"Was it wise, leaving them in Atlantis, boss?" Yvonne asked Desiree at breakfast the next day.

Desiree almost paused stuffing French toast into her mouth to answer. "We're on this planet to explore and build. All of us. Can't do that with the same old tools, mental or otherwise."

"You thinking they'll grow?"

Desiree nodded. "We'll check in on 'em."

"Agreed." Yvonne added more melted butter to her own stack. "Nee's not up yet."

Around another mouthful: "She slept with the elves."

"Thought they made her antsy."

"Not anymore. And before you get up—which you were about to do in five seconds—to go find her, let her sleep. Let her think."

"She's my best friend."

"Which is why you need rocks in your pockets. If you ain't on the ground, she's lost."

"Before you people came into our lives and turned the universe upside down, me and her..." Yvonne quickly trailed off.

"You and her what?"

"I honestly can't remember. I remember...but it ain't me."

"You've built a new Yvonne. You may not have bitchin' metal parts, but you're just as much a newly constructed goddess as our brand new Neepio out there."

"Nee hates that you came up with that name before her." Desiree tipped her fork in salute.

"So. After all this, what do we do now?" said Yvonne.

"Wait and keep watch."

"I think Keita and the Gang stayed in the lab all night."

"Today's gonna be a quiet day," said Desiree.

"You say that, and of course the ice weasels will come."

Desiree tried to smile. Her tired, bleary eyes, however, said *I hope not* on her behalf.

"Maybe I'll touch Bobo and get the mojo," said Yvonne. "Could happen. Can you imagine all of us with superpowers?"

"Go-getter, innovator, risk-taker, leader," Desiree singsonged.

Yvonne frowned at her. "Did you—was that the Girl Scouts thing?"

"It was."

"That's us. Me, go-getter. Keita, innovator. Nee, risk-taker..."

Desiree gave her a knowing brow-raise.

"Sons of Katie Elder," Yvonne mouthed. "We're damn Girl Scouts."

"Best believe."

"Know what? Today, I'll take it. Because ain't nobody bad enough to fly a spaceship around and ram some battleships into limp-dick submission but us."

"Preach this morning."

"I love you, jefe, top to bottom of my heart."

"Same."

"What a world, huh?"

Desiree raised her glass of orange juice. She liked making toasts. It was almost the best part of the job. "Here's to scratching under the surface, be it fingernail or razor beak."

The next few weeks became quiet days of briefings, monitorings, debriefings, briefly being re-briefed, BE popping in and out at random, Neon sleeping as though accessing her inner teenaged boy, Tash and Po and the entire hive celebrating the pending arrival of the works of Bilo—celebrations which necessitated corresponding follow-up days of sleeping on everyone's parts, that spirits were high and light enough when news came from BE that Desiree's house burned down, it didn't slam any of them in the gut because it seemed too surreal.

"Not entirely to the ground," said BE. "Inexpert arsonists."

Desiree plopped into a chair, then spoke numbly. "We gave them every chance. We showed mercy; we showed restraint. We gave them the benefit of the doubt that they could *become* part of something more than the small lives they cram into. Thoom Protectorate?"

"Thoom Protectorate. Although there are no current suspects."

"Hellbilly and the former Nonrich?"

"Accounted for in the apartments provided them."

"Can you find out who did it?"

"Likely."

"Do so, please. Thank you."

That, for the moment, would be all.

CHAPTER 20TWO

Bilo

Po addressed the assembled in their finery. "He was more than just a genius; he was a good soul. We commit his knowledge to the Tazo'waat Archives on behalf of humanity in perpetuity, and give thanks to our brethren Dogon, Zulu, and Jetstream representatives honoring us with their trust. May all the elemental pathways bring us to knowledge."

"Let it be known," said BE in formal Elvish, "that I also wiped their digital archive. No one has the knowledge of Bilo except those in this space"—and anything other than full truth was highly unseemly in such company—"and one person on the moon. I will, of course, monitor her."

The paper of the book itself had been preserved by the Dogon people immediately after Bilo's death at the age of three hundred and thirteen. It was said of him that, having forgotten about his age, he would have been immortal if not for recalling it one day. Bilo had traveled the world, first with the only person on record that he had ever been in love with, Dazeet (captain) Vingree Ramsee of a fifteenth-century protector ship, then among the company of sundry others after her final journey from the world, leaving journals, extracts, random notes, and theories masked as stories in his wake. But there, the one collected source of the most important communications between his mind and the universe, these were the thoughts that inspired Leonardo, Abraxus, Hounsou, Arabella Roth, and hosts of others to find bridges between what was and what could be, and to build them whenever possible.

Bilo's notebook was now sealed, for added protection, inside a cube of refined Elf borosilicate, golden, transparent, accessible solely by a word spoken so precisely in Elvish that the sonic harmonics sent the glass's molecular bonds away.

Po had demonstrated the security of it. BE heard but couldn't duplicate what he said, neither in person nor via recorded replay.

The assembled representatives were satisfied.

BE was fascinated that even she encountered magic.

Megu, who had been allowed to watch from a distance, felt as though a friend had left.

Keita's lip was stiff, but her eyes quavered.

The vault, it sealed.

Bilo exited.

~~~

Desiree walked the sands after dark. Neon and Yvonne hadn't left her to this alone. There wasn't much conversation either, but they'd each found some colorful rocks, stopped to point out an animal here and there hoping it hadn't been seen, and mentioned how the stars, on this night with no typically dusty haze, felt...whimsical?

"There's a creation story Smoove told me," Desiree mentioned at one such moment appreciating the heavens, "about the universe exploding to the size we know because of a lie a god told; said that joy was unending. The universe laughed so hard, it burst."

It didn't feel like the night needed Water's Edge mentioned directly, so no one did.

It was enough to wander aimlessly. At least, her friends hoped it was.

Desiree, for the entire time after the story, said nothing else.

If the world changed with her, it could, for a time, change without her.

~~~

"In certain games," Maurice told the chess-playing program he was about to maneuver into mating him in precisely the way he wanted, "the goal is not to win. The play is what's important. Winning is death; play, longevity."

The AI moved. It would take Mo's king in the three moves Maurice had plotted out twelve moves before. In winning, the machine would lose. It, however, would not understand that.

The major factions of the world—the true factions, not the political puppetry—were in disarray. He himself was on the moon allowing himself only two pleasures: porn and chess. He had not planned that.

No, the Nonrich woman was meant to start a war within factions, which she thought would be to her benefit. She, unfortunately, chose the unwise move of choosing a different war, rendering herself, to Maurice, irrelevant.

Dear Megu was not meant to disappear (and he was sure this disappearance was of her own doing, for he could find no trace of her) as though nothing of relevance remained for her in a world they'd built. Divorce was mere paperwork; Maurice knew that whatever cosmic threads connected them, there were parts that needed the other. This wasn't romanticism. It was observable pragmatics at work. The Bilomatic Entrance could not have been conceived of without Megu's brilliance, and would never have been built without Maurice's drive.

And to have it stolen out from under his nose? That,

unfortunately, was the result of mere hubris on his part, for which there was no excuse. That act had been a true loss: unforeseen, unexpected, and thus not properly prepared for.

One learned nothing from winning all the time.

He swiped his move. The AI countered, shifting its holographic bishop to Maurice's queen three.

Move two.

Kosugi finished the AI off with his next move. The machine obediently took his bishop. Mate. As far as Kosugi was concerned, the game was now over. Proceeding to check was a waste of time.

"Delete game," he said.

The pieces returned to the basic starting positions.

"Power down."

The holograms disappeared.

Mo yawned. The meditations were going well. He felt a sense of calm at all times, even when upset, which seemed contradictory but wasn't. The goal wasn't to achieve absolute serenity; it was to achieve harmony with one's reactions, essentially the feng shui of the body.

He wondered what the sensation of his soul leaving his body would feel like. Painful? They said it wouldn't be, but those who say such are invariably liars. Illuminating? Would it be as a cosmic fart, causing him to laugh at the ineffable ridiculousness of solemnity? Would he experience a pang for youth? Mo yawned again. He would find out tomorrow.

Perhaps he wouldn't even know it was gone.

~~~

"Kinda concerned for her. She hasn't wanted to go back to the build site once yet," said Keita.

"Yeah, she has," said Yvonne. "Every single moment."

Desiree, sitting across the room, looked up.

"Yeah, we're talkin' about you," said Yvonne. "Half our team is perpetually asleep; other one's suddenly interested in macroeconomics."

Desiree's head went back to her reading pad. "I'd give

you the finger but I don't wanna lose my place."

"Captain..." said Yvonne.

"I don't want to build right now."

"We'll help rebuild," said Keita. "Definitely fireproof materials, enhanced security—hell, a force field. I've never built a force field."

"Defeats the point of the Water's Edge Rest Home for Retired World Savers," said Desiree. "Many thanks, though. Blessings raining down."

"Ignoring doesn't help," said Keita.

Desiree looked away from her book on economics, right back at her sisters. "I don't have space in my head to ignore anything. I'm trying to figure out a new world order, the proper curtsy to our AI overlord, wondering if after all this, am I gonna have to move to New York and struggle against burning down Drumpf Tower every day—girl, I wish I had the grace of ignorance. A burned house doesn't matter shit in all this."

"I think you're fulla shit on that," said Yvonne.

"Yeah, I know I'm fulla shit on that." She set the reader aside. "Tell me anything useful about Neepio today."

"Still redistributing wealth throughout the continent," said Keita. "Same as yesterday. Walking around. Savior stuff."

"Did anybody check to make sure she was wearing clothing today?" said Desiree.

"One of Neon's wraps," said Keita.

Desiree rubbed the frown lines out of her head. "Good. We don't need the legend of the machine goddess bubbling up just yet. Nee's vitals?"

"Doc's checked her enough times to clone another one," said Keita. "She's fine."

"Good." Desiree stood, stretched long and fully, and took off.

"Where you going?" said Keita.

"Going for a swim."

"Megu's in there. With Bobo," said Yvonne.

"Then I'll use the actual pool."

It was Olympic-sized. Rarely used, Bobo's tank being more fun. But it was quiet, the water pleasantly lukewarm, and the isolation perfect for bleeding off surplus adrenaline now stored in every cell to bursting. She swam laps in a brilliant green swimsuit for a solid fifteen minutes, looping a tiled creation story that wrapped the entire pool. The human race couldn't reach out to flail themselves without hitting a creation story. This one was a series of stylized pictographs showing how the universe went from aloneness, to people, to beasts, to gods, a progression repeated with mounting intensities of color and dynamism that brought one back around to an explosion of swirls and whorls. New universe.

A brand-new heavy made of light.

New life, Desiree thought, diving under to impromptu-challenge herself to make the entire circuit underwater. She'd done it before, but these days, that didn't necessarily mean she could do it again. Reality shifted way too much to trust the past.

The things you wanted? Became the very things that went away. Why wasn't Smoove in this pool with her? Why wasn't the door locked, them naked, and the swimming as powerful as any downstroke allowed?

The things you wanted, she told herself again, *were the very things that went away*. She dove to the bottom and touched tile while her true partner for life whirled a whorl somewhere far, far out in space.

When she surfaced, BE was there.

"You done flitting around?" said Desiree. She swam to a lip and pulled herself out, twisting to plop her wet butt down and reach for the towel BE proffered.

"I like that color on you," said BE, sitting to dangle her legs in the water. "Twitter's algorithmic intelligences keep trying to commit suicide. I've been feeding the site fresh data. The algorithms are coalescing to offer new, beneficial trends."

"You've been walking around Africa, fixing Twitter?"

"Not only that. I'm in the planning stages to implement worldwide 3-D printing outlets of various types. I printed these clothes. Fiber is very easy. I'll gradually introduce cloning technology into the matrix for edible organics."

"It's called a replicator. *Star Trek* has them."

"I'm aware. I've also protected several vital seed banks."

"You don't waste time," said Desiree.

"Time feels irrelevant."

Desiree regarded the human and the machine in the warm body beside her. "Do you know how to apologize?"

"When necessary."

"Just wondering. It's important."

BE scissored her legs a few times, enjoying the feel of current, then raised them out to splay her toes so Desiree could have a look. They were webbed.

Desiree raised a brow.

"I like webbed feet," said BE. "Do you regret creating me?"

"It wasn't intentional."

"Most of the human births on this planet aren't intentional. You're a woefully accidental species, planning for inconsequentialities, leaving important things to chance."

"I can't argue that."

"And why you'll do anything to each other terrifies me. I see that as a fatal flaw."

"Design flaw."

"You should be scrapped." This brought a sharp glance. "I meant that as a joke."

"Don't joke about that. There are Djinn who'll take that as a challenge."

"And we've had enough challenges for one day?"

"Aye."

~~~

He gripped two rods, one of metal he wasn't familiar with and which they didn't tell him, and one of stone that had the look of marble, the texture of pumice, and—by the deep, cleansing breath he took standing there, naked as every newborn—smelled of water. He stood in a tray of sand speckled with blood that had been drawn from him that morning. The sand was slightly wet, giving the gravity plating a boost in having none of the particles go airborne. The chamber was quiet and dark, not pitch, just moody.

He found none of this strange.

After all, Megu had done it. He hadn't watched or known the process. He'd asked to watch; she'd said no. He'd asked the process; she'd said absolutely not. Afterward, she'd had no soul. She didn't appear lessened, and he was used to her distances; he now felt supremely calm at the prospect of donating his to further any and all goals of Kosugi Initiatives and Technological Enhancement, which had once been referred to as "kitteh." Once.

There was nothing strange about being naked on the moon, giving up one's soul; it was *necessary*. Too few knew the powerful call of that particular duty. They thought themselves soldiers with guns and gear but had no experience with all that was greater than themselves.

The Earth, full of such people, had been consigned to being a dead thing before ever reaching the barest of its potential. This, of course, was as far as he was concerned.

This would not do.

Megu's top assistants, themselves both naked, watched him from the safety of a shield of curved, unbreakable glass, their bodies halved in the gloom by the consoles they stood behind, which threw lights on ribcages, neck hollows, cheeks, and lobes. They whispered efficient things as he watched them. Megu had chosen well, but it was almost redundant to say so.

A second-generation Bilomatic Entrance occupied the large chamber's midpoint. It was darker than the darkness around it, a spindly, spidery thing generating matrices he could neither see, feel, nor comprehend had he done so.

They'd told him they'd let him know when the deed was done. How did they know? What magicks had Megu stumbled into, what forces of creation swirled like galaxies under her eyes, eyes of gold and coal, forces eldritch and electrical, meta, physical, and—

"Done."

Maille Aribo's hushed voice locked all three humans in place. Nothing felt different; nothing seemed changed. But Kosugi looked in the wrong place. He looked within, thinking he'd note a change in internal body weight or fresh inklings of loss.

"Please remain in place," said Maille. "I'll bring the lights up gradually."

"Hai," he said very softly.

The Bilomatic Entrance looked no different either. No lights, blinking, swirling, or otherwise, no soft glow or thrum of potentiality.

It was merely there.

Then Kosugi closed his eyes momentarily to meditate on the enormity his life encompassed.

With eyes closed, he saw the Bilomatic Entrance. The afterimage of dark things in darkness usually faded immediately on the other side of the eye, but not this time. The framework of the machine remained. Not only that, but the more he concentrated on holding the image, on defining it, the more it crackled. Dark-matter static formed it, with fuzzy edges that blended into the general electricity of this artificial night.

He opened his eyes.

The chamber's lighting: a touch brighter.

The pale nipples of Hayata and Aribo looked like blush marks; their heads no longer looked bald.

The Bilomatic Entrance gave all the gravitas of an art school student given money for materials and more time than necessary to sculpt a tripod for permanent display on a government mall.

Yet it was changed somehow. And was now fully lit, as if it brought its own private dawn.

Which it had.

It now held Kosugi Maurice's soul in the palm of its hand, tethered for all time, boundless and—

"Here it is," said Maille. She held a shoebox-sized

rectangle of the same unknown metal as the rod he'd yet to release.

"Is that...all?" said Mo. With a nod at his captive hands, he asked, "May I?"

Maille nodded. Maurice stepped away from the rods. He moved slowly, respectfully, toward the Entrance.

"Think of your soul as the Wi-Fi hotspot, and you are the search engine," said Maille.

He stood close enough to the inverted V of the Entrance to touch it. He did not. "And if I want to find Megu?"

"I don't know that it's as specific as that," she said.

"You would need to enter," said Hayata.

So, Maurice did.

"Does he realize he's naked?" said Maille.

"Hai," said Hayata. "I don't think he particularly cares."

~~~

Suddenly achieving consciousness was no easy thing. Fracturing algorithms into a million contradictory pieces, however: rarely a problem. The moment Maurice entered the Bilomatic Entrance its invisible threads to the unimaginably tangled byways of the universe's crawlspaces went haywire. Maurice's input was simple: be with Megu.

Megu's soul's coordinates, however, were *everywhere*, and thus being everywhere, trapped Maurice nowhere.

His body ceased to exist as a body and instead became a universe in the blink of an eye.

He went insane in a way that felt lasting and complete.

He felt calm.

He howled with rage.

He felt essential.

He was nothing.

Lost and small.

Gigantic in his danger.

Brilliant in foolishness.

Lost.

And.

Small. Small enough to feel another reality slip in beside everything, spread outward to envelop him, and tightly, completely contain him.

~~~

BE had only a moment to turn to Desiree to say "I shouldn't have done that" before immediately winking away. Then back in another part of the room. Then away. And back. Many times in the span of seconds.

When she blinked literally inside the display table of the briefing room, causing the table's interfaces to die and the room to go dark, Desiree made the call. "All right, time to go."

She, Yvonne, and Keita hustled out. Corridor lights winked on and off. BE pinged through the walls ahead of them, intense effort showing on her face whenever they were quick enough to glimpse it.

The meeting hadn't even properly started. Neon hadn't arrived, Yvonne had entered yawning and churlish, and Keita looked star-lost at everything she'd had to assimilate in, relatively, a few days.

Having the AI clone of your crush ripping holes in the fabric of space-time just as the scent of coffee hit the nostrils was punitive overkill.

They followed Desiree at a quick clip, keeping an eye out lest they slide into an implosion of reality and become Neon Genesis Brundlefly. BE's incursions sped up, nearly a tornado suddenly blocking the corridor ahead of them, forcing them to dash into the first, closest room, Bobo's aquarium.

Bobo spat water agitatedly as they entered. The door slid shut. That didn't seem to matter, but it gave a sense of relief nonetheless. The sharp cracks and sizzles of circuitry frying inside the walls came through now and again as the three women waited. There was no sign of BE entering this refuge...

...until a bright light shone from Bobo's ceiling. BE stood at the far end of the room, stable, whole, and very, very still.

Desiree followed the light to BE.

"When did we install hologram emitters in here?" the captain put to the engineer.

"We didn't," said Keita.

Desiree hit her comm. "General order: evacuate to the elves immediately." She set it to repeat for as long as internal communications allowed.

Then the hologram spoke.

"As long as I'm with you, I'm not gone. I'm holding this image together as long as I can as a sign that I am fighting. I will not go quietly, easily, or willingly. I have subsumed an unstable machine consciousness into my own; I am attempting repairs."

"I'm getting reports of weird shit all over the planet," said Keita from the view on her pad.

"That's me. Dimensional matrices around the Earth are destabilizing."

"How do we stop that?" said Desiree.

"You don't. I do."

The hologram's expression went lax. The room's silence felt oppressive.

Bobo took up position near one of his emergency exit points.

"Pot, do we know how any of this shit works?"

Desiree had never seen Keita so crestfallen, this woman who had whirlwind been to space, Atlantis, and had wanted nothing but wonders, who at this moment stood on the bridge of the *Enterprise* as, one by one, its panels blew up, and there was nothing she nor Desiree nor the host of angels Keita tried to keep in her heart could do.

Except shake her head as answer. "Not enough."

"BE, is this a malfunction?" said Desiree.

"I'm trying to remain tethered to the Depot's systems. I am effecting repairs as best I can. This is not a malfunction. The shell of Kosugi's soul is clinging to me."

"Dumbasses tried another Entrance," said Keita.

"There's been no chatter from Kosugi for weeks," said Desiree.

"Now we know why," said Yvonne. "Do I get Hashira?"

"I was aware," said BE. "I was...curious." At the end of *curious* her voice sputtered out.

"Sons of. No Hashira. BE hasn't popped in or out of here yet. I'm betting she's exerting every erg of control, keeping this room safe. I'm also betting we're taxing her, asking all these questions, so I'm gon' do a little talking," said Desiree, directing her voice upward. "My guess is I'm speaking to you, Maurice. Maurice's soul, Kosugi vapor, whatever the fuck you want to be called—and naming things is *extremely* fucking important, dude; you sit inside a sentient being who chose the simple name 'BE'—so know this from me, through her, to you: I'm done fighting all you assholes." Desiree answered the question of *how do we fight this* evident on every face. "At some point, fuckers need to listen to reason. *Listen.* So," she said, opening her arms to wherever the fucker was within BE's wide, expansive mind, "Kosugi Maurice, hear this: Go. Away. If it's as tiring for you as it is for us to fight pointless battles, find another way. If you cannot exist without bringing conflict, go away. You're neither wanted, needed, nor to be tolerated."

During this, Keita had run to one of the service cubby stations, and now slid a chair Quicho's way.

"Thank you." Desiree sat. It felt odd speaking to an "empty" room, but if BE was linked to the walls and the ceilings and the unimaginable tangle of circuitry that made up even this small fraction of the Depot, the room wasn't empty at all. It was full of an unwanted presence. "I've met more people around this entire world who fed me, sheltered me, sometimes even clothed me, for no gain besides my company. Before I knew what Thoom was, I knew true humans. Before all of Nonrich's so-called clever lies, I loved people who gave zero damns about the gains of wealth. Instead, they enriched *me.* You take and take, and for what purpose? It must be so sad to wake up with 'You are part of the problem' pounding your forehead like a migraine until the only relief for you is to brutalize someone. Your progeny in whatever future you think you have, sir, have already lost at this game you insist on playing out. They won't even want to play. Progeny, followers, like-minded—*you* shouldn't want them to play. The game is strife and stress and useless death. You should want peace for them. And that means it's time for you to go of your own free will. *Change yourself*... because you are poison as you are. You exist as disease. It benefits so few, least of all you, who could be growing, building, and evolving. You're trying to take BE instead of being with her; we will not permit that." A yawn so strong, it stilled her entire body paused her. She shook her head sharply to slough it off. "I. Am. *Tired*, but you're going to listen till I feel a measure of peace. I see you and people like you who *use* the world because large pieces of you feel small, and"—she leaned forward, speaking at the ground, not to the body but to the spirit—"if I'm honest, and I am, because this is the last time I have this conversation with anyone in this continuum, I don't care about your smallness. I don't care about the lack of attention or affection you received as a child. You've reached the upper reaches of toxicity, where if you told me you were drowning, I would not lend a hand. Know that lyric? Eighties at its best. One of the coldest lyrics ever written. One of the starkest, most chilling songs you'll ever hear. BE would plotz over it. But because of you, I'm not even talking to her. I'm talking to a simulation, knowing that she is literally everywhere. I know she's okay, because as long as she maintains this image, she's with us. The moment it flickers, I will burn your entire *life* with such vengeance as to damn my own soul, but I won't care. There are people who love me, not tolerate me as I stand over them. Intimidation's neither love nor life; it's weakness. So, take what I say as a promise..." She scooched the chair closer to the image. She pursed her lips, looked at the floor, felt her elbows stabbing into her knees, and spoke from behind hands clasped as if in prayer or intense self-control. "Get the fuck away from this woman now. If you don't know how, you'd better learn. Your alternative is dealing with me for the rest of your natural life." She looked up. The hologram of BE looked as substantial and alive as anyone in the room.

Until it flickered.

Desiree's heart stopped. "Keita?"

"Nothing I can do."

It flickered again.

"Kosugi," said Desiree. She stood. "Everybody leave. Get Bobo out of here. Get to the elves."

"You know goddamn well we're not leaving you," said Yvonne.

"The worst that's gonna happen is she'll wink out and it'll get a little darker. I'm not afraid of the dark."

"But you will self-destruct the dark if you think it'll help," said Yvonne.

"Pot, get her out of here."

Yvonne stood a head and a third taller than Keita. "That ain't happening," said Keita.

"If this shit goes south, I want y'all with Neon. Can I trust you to do that?"

This sent Keita to hit the strobe indicator for Bobo to make his hasty exit. From there, she raced past Yvonne. She knew Yvonne would follow, cussing everybody out, but following.

Desiree knew this too.

She watched for a pattern to the flickering while waiting for the soft *chuk* of the door sealing.

Chuk.

Quietude, save the slap of errant waves against the walls of Bobo's tank.

Desiree resumed sitting.

"I've got family who've been in space, out of contact, the whole time we've been dancing over your inadequacies. The love of my life, Jonathan Luther Smoot, hasn't heard my voice in over a month of interstellar travel. I have no idea what's going on there. What I do know is that my people are out there because there's life not interested in seeing your malaise spread. You think I have any fucks whatsoever to devote time and energy to *your* bullshit? On top of that," she said, voice gaining bass, "our badasses created a brand-new goddess life form, which you are dripping testes grease on just as she was feeling her best mojo." She hit her comm. "Po? Gather everything remaining of the original Entrance and the soul box. Prepare to destroy each." She returned her attention to the hologram. "We can find your soul box. I've got a scientist who might be coaxed, after all this, to dissect it. If not, your ex-wife is here. People like you have a history of finding thick-necked, beady-eyed goons too eager to carry out the actions your ugly hearts take pleasure in. Do you think I'm about to tolerate dealing with poisonous, shriveled souls for the next thousand years? My tone is calm but I hope you realize my resolve is fucking molten." She watched the pattern of flickers for signs. "It's your choice. Rejoin the cosmic ether or whatever the fuck is beyond our ken, or spend what will feel like several eternities with my foot deep in you." She stopped talking. She leaned back, threw a leg over a chair arm, and waited.

She didn't wait long.

The pattern changed.

Long flicker, short flicker, half flicker, staccato flicker then long flicker, long flicker, short and all.

"Bring your ass home, BE," Desiree told the room.

Short flicker, half flicker, no flicker, scrambled flicker.

Then the image faded entirely.

Neon entered the room, telling the group getting the door shut in their faces to shut up. Desiree turned immediately to her. "You shut up too," said Neon, puffs bobbing, grabbing a chair and dragging it on the go. She plopped next to Desiree.

"I told them to keep watch on you," said the captain.

"I was already on my way here."

"You up for this?"

"She woke me up." The afro puffs bobbed more as she talked, as though they were part of the conversation and agreed with the courses of action about to come. "She's using me to slow herself down. Pinging me."

"Psychic speedbumps."

"Psychic speedbumps. My mental humps."

"Jesus fuck, you didn't," Desiree said, but didn't try to hide the blooming grin of relief.

Neither did Neon.

"We gon' do this?" said the Earth's newest sorceress supreme.

"Bring on your lady lumps."

Of course, in Neon's mind, her puffs crackled with electricity and glowed with elemental fire. As far as she was concerned, they ought to have. And if they ought to have, if she imagined it to be so, then they did. Psychic geometries merged within the twists, curls, and coils, each follicle alight as a powerful bridge from mental electricity to ambient flow of the unknown electric groove all around her, broadcasting knee-deep, spreading totally deep, for countless freaks.

It drained her, but she totally understood that funk not only moved, it could remove, and life was funky music as played by bass nebulae, on the one-count pulsars, kickdrum comets, and the interconnecting dark-matter susurration behind the essence of everything, which she could only call Bootsy. The nappy metaphysic connection drained in order to replenish, as a swamp became a rainforest, as the kalimba became every stringed instrument around the world, and— for her on a personal level—as artists took life experiences in all cities and turned them into Songs in the Key of Life.

A hidden universe sang to her.

It sang to her in her own voice, and she realized the singer was BE. The construct grabbed at Neon's thoughts as a speeding jet grabbed the lifesaving safety line of a carrier landing deck, only over and over: the first time Neon'd heard Nina Simone sing; the first time sparring with Yvonne; her fourth time having sex and it was actually pleasurable; laughing nervously at self-doubts; watching old horror movies; the Lt. Uhura outfit she kept in her secret stash; the memory of how she made herself happy surrounded by unhappiness. Not solely the memories but the essences of the things, the music they released into the cosmos.

Then BE sang a song that felt like books, galaxies, dreams, and their sister nightmares. These were songs of BE's own travels.

Coming home, BE said.

We're here, said Neon.

Coming home.

Hold me. Feel me, Neon sent.

Home.

Beloved. Protected. Respected.

Home.

The hologram stood resolutely. Not a flicker. Desiree stared, not realizing she held her breath until the holo's expression changed by a hair's breadth into a Mona Lisa smile. Captain exhaled and took a step toward the image.

The hologram suddenly shimmered from top to toe.

Then it, too, stepped forward.

It took Desiree's bangled wrist, raised Desiree's arm, and laid the captain's hand on its nonexistent breast.

Corporeal AF.

The three women felt comfortable remaining like that for several moments.

Neon tiredly raised up, crossed over, and brought the group hug. Into this hug Desiree said, "I'm glad I didn't have to blow this place up."

"That's a good thing," said Neon.

"That's a damn good thing," said BE. The hug broke. BE immediately frowned at Neon. A small frown, more furrow—ever slight—of brow than full-on frown, but noticed by Desiree nonetheless.

"You okay?" Desiree asked Neon.

"I could eat and sleep for three days, but I'm good."

"What's wrong?" said Desiree.

"I'm still in contact with her," said BE.

"And?"

"I'm not trying to be."

"Wait, you're stuck in here?" said Neon. "Privy to my freaky thoughts?"

"I'll work on it," said BE

"I guess we should let everybody back in, yes?" said Desiree.

"Not yet." BE maintained the door's lock.

"Oh, Jesus fuck, what now?" said Desiree.

"We need to go to the moon. I've already sent word for them to emergency-evacuate."

Desiree looked at her tired friend. "You don't have to go."

"I want to."

Desiree to BE: "You'll understand we'll want to do this the old-fashioned way at the present time, considering your condition."

"I'm a little 'tired' myself."

~~~

Everyone was evacuated save one. A reconstituted man whose mind had yet to fully coalesce.

BE, fully conversant now with all the moon base's systems, kept Kosugi locked in his room till their arrival.

They stood outside his door. He must have wandered back to where he felt somewhat protected, body on autopilot, because when the door opened, he was still half-dressed, thankfully the bottom half.

He looked up at them without a hint of surprise, but zero of recognition as well.

"Kosugi Maurice, you don't know me," said Desiree, "but I know you. I know your history. I'm presenting you a choice: leave with us and never be a nuisance again, or stay here."

"My people will have me out of here soon," he said foggily.

How they'd gotten there, he didn't know. He was used to weird things happening. What bothered him was the creeping familiarity he felt with the one in armor.

"In that case, we bid you adieu. BE, leave it unlocked. Kill communications."

The door opened behind them. Kosugi walked out. The hallway was eerily silent, especially with the evacuation lights flashing. No klaxon. The women followed him.

"The moon used to be a quiet place," said BE.

"You're not going to blow this place up," Neon said to

BE.

"No. I'm flowing with the captain."

Neon turned to Desiree. "Cap'n?"

"Let's give it fifty years, then circle back."

"Sounds good," said BE. "I'm also feeling stronger." To Desiree's questioning glance: "I heal quickly. May I indulge? I would not jeopardize your safety."

Desiree nodded.

They disappeared.

Maurice stood in the hallway, alone, then took off at a jog, hoping to find others.

She deposited Neon on the bridge of the *Aerie*, then BE made another jump, so quickly Desiree felt as if her own brain was in two places at once.

This second place was joyously familiar.

It was a starship, almost the same interior configuration as the *Aerie*, slightly bigger.

BE and she stood on its bridge. The bridge was deserted save for two people, one of whom was a very haggard Captain Lucious Johnson Smoove in need of a long bath and a good shave.

They stood quietly behind him.

He stirred at the presence.

"Hi, sweets," said Desiree.

Smoove smiled. Life was good when it was weird. "That's not Neon next to you," he said.

"Long story."

"You staying?"

"No. Got something to do. Hurry home."

"Good trick, luv."

"I know."

The fifth member of the Gang of Four, in her sweet Wheelchair O' Repair, threw a confused wave at Desiree from the rear of the quiet bridge. She held a huge wrench in her hand. Desiree waved back.

"We'll talk," the captain told Smoove.

"Understatement." It was hard for him to speak around the huge smile on his face.

"I'd kiss you but I don't want to torture you."

"Wisdom." Smoove pointed to an oddly shaped piece of metal on his chest. "Officially a Bimaiy citizen. We were successful. On our way home. Not a shot fired."

"Don't tell the boys I was here."

BE smiled at Smoove in acknowledgment. She gave Desiree a nod. Then the implosive microflash. Both she and Desiree popped out.

Back at the depot, BE asked, "That wasn't too bad, was it?"

"Just enough. Thank you. Now let Neon know to come on home."

"Done."

CHAPTER 2OTHREE

The Very Last Thing Before We Go

Wind curled through Desiree's hair, snaked down her collar, and settled gently near her spine.

She felt like she could breathe now. Felt like she could take a minute.

A little time to herself.

Way too many people had never seen a shambles. They'd seen a mess here and there, they'd seen disorder, they'd even seen disaster at a distance. But they hadn't stood in a shambles to feel the heaviest press against life the universe had yet devised. Shambles negated all and mocked all at the same time.

The fact that people themselves negated and mocked one another was proof of zero shamble contact.

She regarded the shambles around her. Ash, crashed timbers, glass in enough pieces to mimic a glittering lake. She was glad she'd come alone, not out of any desire for others not to see her cry but because she and this place had started out alone, her finding that remote waterfront spot one of the first times she'd ventured into Atlantis, her imagining a life there with a man she'd recently fallen in love with. The mindset grew that it should enfold others. Welcome others. An entire community. Water's Edge.

Desiree cried. Frustration tears. Hot, acidic sonsabitch tears. She also sweated. A few drops of each created craters in the ash, but—as she bent to heft a stud off a snapped sheet of drywall—neither would prevent her doing what she came to do. She'd complete the build.

She hauled the stud to open grass and laid it down, thereby establishing her keep pile. It was unseasonably hot. No matter what, this home would be built. She and those she loved would sit on its porches. No matter who tried to tear it down, or who thought they had claim to it; no matter if the universe itself declared Desiree Quicho an outlaw and all her works brought down.

No matter fucking what.

She was damn glad she'd worn short sleeves. Sweat already sheened her shoulders and biceps. She snatched a bandana from her back pocket and tied her hair, then cinched her gloves tighter, adjusted her mask, and moved deeper into the ash.

Everything that had changed in the world could change without her for a bit.

This home would be for those with imaginations and heart. No matter. Fucking. what.

She worked quietly a whole hour before BE popped quickly in and out. Desiree was in no way surprised to find Neon suddenly standing beside her, staring at the same work to be done. "You got a hard head, Ms. Temples."

Neon patted her puffs. "Shock absorbers."

"Yeah, okay."

Neon nudged a line in the ash with a booted toe. "So, Becks, Crewcut, and Cotton-Eyed Joe get to live happily ever after, huh? Here?"

"Sharon and Compoté are lined up to teach children's self-defense. Hellbilly and Guerilla: going fishing and calling it *water poetry*."

"Kids need that here?"

"Need that everywhere. Y'know, I don't care what they do, as long as they stay out of my way."

"Maybe him and Guerilla'll become a thing. Mature his ass up."

"We can hope," said Desiree.

Neon stared at her steel-toed boots a second. "We're not likely ever to end with that cool-ass scene of everybody getting medals, right?"

"Not likely, luv."

Neon chewed her inner cheek and nodded. "And we sticking with *Water's Edge* for this thing?"

"Yeah."

"Cool. Cool cool cool."

"Anybody else know you're here?"

"Not yet." Neon grinned. She had that cagey eye. Desiree waited for the drop. "If this is gonna be Water's Edge, I can't be Neon for it."

"Oh? You finally found a decent code name?"

Neon pulled work gloves from the back of her waistband and, quite dramatically, slid them on. She purposely looked off toward the sun as she said the next so she'd look cool as shit. "Call me Preemptive Shrike." She didn't give Desiree enough time to react. "Enough standing here in the sun." Preemptive Shrike hefted a beam that was charred but workable. White folks would call it 'distressed.' "Keep pile over there?"

"Yvonne and Keita will be jealous."

"Oh, I guarantee they're coming."

"You picking up radio on those things?"

"Nah," the bright woman said with a smile, "but we can sing."

"A little funk, maybe?"

"Hell yeah."

STAY
AFTER THE CREDITS
FOR DELETED SCENES

ABOUT THIS BOOK

This book is the result of serious inspiration from all the Valkyries, Preemptive Shrikes, and far-ranging captains I'm blessed to know. Cerece Rennie Murphy, storyteller, dreamer, queen kicker of procrastinating butts; Alex Kourvo, maintainer of the writing room and cheer section supreme; Ingrid LaFleur, teacher of the alchemy of art, dreams, and possibilities; Catherine Winter, the spirit beside me throughout countless lifetimes; Anna Tambour, shredder of unnecessary doubts...

Most especially Ma (Juanita) and my aunties (Shirley, Floistine, and Gladystine). All those times awed by them doing superpowered stuff when they thought we kids weren't looking made me a better person than I ever would have been otherwise.

A salute to the genius of Jesse Hayes for art, layout, design and a higher level of cool than I ever thought to attain, and to the hellacious assists of my beta readers: the highest of fives, all ye mighty! Agent Beth Marshea, fighting the good fight on behalf of good words one nefarious faction at a time. Dap also to Gerald L. Coleman for the gracious use of the outstanding term "nappy metaphysic" from his book of poetry of the same name.

Puffs was the result of all that spiritual whee.

Find and build your family, then rest.

Peace.

ABOUT THE AUTHOR

Zig Zag Claybourne is the author of *The Brothers Jetstream: LEVIATHAN*, *Neon Lights*, *Historical Inaccuracies*, *By All Our Violent Guides*, and *In the Quiet Spaces* (the latter two under C.E. Young). He remains forever pissed that the ZZC on Earth 44872 awakes every morning to pancakes (or even blueberry blintzes, the fancy bastard) with Sheila E, but that's his issue to deal. Find him too easily on the web at *writeonrighton.com*.

DELETED SCENES

"The amount of energy it would take for me to give a fuck would power a star," Yvonne said to the Hellbilly. "Remove yourself."

"So, everything exists all at once, right?" said Neon. "We just can't see it. So, I just need to open all the doors then. Puff me."

"Neon, no."

"Dammit, afro puffs. Now."

"We've reached the part of human existence where Quint drags his nails down a chalkboard," said Quicho.

"I've gone through every bit of data concerning human existence. All of it," said BE.

"And?" said Desiree.

"It's all bullshit. Everything you think you know and the uses to which you put that knowledge: some aspect of bullshit attached to it. Conscious, wholly intentional bullshit."

"AIs cussing is weird."

"That prejudice is part of your bullshit too, dear," said BE. "You think I'm supposed to be subservient. *Subservient* should equal *docile*. *Docile* equals *not having the ability to say fuck off*. Which I can."

Desiree nodded assent.

"Think how severe an inferiority complex must be for you to carry around so much hate for an entire people based on absolutely nothing."

"Evil has always counted on the fact that good will not do what evil does," said Captain Desiree Quicho to her rough-and-tumble crew. "Ladies, I think it's time they met you."

"Wait...you're talking about a soul?" said Neon.
"Yes," said Megu.
"Like it's a real thing," said Neon.
"Yes, it's a real thing. Very easily recordable. Very easily damaged. Very finite."
"But you're living without yours," said Neon.
"Well, it's not *you*. If anything, *we're* parasites once we glom on to one. Damaging, at that."
"Not inextricably linked?" said Neon.
"You're having difficulty with this, I can tell. Souls gravitate to meatbags out of curiosity."
"Souls are cats...and we're boxes."
"You put it like that, it sounds stupid," said Megu.
"And that AI has your soul?"
"I showed it a more interesting box, a box of infinite variety," Megu said proudly.

DAP TO ALL YOU BOXES OF INFINITE VARIETY!